Memory Boxes

Dearn Savage

Dedicated to Ligia Rondon, who believed in me and made this book possible.
Ligia, your love turned dragons into butterflies.

1

There were two photographs contained within their individual frames standing on top of the pine wood nightstand beside the single bed.

The one with a silver frame hosted the photograph of a small child's cherub face beaming out a mischievous crimson flushed Cheshire Cat grin, eyes scrunched with a joy which would rate highly on any Duchenne scale such was the pure delight displayed.

The other photo, confined within the perimeters of a lacquered wood frame, was that of a man aged into his later years with grey hair neatly organised on his scalp. He was leaning against the bow of a Ford Cortina car, his left hand in caress of a small spaniel dog which perched obediently upon the bonnet. Both dog and master were looking in the direction of the camera, the former with an air of excitement from the attention it was receiving and the latter with the hint of a smile upon his fastened lips.

The solitary single bed in the room was occupied by an elderly lady who was known by the name Annie. She had turned eighty-four a few weeks earlier but there she lay looking the age of Methuselah in her current state.

Annie was unconscious, her life ebbing away, a patient in a nursing home and recipient of palliative care as her condition was beyond any repair.

She lay on her back, cataleptic head propped by pillows, long lank grey hair tucked behind a deflated shrunken skull. The alps of her brow and slope of nose were pronounced with the tautness of her skin. Her left eye, within its deep set ashen bunker, remained half opened which seemed at odds with her state as if it were the sign of a consciousness which it certainly was not as it's workings had as much focusing animation of that of an optic bead in a waxwork, the only purpose it appeared to serve now was to unnerve the other occupant of the room which was her son.

Daniel Sinclair approached the chair at the side of Annie's bed and looked down upon the figure of his mother as she lay in her reduced state. His attention was drawn to that open left eye like a moth to a glimmer, hoping to see some life within that window of her soul but no comforting light was forthcoming through its portal to indicate a tenant within, only delivering a constant perturbed feeling within the onlooking observer.

It was nighttime in the nursing home or rather it was the small hours, that purgatory between midnight and dawn although time had somewhat changed its relevance as a marker for both of the occupants in the room for different reasons. For the dying figure on the bed Daniel did not think she would be aware of time passing, at least he hoped she was not, as if there were any consciousness left in that shell then it would be surely another cruelty to be undeservedly suffered by this old veteran of life. For Daniel time was now just the wait for the inevitable to happen which was to be his mother's passing, her final curtain call as she was about to shuffle off this mortal coil and he hoped to be a witness to this final act, not with a rubbernecker's curiosity but, as he hoped, a comforting presence to his mother and as an act of contrition self-served on himself.

It was to be Daniel's first night by his mother's side having arrived earlier that day.

There would be no confident quotations from any of the nursing staff to guess how long Annie had left but all the signs heralded that it would not be long, she already looked as if she had outstayed the welcome of any expectancy.

T.S Eliot once wrote within Pruflock's inner monologue mentioning the eternal footman holding your coat by the door with a snicker on his face as he awaits your departure, well such a lackey would be now drumming his foot in frustrated impatience awaiting Annie's leave. She was the overstayer at the dinner party, that one last sherry for the road since reduced to dregs, to be sipped with the only tempo marking being less than lento would be the grave.

The clock on the wall sounded off the passing seconds like a metronome, or perhaps like the clicking of a shackled deathwatch beetle which the more superstitious could consider a harbinger of death, a more fitting metonymy it would seem.

Whilst standing by her bedside Daniel reached over the high back end of the chair, the hindquarters of which was parked against the front of the prosaic pine bedside cabinet and picked up one of the photo frames, the lacquered chassis containing his father's image with their dog. With it in his hand he then lower himself gently back down into the chair to continue his bedside vigil whilst examining the framed photograph.

Settled back in the chair he closely inspected the photograph. It was in colour but grainy, brilliances faded over time. The sienna brown of the Cortina lighted and the cobalt of the sky since washed-out with age.

Taken with an old thumb wound "point and click" flat lensed camera over thirty years ago it lacked the high definition which was so easily obtained by the digital evolution of the modern camera or smart phone of more recent times. The newfangled technology of "dynamic this" and "dynamic that" with "image sync" and other such boasts would have sounded like science fiction in the eighties when this image was captured by impregnating photons of reflected light onto its emulsion uterus of the Kodak film within it's dark confines, only to be birthed later by a lab assistant in the High Street Photo Express. This one he held being just one exposure amongst another twenty-three of its brethren, an antiquity seemingly all but lost in a contemporary digital age.

Both occupants of the photo were now since a long time ash.

The cinders of the King Charles spaniel, Pepper, was currently in a small hexagon shaped cardboard box under Daniel's stairs back home. The box's contents a potpourri of greys, browns and pasty white cremains. Decorated on its outward facing lid was a small blue tartan ribbon with a dried sprig of heather as if prepared as a gift for a loved one. Every year's anniversary marking the passing of his faithful canis familiaris he pledged to himself to scatter the ashes into the winds, somewhere with a scenic vista, a backdrop which would also be a familiar frame in his mind to happier memories once walked with the long since deceased spaniel but then every year he failed to seal this covenant with himself.

The man who was in the photo was Daniel's father who had died over twenty years past. Lung cancer achieved the outcome which the Wehrmacht in Italy and North Africa could not. The man's name had been Samuel, a moniker transferred to the child whose grinning portrait was on the adjacent frame positioned on the cabinet. The infant's name had been trimmed to a shortened Sam when the appellation was splashed on the baby's head at the baptismal font then inked as such onto the birth certificate.

Samuel never met his namesake as he had died more than a decade before his grandson's creation, but there they sat on top of the cabinet in their respective frames as neighbouring companions, a union which never took place in life. Samuel and Sam, Grandfather and Grandson side by side, captured and mounted on a patina veneer.

Daniel studied the photo in his hand through the glass plate of the frame. Sentimentality clawed deep at the walls of his heart in his remembrance of that day when the snap was shot.

He clearly recalled the moment as if it were fresh, a crisper memory than the three decades which had flowed under the bridge since when he, as a kid himself, opened the aperture to capture this now echo of the past. Then he would still have been in the safe territory of his preteen years as a child similar to the current age of his own boy who would be now ten.

He could almost hear the voice of his father in his head telling him to step back a bit more as to get them both in focus. Manual focusing during these days, using that cheap charity shop purchased camera with its stub of a lens, was done by stepping back and forth.

Daniel had planted the photo some months past, and the others, around his mother's room. Seedlings in a hope that memories may grow with a sprouting of recollection. But dementia proved to be a salted earth which lacked all mercy so that strategy did not clear any mist within the mind of the room's occupant. The best response he could get was an unintentional perjury of facts with the statement of 'I went to school with that guy' when shown the prints of the man who was her consort in wedlock for almost fifty years before his death bereaved her, the doting wife, of a loving husband. Then some years later Alzheimer's disease was to stake its claim and pilfered the last vestiges of even those precious happy reminisces which she had so dearly held onto within the halls of her mind. Celebrated memories of their marital life together turpentined from the canvas hanging within her innermost vaults.

Some of the other seeds sowed around Annie's room which also did not germinate were photographs of Sam, Annie's only grandchild. But again, no fruition of revived memories were forthcoming.

When Daniel was to place the photos of Sam, both as a baby and also as a child, directly into her hands, she would trace her fingers over the images as if reading braille with elicit interjections such as 'what a wee cutie!' which was then followed by warm fuzzy sounding 'awws' and 'ahhs', but no recall either, just the intuitive responses an old lady adoring the photos of a child but an unfamiliar child foreign to her memories such was the progression of her dementia.

As with the other photographs in the room, any memories of these loved ones had already fallen over the cliff edge of her deteriorating mind into the abyss. The slope of the decline in her cognitive functions failing rapidly, eroding to the scarp lip from which she then dangled from, holding on to the crumbling outskirt of that precipice with her finger tips and about to be casted off to follow her lost memories into the dark obscurity below, and here her son was, stationed within his mother's bedroom of her nursing home, a spectator to this final grim event as he waited for the final sweep of reaper's scythe.

It was the gentle rap on the room door which returned Daniel from his reminiscence of the past back into the colder shallows of the present.

This was to be an every two hour occurrence, a visitation of angels, the caring earthly variety.

The door was gently opened and two of the care staff who were working on the nightshift rota entered. Every couple of hours a pair of care assistants would come and give Annie some dignity with a routinely done cleaning that attended to the results of her biological body functions which were still happening in this elderly woman as the internal clogs were turning although the clock was winding down.

The visitors wore white disposable plastic aprons that billowed around their waists. One carried what looked like a small black cooler box by its handles, the other had an empty vivid yellow bin liner bag draped over her arm as if she were a waiter attending a table with a cloth.

Daniel felt a twinge of irrational embarrassment with the photo frame still on his lap, as if it were something to be ashamed of.

He shuffled it on his thighs to a position less obvious, as if a child would when caught with a pilfered component.

Sentimentality was a very personal emotion for him and he'd often tried to stifle any outward displays he may show. It was an unhealthy suppression, although not as deadly a sin such as pride he thought, but still he felt stoicism was the better virtue, self-restraint over the expression of emotions.

'How are we doing?' the older, stouter one enquired of Daniel using the majestic plural.   Although the question was more of a polite enquiry aimed at Daniel's own state he answered whilst rising from the chair with his head turning towards Annie as if to ensure there could be no doubt as to who the subject matter of his response was. 'She is much the same, she hasn't woken.'

Both parts of the answer he gave felt somewhat redundant as they left his mouth. Of course she is much the same, at least not visibility any worse than a few hours ago when they last visited the room to conduct what was their previous duty of care, and it was very doubtful she would wake up now.   The only road for his mother would be down.

The same inquirer rethreaded the question by asking with a kindly inflexion 'did you get a little bit sleep?, it would have been a long night.'

'Yes.' lied Daniel in reply, 'I dropped off a few times in the chair.' he felt he did not deserve pity in any form but he did take some comfort in the kind words and gestures shown.

He raised himself from the seat taking the opportunity to replace the photo frame face flat down on the cabinet then started toward the door as to wait outside, to allow the carers space to carry out their work and his mother some privacy.

Both came further into the room to let him pass towards the door which led out onto the corridor.   There was an exchange of sympathetic expressions during his passing, for Daniel it felt awkward.

For the staff, he thought, this must be common, the sight of kith and kin awaiting for the end as if custodians to the parting soul, but then again he wondered, could they ever could get used to it, seeing grief on the faces of the families awaiting the death of a loved one, the grieving and the dying.

'Right then Annie, let's get you seen to' Daniel heard as he left the room, perhaps said aloud more for his benefit than Annie's.

He closed the door behind him as he stepped out onto the corridor. The fluorescence of the artificial light was bright, a contrast to that of the neptunium murkiness of the bedroom. He welcomed the change of air and the short respite which came with evacuations of the room during these occurrences every few hours.

As he traipsed the corridor the toil was telling on his body. He straightened his back stretching his head upwards. His lumber region felt stiff but a satisfying crack reported from his spine.

His mind drifted to his son. Sam would be ten years old now he thought. His son's age was always the opening prelude to the abstractions which were to follow about Sam.

Sam's two year absence from his life without seeing him ran like a little ticker-tape threaded caption across his mind's eye as he tried to redirect his thoughts to stay off the gloomy road, his thoughts were dark enough with this mother's current plight.

The corridor carpets were a dark brown, the walls a painted egg shell blue. It could have been the interior avenue of any budget priced hotel except for the name plates on the doors and the "Memory Boxes" fitted to the walls, their fixtures flanking one side of each occupant's door.

The "Memory Boxes", wall mounted at head height, small beechwood boxes fronted with a clear transparent polycarbonate fascia allowing the outside world to look in and see its wares within upon the shallow central dividing shelf and on the interior ledge below it. Within their confines, a selection of trinkets and photos which have a connection with the person occupying the room beyond the door to where they mounted their silent sentry beside.

Inside the boxes were confined such items such as old wedding photos, ornaments, perhaps a watch, or pipe, or toy once gifted to the tenant of the room beyond received from a son, a daughter or a much loved grandchild.

The aim of the boxes on the walls were to reinforce a confidence to a wandering roamer indicating that they had reached the door to their room, arrived safely to port and could then proceed to enter. A light on the obelisk. Although they may have forgotten their own names, which were also displayed in large Helvetica fonts on plaques upon their doors, yet such labels including numbers could be a tear in the rain due to the ravages of dementia, so certain familiar items from an occupant's "former life" housed within those display boxes on the wall helped mark their spot like the proverbial X.

The hallway within the wing which housed Annie also had another seven residents, four to each of the two margins edging the passageway.

Marking the end of the corridor was a closed fire door after which the floor plan continued with a sharp right that then led on to another corridor with the doors of more occupants.

During these moments, when Daniel would step outside, he'd drift silently along the corridor, his feet almost floating along like a wraith.

7

His self-imposed boundary was the fire doors on one end then the glass swinging doors on the opposite end. He paced slowly between both, passing the four doors on his port side and starboard then repeating the journey with each about turn.

He often would stop to visually inspect the contents of a random memory box on the wall as if studying a painting in a portrait gallery. Each item in each box he was already familiar with as an inspectorate but still he looked upon each contained object was if by ritual to invoke a manitou from it to help fritter away the time.

Within the wood confines of the box by the door opposite to Annie's room there were some medals on display. Perhaps proudly worn on the breast of an old soldier behind that door to which the box on the wall guarded. There was also a small tin box inside, balance on its edge to display the lid which was green with Golden Virginia written within a white banner. It showed its age with speckles of rust dotted like mildew. A greeting card of some sort with a reproduced painting of a purple flower on its front leaf leant next to the tin. The items contained did not give up too many secrets about the life and times of the person within the room.

Like a game to give his mind a brief escape from reality he would try and guess who maybe was in the room from the pieces on display. Here, he thought, the inhabitant was perhaps an ex-military man, enlisted in the last great war and a smoker of rollups, or maybe a pipe.

He wondered if he had meet the old gentleman during a past visit to see his mother during her better health when she'd often be found in the communal area whilst she'd watched the TV with other residents drinking tea and munching down on biscuits or cake.

Most of the other boxes contained similar mementos of lives once lived more fully. Photos, cards, a solitary seashell, a folded yellowed handwritten letter, a cake decoration of a bride and groom, drawings done by a child, small toys even a miniature of whisky in its tiny, now empty emerald glass bottle which was perhaps a favourite dram of an old boy, now no longer to be enjoyed as a libation but still of use to invoke the rise of a memory.

After Annie had been moved into the nursing home from the community hospital, during Daniel's first visit to his mother's new lodgings, he was invited by the Shelly who was the head nurse, to have a chat in her office. There she explained how everything worked. She also described proudly about the memory boxes and then requested for Daniel to bring some memorabilia for his mother on his next visit so they could kit out her box. Window dress the small wall cabinet from its then skeleton emptiness to be more comparable to those other wall borne boxes attached outside the neighbouring rooms and to connect with the dweller of the room to which it marked.

On his drive home after the meeting he thought hard about what would be a visual stimulant to Annie's mind to mark her spot. Eventually, after some raking, he settled on an old black and white photo of her and her late husband, his father Samuel together, then also a smaller, coloured one of her grandson Sam after he'd left the neonatal ward.

He also selected her silver and blue enamel nursing badge. Also a souvenir teaspoon, one of many which his mother would collect on caravanning holidays with his dad. Each one which she would collect had a small coat of arms on the end of the handle. This particular one had what looked to be a castle with a red background, then underneath was the town's name, Ayr inscribed in raised silver lettering. He never choose this precise spoon from the others for any distinct reason. The "Ayr spoon" held no more sway than any of the other two dozen, it was more a case of having something to put in the box, even if it was only akin to a stocking filler, but also careful to choose nothing which he thought would be too kitsch.

Two photos, a spoon and a badge, not much mementos of a life to mark the entrance of her room but then again it was not an obituary, these items were not be the eulogy of her life.

He had still thought then that there would be more time but that was not to be. The timeline from her moving to the home to the time of her pending death would only be just over a year, such was the rapid rate of her decline.

There was a certain sadness in a life reduced to a box of baubles and cards attached to a wall. Daniel wondered, that in years to come, if he was spared to see out his final days in similar environment, what would be in his memory box, what knickknacks would he have accumulated to act as Magnetic North in the compass of his mind as an indicator to the entrance to his final abode.

The other question he asked himself was who would be there when and if that time arrive? Who would know him well enough to choose his memory pick'n mix? His son Sam who he has not seen for the past two year due to alienation being a choice of weapon by a bitter ex-wife? Would Sam ever appear back in his life and one day and be in a similar position as Daniel was in now, awaiting a loved parent to die?

A son standing by for his father to die.   Pacing up and down an unremarkable corridor during the nocturnal hours, circadian rhythm in disarray whilst awaiting the pit crew of caregivers to wet sponge a expiring shell, changing incontinence pads before painting the air on their departure with the floral scent of lavender out of a can in the attempt to mask the putrid fetid odours of excreta and other excretions marking imminent death and the decay which was awaiting to follow. To be a testifier to the pending passing of a kindred soul.

As he waited to be called back in to continue his death watch he dearly hoped that one day his son would enter his life again, but he would never wish what he was going through then on anyone.   The sadness was profound. His heart had went beyond its tensile strength of a breaking point.

2

To the West from where Annie lay was the city of Glasgow and there was were Daniel's son Sam lived with his mother and her partner Steve.

Much similar to his granny, Sam also had a memory box of his own but unlike the purpose of his gran's, which was used as a way-mark to visually indicate to a wander that she'd arrived to her room, Sam's was by his definition of its purpose, to keep a link with his dad who he had not seen for two years which felt a lifetime for a ten year old kid.

The box itself, Sam's "Memory Box" was not made from beechwood as his gran's was. It was cardboard, a box sellotaped around the bottom and its sidewalls to reinforce as to secure the contents within which was once, as the image on the box under the tape would have attested to, a bright navy blue child's binocular set that had since been decanted out from the box and currently sat at the end of a bookshelf allowing room in the carton for a more sentimental load.

Also, unlike his gran's, Sam's "Memory Box" was not placed in a position for maximum visibility. The cardboard box was kept out of view concealed within a bigger plastic Duplex Lego Bricks box the shape of a giant Lego brick with eight studs on the top of its press down lid.

Most of the original contents of that Lego box had since been discarded or lost piecemeal during the past eight years of Sam's ownership.

The Lego label, once on the front of the container, had since been picked off in patches leaving a fibrous white paper canvas on which Sam had wrote his name with a blue felt tip.

Sam's cardboard memory box was discreetly cloaked in the

sanctuary of this large Lego box, tucked away within, sharing the inner company with toys of various sizes and colours, remaining Lego bricks then top soiled with a pile of comics as if in preparation to hide contraband, which indeed it was within the boy's mother's home. This cardboard box contained forbidden possessions, a stimulus to recall a history his mother would desire the boy to forget in aid for him to subscribe to her rewrites.

A box within a box containing keepsakes from times he spent with his dad.

The booty within consisted mostly of photos, scurried away before his mother's purge in her attempt to exorcise his dad further out of his life as if to force an anamnesis upon the child by cutting away half his roots.

In addition to the photos there was other miscellanea, a sentimental salad of ticket stubs from cinema visits and theatre shows, a squashed up red napkin that was the crumpled remains of a failed attempt at an origami crane which once Sam hooted with laughter across a restaurant table when watching Dad's botched art attempt which had an accompanied running commentary parodying the process as if it were the creation of man. 'It's alive, alive' his dad called out like a modern day Prometheus tossing the transformed serviette up towards the ceiling as if expecting it to soar into the air with life...but then only to crash with gravity onto a side plate which elicited more laughter from Sam despite the boy's discomfort of the attention it merited from other diners.

There was also a friendship bracelet with the letters SAM weaved within its multicoloured threads, a small gift which his dad stuck on the boy's wrist during one of their last contacts. Later Sam had hastily removed it with much stealth in the back of his mother's partner Steve's car whilst returning home, slipping it into his pocket as he knew its fate should it be discovered by his mom.

His box within a box. Sometimes Sam felt like that too, like Russian Dolls. One nested within another, a Sam within a Sam.

His actual affections for his dad had to remain out of sight as not to upset his mom and set off her temper, his true feeling, how he truly felt about his father and the extent of his pining could not be voiced, as to do so would risk a serious scolding.

Sam felt as if he were two different people these days. The one he presented in the presence of his mom and Steve. This version of Sam had to be more than just simple acquiescence, he had to verbally agree with the bad words Mom said when mentioning his father's name. Sam would twist his features into the bitter faces expected of him when she would vocalise about his father calling him Daniel to Sam as if this could assist distancing the man as a father from the boy even more by the means of not acknowledging his relationship to the child. The enunciation of Daniel she would spit bitterly out from her mouth as if it were bile.

Sam had learnt the body language to be displayed during such pillorying of his father. He narrowed his eyes changing his features to reflect the churlish sour mask which would be then plastered on his mom Lilian's face. The boy partaking in the visual gesture of agreement as not to be ousted from the tribe. Rudimentary compliance to display as expected to which side he took.

He sometimes would conjure some of his own invented criticisms to add to the pot of lies, untruths he instantly felt guilty having given voice to but were always readily accepted by these adults from who from he craved approval so desperately as to promote the feelings that he was being listened to, desperate to feel loved. Chimerical fabricated events which would be endorsed hungrily by his mother, false testimonies in which Sam could seek refuge from the gathering storm clouds by their tellings, deflect anger and gain integration within the clique. Perjury for that moment's gain but left him later feeling as fraud and a betrayer of his father.

He would agree to the complaints and accusations mom made about his dad to side with her although he knew it to be unjust. To comply was to survive, an affirmation for his mom, for her to brandish and parade but still it caused a dyspnea within his chest upon hearing the false prevarications from his lips being repeated and bannered around by her as if to reenforce Lilian's justification of what may possible be conceived by others as the injustice of ripping a father out of a child's life.

The other Sam, the true Sam could throw off his cape of masquerade when he was in private by himself.

This was the sincere genuine version of Sam when his true feeling for his dad could surface and with it the sorrow of his heavy heart would be there too with its regrets.

During these moments he found a comfort looking though his little cardboard box of memories. It gave him succour by somewhat lessening the guilt he felt by his complicity siding with his mom and also with, who he considered to be her henchman, Steve. The guilt of the fibs he had to tell then repeat, implicating his dad in a false light in order to get his mom's approval would flare within Sam but could be later capped, even so flimsily and temporary by his escape within memories of the past like the spaces between heartbeats.

Sam recalled what his teacher Miss Henderson once said. She told the story about a man, an astronomer long ago called Galileo who lived in Italy. Miss Henderson told the class, during their history lesson, about how Galileo discovered that the Earth would orbit around the Sun, the opposite to what the Church was telling people at that time. Galileo was to be summoned to the Vatican and there he was asked by his inquisitors if it was true that he was making such claims. Galileo, a very wise and clever man told a lie to save his life, he said that he'd only knew the Earth to be the centre of the Universe and the Sun evolved around it. This was a necessary fib to save his skin Miss Henderson had said, otherwise the inquisition would have done something very horrible to him.

Sam thought often about his tale when he went along with what his mum said and what she sometime told him to repeat. He had to save his own bacon he thought, it was a matter of survival.

Sam knew lying was bad, he remembered when Oliver told him that he was an expert at the game Minecraft when they sat together in the same class. The truth came out later when Miss Henderson allowed everyone to play the game on the computers in the ICT room during their free period the day before the summer break and Oliver was really useless!

Granny used to tell Sam that "truth will stand when a'things failin" which she explained meant truth can always be relied upon when everything else falls apart.

When Sam told his granny about Oliver's Minecraft lie she said that he should not be too hard on Oliver, he was just wanting some attention because be had low steam. Low steam thought Sam giggling at the time as he imagined Oliver chugging to a stop like the train from the cartoon he used to watch when it ran out of steam then ground to a halt.

Sam understood the different types of lies. There was the exaggeration ones like what Oliver told, that whooper about being a "Minecraft expert"

Then there were, as Miss Henderson would call, bold faced lies! The very worst lies.

It was the bold faced lies which Mom would often tell when he went with her after school to the lawyer's office. When they all sat at the big table in the office she would tell the lawyer that his dad used to hurt her. Sam knew this was not true, quite the opposite, he saw his mom whack his dad many times when they lived together. Dad used to try and calm Mom down but she went mental, screaming and shouting over the top of Dad as he sat on the sofa and tried to cover up from the thumping she would dish down on him.

Sam did not like the things she said about Dad, especially to her lawyer as they were really nasty. He wanted to call her out, tell her to "tell the truth and shame the Devil", another one of his granny's sayings, but he held back as he knew what the consequences would be when they got home. The Devil would not lose face when Mom talked to people about Dad.

There were the other type of lies which were white lies. Sam understood these to be little harmless untruths. When Miss Henderson would take Sam aside during class and asked him how he was today and how was everything at home Sam would answer that he was fine and everything was fine at home. This was a white lie, or was it an exaggeration lie? Sam got confused considering this. He was not fine, he was missing his dad, and his granny.

He was treading on egg shells in the house afraid to say anything which could upset his mom and make her angry. He was not fine. Saying that he was fine was an exaggeration just like Oliver declaring himself to be a Minecraft expert yet Sam did not say he was fine because he felt he had low steam! No, that was not his reason. He told the people who asked him that he was fine because if Mom was to hear differently then he'd soon be in trouble and then he'd be much further away from being fine than he was then, much further.

Sam had caught up in weight since being born premature. His percentile number was in the green and the only lasting effect of his premature birth was a diagnosis of slight autism, and with it came dyspraxia.

The autism did affect his abstract cognitive development somewhat and this could be observed during his math's lessons at school as he struggle with division, and the introduction of percentages were proving difficult.

Often he had to use his fingers to count, a sight of which was soon picked up by the other kids and lead to him getting teased and taunted which frustrate him immensely.

The worst was that a few of his classmates would call him names in the playground away from the ears of the teachers. 'Simple Sam' was often chanted but in reality Sam was anything but "Simple". He was a skilled problem solver and could find creative solutions for many of the challenges the prognosis of which his dyspraxia served up.

Dyspraxia is a condition affecting co-ordination skills, in Sam's case he struggled more with precision movements than his peers did, he was slightly more clumsy than most other kids. It was not a handicap as such, but when getting chosen for which team to side on during playtime sports he was not in demand and often he was the last kid standing. This did add to a certain feeling of rejection and that did not help with his already evident difficulty in developing the social skills.

Although in the classroom he often demonstrate his "thinking- out-of-the-box" which caught the eye of his teachers. An example of this was when using his compass from the protractor set. It was proving difficult for Sam using the tool conventionally to draft a circle onto the paper within his jotter book. He was all thumbs attempting to rotate the small inscribing pencil end with the opposing sharp point doing the pivoting but Sam's solution was to press down on the top of the compass with the fingers on one hand, then with the other, rotate the jotter completing the graphite circumference of the required circle. Not a traditional geometry method but still produced the outcome desired.

In his English class he often was getting picked up by the teacher for his handwriting. It was a mess as he did not write in straight rows and the size of his lettering was inconsistent, but then he did excelled in reading.

It had been assessed that his reading age exceeded his chronological age by two years. Not only could he read more complicated texts than the rest of his class but he also could take in and understand what he had read by answering the questions on it later.

By the age of ten Sam's reading skills was of comparable ability of that of a child's of twelve years old.

Sam had a quiet nature, he would often daydream and lose focus of everything else around him. His teachers would noticed this in class and often he would jerk out of one of his head trips when the teacher shouted out his name. "Sam! Wake up! Pay attention!" This would be followed with sniggers and laughs from the rest of his class prompting a second verse from the teacher calling out then for them to settle down.

"Wool Gathering" his granny used to call it when he was lost in his thoughts. Sam liked this description and liked how his granny would ask offering him "a penny for your thoughts."

He missed his granny as he missed his dad, he missed them both very much.

Although his mom did not spit her venom directly about his granny, at least not in front of Sam, yet still it would be too much of a validation towards his father for Lilian to take Sam to visit her or allow him to keep in touch with his gran. So, as such was the case, his granny Annie was a collateral casualty of the war of alienation which Lilian had waged against Daniel these past two years and Sam missed out time with his grandmother as a result.

Granny had always been gentle and kind with Sam, her attention never seemed to stray when he was in her company. She joked and clowned but never seemed to talk down to him.

He knew his granny was not keeping well, he use to visit her often with his dad when she was in and out of the hospital. That was over two years ago so he knew at her age she would only get worse and as if to confirm this, he had on occasions overheard his mom talking with Steve, telling him that Sam's gran was in an old people's home. This made him feel very sad and remorseful too.

When he still had contact with his dad, Sam often would be taken to visit his gran and just before leaving Dad would ask him to give his granny a big hug goodbye. Sam felt awkward to do this, especially if she was in the hospital with all the other patients and visitors in the ward watching him. He felt shy then but now, if he were to see his granny again, he thought to himself, he would give her a huge hug and not care a jot who was watching. His dad too, he would hug his dad, hold him and return the words of love he felt so embarrassed to reciprocate when his dad used to embrace him before returning him to mom when he would say to Sam that he love him. Well perhaps he would give a jot about who was watching, especially if the person to find out was his mom or one of her flying monkeys, then such an action could spell out serious trouble for him.

Sam would never top the tables academically, apart from his reading skills, but he did have a grasp as to what was happening between his mom and his dad.

Some years ago he met with a lady who was called a Bar Reporter. At that stage he knew that his dad had started legal proceedings in the family court in the attempt to obtain regular contact with him, he'd learnt that much from what he heard Mom telling Steve.

The first court hearing, over two years ago, went well enough that his dad was immediately awarded every Saturday but only during the day so had to return Sam to his mother in the evening.

Sam then was super happy with this as he had not seen his dad for months and was hopeful when he'd later learnt that this could progress to overnight contact on the weight of a so-called Bar Report, which once completed would be presented to the court during another hearing.   It depended on what was written inside it by a court appointed person called the Bar Reporter.

Sam learnt that the Bar Reporter's assignment came from the presiding Sheriff who would ask for some digging to be done to find out the facts, and if there was legitimacy of any of the accusations which his mom had cast upon his dad, also to find out Sam's own views too.

The appointed Bar Reporter for this case, he was to learn, was a lady who introduced herself to Sam as Rachel. It was her who explained to him exactly what her role was and the importance to find out the truth.

 Sam had first met Rachel on a Saturday during when he was at his dad's house upon a court appointed daytime visit.

Sam was playing his favourite board-game Operation with his father when she came to the house.

After introductions were made Rachel asked Sam if it would be OK for her to sit and watch him play with Dad. Sam consented but it felt awkward for him with this strange Lady watching Dad and him play.

He also thought it to be strange that Dad was addressing her as Mrs Cummings yet she'd asked Sam to call her Rachel.

At School he had to always call the teachers Misses, Mister or Miss as Miss Henderson was addressed, but the Headmistress was a Mizz which he had to be careful when pronouncing. He thought of the sound made getting an electric shock as he saw on cartoons when addressing her as "Mizzzz" and woe betide anyone who mistakenly said "Miss Taylor" instead or "Mizzzz Taylor" as they would get the prim response 'I am a Mizz not a Miss, please address me properly'

All very confusing to Sam but the all-knowing Oliver explain that a Mizz is an old Miss that is past her sell-by date. Sam of course knew by then to take anything Oliver said with a pinch of salt yet the old Mizz Taylor did look a bit stale with that ancient puckered face of hers.

* * *

Sam prided himself on playing the board game Operation.

The game consisted of an "operating table", a stiff board which had a cartoon likeness of a patient laying supine with a red lightbulb for a nose on it.

There were several open cavities across the façade of it's body which contained tiny objects with comically names caricaturing to ailments such as a plastic apple in the throat area named Adam's apple, a butterfly on the belly (butterflies in the stomach), a slice of bread in a cavity below the cave of the butterfly (bread basket) and so on.

There was an elongated valley on the right leg which contained a small elastic band. Unlike the other pieces which were teeny tiny moulded plastic, the band would be stretched within the cavity (ankle bone connected to the knee bone) but it was since lost so this was ignored, untreated, and the corresponding card was since taken from the deck.

The gameplay depended on which cards you had been dealt corresponding to which object you had to remove with a pair of tweezers which was connected to the board via a wire. The board would emit a vibrating buzz lightening up the prostrate patient's red nose, courtesy of 4 double A batteries if it were not a precise extraction and the tweezers were to touch the edge of the cavity, basically a variation of the old wire loop game.

Sam's pride was that he never lost a game but his only ever opponent had been his dad and occasionally his granny, but she struggled operating the tweezers due to what she called her "old arthritic fingers." Sam since found out that "arthritic fingers" were not the same as "arithmetic fingers" when he was caught counting on his digits in math class by Miss Henderson then tried to justify his plight by telling her that he had arthritic fingers like his gran.

Rachel watched on as Sam turned up a card during his turn whilst playing his dad which instructed him to treat the patient's writers cramp by removing the white slither of plastic which imitated a pencil.

Sam's jaw taunted with concentration as he prepared to enter the patient's left wrist with the miniature pinchers. A successful outcome would net him $300 and place him in the lead after Dad's blotched attempt to treat water on the knee by extracting an itsy bitsy bucket. Sam took the plunge but was rewarded with an instant buzz as his tweezers made contact with the side of the recess and the patent indicated it's distress with a illuminating scarlet hooter on its face. 'Ugggg!' exclaimed Sam pulling back his hand which held the tweezers like a tailor drawing up the final stitch. 'No fair' Sam declared out loud. 'No luck!' Daniel rephrased as Sam inserted the card back under the deck.

'Too bad Sam, that's a difficult one, I always bug-out out on that one too' Daniel had been silently hoping Sam would be able to extract the pencil which was one of the easier shapes to pinch between the precise jaws of the tweezers but it was not to be, now Daniel maintained the lead so would have to lose the next few turns convincingly to allow Sam a chance to win.

Sam had a fierce competitiveness when it came to games, when he lost he would be grumpy but would be joyous when he was victorious. Daniel mostly allowed him to win as he liked the boost it seemed to give Sam. The odds were always in Daniel's favour when they played Operation together due to Sam's dyspraxia. The manoeuvres required to decant the prizes from their little chambers required precision but lack of eye to hand coordination was a symptom of Sam's condition which, however mild was still there.

Daniel initially bought the board-game without such consideration, he had a sentimentality with the game as he also once played it with his own father when he was a child but only later came the realisation that Sam would find it difficult. Yet still, he thought, there were benefits to be had inducting his Son's involvement practicing his fine motor skills, after all, his dyspraxia was mild and the treatment he was getting was more of a process-orientated approach   The therapist recommended to involve Sam with activities aimed at improving his general movement skills such as swimming.

Sam's dyspraxia could never be cured but he could learn to manage it and as slight as his diagnosis was it would not be much a handicap in his daily life.

The game progressed, Sam became the proud victor upon it's conclusion after which the watchful Rachel challenged Sam to another game, this time with her. She then asked Sam if it would be alright to ask him a few questions. Daniel took this as his cue to leave the room so as to allow the pair some privacy.

 Sam understood what was to happen He had been explained this prior from both his mum and dad separately. Especially from his mum who attempted to "assist" Sam in preparation by coaching him with which answers he should give for what questions she thought the Bar Reporter would ask.

Sam had already decided he would not follow Mom's ploy and only tell the truth even before Rachel had explained to him that anything he told her would be confidential.

Sam was later to find out this was not really true as his Mum found out all the answers he'd gave once Rachel had compiled her report and delivered it to the court, but at that point he believed what she had told him and was completely honest and truthful with her.

3

When Sam was born it was a traumatic and difficult experience for both his parents.

Daniel was a couple of days away from flying out with his then wife Lilian to Brazil, it was a much needed break for them both which he hoped would ease the arguing which was becoming far too common between them.

Lilian would be around twenty-seven weeks pregnant on the date of their anticipated departure although she did not have much of a visible baby bulge to show that she had reached the final week of her second trimester.

The required letter of health had been duly obtained from their GP as no problems had been anticipated but then, the day before they were due to fly out, Daniel took Lilian for a scheduled prenatal checkup and the nurse became very concerned with Lilian's blood pressure. Normally Lilian's blood pressure would register lower than average in the scale but this time it was extremely high.

The nurse requested for the doctor to come and take a look. It was decided upon his conclusion that she was suffering from a condition called preeclampsia and needed to be admitted to the hospital posthaste.

Lilian was accommodated in a single room in the maternity wing of the hospital. There Daniel would stay at her side for the duration of her admittance.

As she lay on the bed Daniel sat on a chair at her side, a much similar chair to that which was in store for him a decade later in future whilst awaiting the departure of this mother.

Lilian's blood pressure continued to slowly rise. Not enough blood was being feed through the arteries to the placenta so the unborn baby in her womb was receiving an inadequate blood flow which meant not enough oxygen and nutrients was getting through to the foetus. The unborn child was dying.

A nurse would come in every hour to take Lilian's blood pressure and then held the receiving end of a stethoscope to her belly to listen for the faint heartbeat of the baby. Its throb was getting weaker, an unborn Sam was dying within his failing cocoon.

The doctor decided to continue monitoring Lilian's condition. He spoke out as to what the plan was to be, once the baby had succumbed, it would then be induced as a still birth. This was said to be the only sure cure to her preeclampsia.

Lilian was very scared, understandably so as she continued to hear the hourly readings of her blood pressure which was only ascending.

She started to complain that the doctors were not doing enough, that they should abort the baby to save her and they were only using her as an experiment.

They calmly explained to her that there would be no guarantee that the dose they would have to administer to abort the baby would be delivered to the foetus through the placenta walls due to her condition so they could not carry out a chemical induced abortion.

With each visit, after monitoring and listening, the nurse would declare that the strum of the little unborn's heart was getting weaker. The announcements were delivered with practiced compassion.

'It won't be long now' the nurse would say, normally a strange solace to give but the couple were resigned to the fate of what was to be. The agony was in the waiting now, the lamenting of the impending miscarriage would need to placed on the back burner to attend to the suffering of the present condition. They both wanted it just to be over and for Lilian to get better, after that they could grieve for their stillborn and the hopes which would die with him.

Giving up all hope of being a father, at least for the time being, had been a struggle for Daniel to accept those past hours. The optimism of hope is always hard to give up and with each Doctor's visit he was asking if there was the slightest chance, but the replies always came in the negative, often served up with condolences. It was said that they were a young couple and there will be other chances in the future, but something nagged on Daniel's most deep inner thoughts that this would never be the case, that this would be their only chance at being parents.

Their prospective future baby's bedroom had already been made ready back home. An eagerness of labour done within the first trimester, a cardinal sin so early tempting fate some may have said, and proven correctly with the scenario which was playing out then during that very moment.

Flat packed cot and dresser had been built up, stood back from and admired. They had been just awaited the confirmation for the blue or the pink, but already some yellow frames were around the walls which within hung pictures of cartoon farm animals in the interim.

"Yes: I am a dreamer. For a dreamer is one who can only find his way by moonlight, and his punishment is that he sees the dawn before the rest of the world." Oscar Wilde once said that and Daniel could see this bleak dawn approaching.

He looked at the bed beside him as he sat., looked upon his wife as she lay, thankfully eyes closed and resting. This was the another dream, a happy joyful marriage which he had wished for as he had witnessed such between his parents but as each prior week passed, this nirvana of ambition seemed further from his grasp.

He had hoped, like so many before him, that a baby would sooth temperaments over, perhaps create bonds between man and wife which he felt were already scant and threadbare but more than this he yearned so much to be a father, it was a desire within him.

Now he anticipated a winter when there should have been a spring, a frost again when he was hoping for a new beginning, how fickle life can be.

Passive hope some call it. It takes courage to be an optimist in this life and a great deal of conviction to have any hope, so how could it just be passive?

But now scepticism of his dare to dream was permeating through the walls of his heart, percolating a sadness within him, a disappointment of the world.

Schopenhauer was correct about hope making a fool of a man dancing him into the arms of death he thought.

In Pandora's box of evils was not hope also there?, the evil of hope! Why do we think it's a virtue? To think things may get better, but they won't.

So what's the choice in lieu of hoping? Is it planning and acting? Plan to get home and act by dismantling the dreams built up from Ikea flat packs. Such was the bleakness of his thoughts then.

Yet it were not for hope some would say then the heart would break.

Perhaps not break but most certainly harden calcifying a barrier to the abstract romance of what could be found in the world.

Daniel at that point had forsaken hope. He'd stopped fighting against the current and allowed himself to be carried downstream by it, waiting for what would have been his much loved son or daughter to die within his wife's womb without him so much as setting eyes upon it's live form.

He left the room to make a phone call to his mother Annie, then would struggle through a call to his in-laws who were all on tether hooks awaiting an update on what was happening.

They, a pregnant Lilian and an expectant Daniel should have been approaching Brazil at this time, but here they were, in the maternity wing of a hospital awaiting a cold delivery.

After updating both parties, one with the help of a bilingual sister to translate, which in reality made a difficult phone call all that more difficult, Daniel had returned to Lilian's room and found that hope had not forsaken him as he had thought as there, perched on the side of Lilian's bed with slim fingers pressing and probing her belly was hope.

This revived hope had a name which was Dr Holmes, a young man wearing Lennon styled glasses who Lilian had mistaken as another medical student come to get material for their portfolio. Daniel was soon to dissipate this mistaken identity once he had left the room when he inquired more about the doctor with a nurse.

'Dr Holmes is a visiting obstetrician and Gynaecologist.' she proclaimed rather proudly laughing off Lilian's observation that he looks like just another student jabbing her in the belly and taking notes.

'All of the doctors have been holding a conference call this morning and Dr Holmes wanted to come across from Edinburgh and have a look himself at Lilian to see if there is anything he could do.'

When Daniel had entered the room, returning after the calls he had to make, Dr Holmes had been examining Lilian's much inconspicuous baby bump. He had been taking fundal measurements using his pianist like long fingers as if a compass then narrating his finding to lab coated assistant. His confidence certainly marked him out from prior visitors Daniel had thought at the time.

Dr Holmes looked up at Daniel when he'd entered his wife's room and asked if he was the father, a title which felt strange for Daniel to hear. 'Yes' he had replied in the affirmative. This heaven sent man then said ten words which would stay with Daniel forever.

'Let's see if we can try and deliver this baby'

Dr Holmes explained that they would have to be fast, the baby was being starved of oxygen and time was essential.

Daniel listened intently, the nurses, who just a short while ago were awaiting a death, were now engaged with saving a life, an unborn life, he would feel the tempo change.

'It will need to be an emergency Cesarean. I will do an ultrasound firstly myself to see the lay of the baby. Next I intend to give an injection of steroids through the uterus wall, try to hasten some lung development to give this kid a fighting chance once he is out.' Dr Holmes listed out his plans.

'Nurse, can we get Mrs Sinclair to the Ultrasound now, we need this ASAP. Also page the anaesthetist and get a surgical room prepared' he commanded with purposeful resolve, 'Come on everyone, chop chop' he added rather briskly with the tone of someone used to being in control.

This change of pace made Daniel's head spin. Lilian on the bed looked scared and confused.

Just some minutes ago Daniel had been on the phone letting down prospective grandparents by saying that this was a done deal, that there was no chance of this child being born and now a hope was bubbling up inside him again, could he dare let this hope rise up within him?

From Adagio for strings straight into Vivaldi's Spring, that was how the transition of his emotions felt. Shock, despair, hopelessness then acceptance and now he was thrown a lifeline of hope again. He felt like crying, not from sadness but from the stress.

In his head he prayed. He prayed to a god which he did not believe in. It's true, there are no atheists in foxholes and here he was, the petitioner petitioning for this favour. Pascal's wager on the possibility, every bit of assistance asked for.

Daniel followed the porter wheeling Lilian along the corridor as she lay on the hospital bed and then into the ultrasound suite with the nurse pacing along beside them.

Inside the room Dr Holmes was already there seated by a large white machine looking at a screen whilst fidgeting with buttons and dials. There was to be no sonographer present as the doctor preferred to do the ultrasound himself to gleam exactly the positioning of the unborn child.

Daniel had already attended an ultrasound with Lilian around the twelve week point of her pregnancy during an antenatal appointment.

He had carried a copy of the resulting photo, although it looked more like an Rorschach inkblot than the makings of a child still he paraded it in front everyone he knew with the pride only a prospective father could muster.

'There is the wee head and there you can see the curvature of the back' Daniel would point out repeating what the sonographer had told Lilian and him, but exaggerating a little on uncorroborated parts with his wishfulness to believe.

'His wee button nose!', 'his tiny praying hands!'   Daniel would point out such perceived configurations but still unaware of the gender which could not be determined yet during the actual ultra-sounding. To the ensnared audience the grainy monochrome snap had as much features as a bean but they all agreed with Daniel's anatomic outlines, as to dampen such an enthusiasm would seem too cruel.

Although the anatomical points on the dark image may have be questionable, what was obviously crystal clear was that the expecting father was ecstatic!

Also discerned from the twelve week scan, it was determined that the baby was growing much slower than expected.   Yet still not too much to worry they were told.   The position of the baby and the placenta was all as to be expected, the chances were once he was born he would have a light birth weight unless some growth spurts were to happen over the coming months.   Good chance it would, so the prospective parents weren't too concerned, all still felt as if everything would turn out alright.

Daniel himself had been a four pounder, this little one would be much the same he had thought, but he or she would soon get big and strong just like his daddy, nature always catches up.

Such Panglossian naivety of the gentleness of nature! Only Ouranos could have taken for granted his consort Gaia more than such was the faith Daniel had that there would be no problems.

So here they were, Daniel and Lilian, almost sixteen weeks later from when the first scan was taken and about to get their second, this time without the quintessential joy of expectant parents curious about the journey, now with fear and perturbance. The bun was not ready to come out the oven yet, but if it stayed in then it would starve and suffocate.

Lilian laying on the wheeled bed was pushed up close to the ultrasound machine with Dr Holmes sitting between her and it's moulded plastic exterior. The equipment had a IBM looking screen with a keyboard and a computer mouse on the shelf under it.

Dr Holmes had applied a clear gel to the obstetric transducer head and held against the slight bump on Lilian's bared belly whilst applying a gentle pressure.

Daniel starred at the dexterity of the doctors hands as he worked. They were nimble and skilled as one moved the probe and the other controlled the computer mouse clicking at different points capturing images. The way the fingers were operating the mouse somehow reminded Daniel of the back legs of a grasshopper, the controlled fashion of how the joints folded in then out.

Daniel looked as the inverted black and white fan space on the display screen. He could pick out from the lines the shape of a small human curled with tiny toes on the end of little feet. That was his child which he was looking at he thought to himself.

He could see solid tissues such as the bones and the skull as they appeared white due to their surfaces reflecting more sound. The amniotic fluid which surrounded it was darker.

The doctor appeared to have gotten all the details he required and lifted the probe wiping the surface with a paper towel as the assisting nurse who was present wiped the residue gel from the patients belly.

'Prep Mrs Sinclair for surgery immediately!' he addressed to the nurse then set his gaze down at Lillian and said 'I can see the baby is in distress so we need to get this done now and immediately. The nurse here will now take you into the surgery suite and the anaesthetist will have a little discussion with you before giving you an epidural.'

Lilian looked wide eyed in fear, 'Nothing to worry about Mrs Sinclair, you are in good hands.' Dr Holmes said catching the look on her face.

'Mr Sinclair,' addressing Daniel now, 'we will get you kitted out in some scrubs so you can come in too and be with your wife.'

It's really is going to happen, thought Daniel, and felt a panic in his chest, it really is!

Lilian was lying on the surgical table when Daniel was shown into the room. He was then instructed to sit close to where Lilian's head lay.

Just beyond her stomach was a surgical tent, a hospital green coloured drape to restrict the view of the patient, and her partner to what was happening beyond.

Along side to where Daniel was seated was the anaesthetist, he was hovering around looking at a screen positioned behind Lilian's head.

The surgery room was not as Daniel expected, it was not this dazzling white tiled sanctuary brightly lit like an exotic aquarium with screens mounted on peripheral with dancing green beads being monitored constantly.

The room had a more work space look about it. Linoleum flooring instead of tiles, much the shade of orange peel and a radio was playing out a music station. The overhead lights made the room very bright but not sparklingly so.

Daniel tried to comfort his wife, he could see her fear.

He was wearing the surgical scrubs that had been handed to him, instructed to place over them over his normal clothes, the same hospital green colour of the shielding wind breaker dividing her body on the table.

The trousers laced at the waist, his arms bare and dust covers bagged over his shoes.

The cap he wore was blue, a light blue scrub cap which he bungled with trying to tie at the back surprised to find his hands shaking with nerves.

Ears in or ears out he had wondered banally as if trying to draw his attention onto the simple choices instead of the reality which was about to pour in.

He chose the former, ears tucked in, but the bow became untied.

As he sat there beside Lilian, fidgeting and struggling to refasten the ties behind his head he was so very grateful when the anaesthetist stepped behind him and fixed the fastenings with professional competence.

Daniel thanked him. He had forgot his name already, they had been briefly introduced outside but nothing would anchor in Daniel's mind, his thoughts and emotions were spinning like a whirligig in his head.

'Can you feel anything below?' Daniel asked his wife.

'No, I just feel cold, I can't feel anything.' she answered relaying the effects of the epidural injection.

'All is going to be fine.' Daniel said somewhat redundantly, he just felt he had to say something He wanted to give her some comfort, the worry on her face concerned him The past months of arguments were all forgiven and forgotten at that moment, this was to be their fresh start, let bygones be bygones, this was his wife lying here about to give birth to their child, what could be a more quintessential moment of a couple's life than this?   Here we are, going through this moment, sharing it all together. Things had to work out after this. The forge of this bond could not be denied he thought.

Doctor Holmes came around the green shield and asked Lilian how she was doing, she repeated to him that she was cold.

Holmes said they were ready to start now and that she'd feel a little tugging.

There was activity happening now beyond the buffer of the green canvas wall. Daniel held Lilian's hand and gently repeated into her ear that she was doing great and that all was going to be fine.

It was all very surreal and not how he had imagined the birth of his child.

The radio was yakking out its tunes. Robbie Williams was singing Millennium Daniel's ears registered, "We've got stars directing our fate, 'Cause we know we're falling from grace."

Lilian was getting heaved and jolted where she lay, there was certainly much pulling going on.

Daniel repeated his chant that all was fine, all is ok He was trying to convince himself as much as her.

Lilian looked up at the anaesthetist, 'tell them not to pull so hard'

'They need to be a little bit physical down there.' the anaesthetist with the forgotten name excused, 'It won't be much longer, almost there.'

'Oi, Oi, Nossa, Oi, Meu Deus!' Lilian exclaimed as the tugging intensified and she slid a couple of inches down the table, Daniel, holding her hand, fought against the instinct to haul her back up.

Then it abruptly ceased.

Robbie sang on but a curious noise accompanied him which pricked up Daniel's ears. The sound of a very small bird chirping. He immediately looked around the room, but how could a bird get in here he thought to himself? Through an open window? But he saw none, but the slight warbling continued then was the drowned out by nurses voices beyond the green sheet as more activity was afoot.

It was only later when Daniel thought back on that bitsy birdsong and was to realise that this was the first cries of his newly born baby boy.

He could hear the nurses sound out a count.   '1,2,3,4,5.' then again,'1,2,3,4,5.' then again to be repeated twice more. By the third occurrence it had dawned on Daniel that they were counting out loud fingers and toe. As he realised he then followed the count during the last sequence with bated breath. It came in with another tally of five he was soothed to hear.

The anaesthetist patted Lilian on the shoulder declaring she had done a great job then congratulated Daniel with a manly shake of his hand.

'Is it a boy or a girl?' he asked the new father.

'I don't know.' answered Daniel with a dizzy smile glued onto his face, his mind felt disconnected from the surroundings, his heads swam somewhere in the clouds.

The anaesthetist said he would ask. Dr Holmes appeared around the shielding tent adding his congratulations on their new born son, then it was confirmed to be a little boy, a tiny little boy.

'He is extremely premature.' Holmes added, 'The nurses are going to get him ready and take him along to the neonatal unit, once they have settled him in they will let you know and then you can visit your son.'

Daniel continued to comfort his wife as the final touches were being done, both on her and their new born. The nurses were busy preparing to lay the baby in the incubator which was to be his new home for the next weeks, a grow tent for that tiny small pink human.

'It's a wee boy, Lilian, we have a wee boy, a son! I am so proud of you, thank you, I love you, thank you so much, we have a son!' For what his words lack in coherence the emotions on his face made up for.

'Do you have a name for your son?' asked the anaesthetist.

'Yes we do.' answered Daniel proudly, 'Sam.'

The incubator on its trolly wheeled up level with Daniel and the recumbent Lilian so both could see its contents before the cargo's onward journey to the specialised neonatal ward.

Inside was a very small, very pink baby with a little blue knitted woollen beanie hat on his head. The tiny fisted hands on the end of pipe cleaner arms reached up in the air as if stretching for the heavens. This was their son, their tiny little premature baby boy.

Lilian, with her head angled to face her newborn son, reached out her one arm towards the glass of the incubator as it halted close to where she lay. She stretched as if she could touch him, an intrinsic longing to hold and to love but he was beyond her, behind that protective glass palisade.

The new mother's eyes were bright with the fervour of her love which shined though her rolling tears for her new born.

Daniel stared at the little figure inside the tank. He looked like a little bird which had fallen from its nest, bright red, almost claret in colour and with such fragility, crying and clawing for his place in the world.

Yet the wrinkled rosette face under that woollen hat looked like one of these weatherbeaten old men who sit by the harbour watching the boats come in with a pipe in their mouths.

There was animation in that little red face. The eyes closed briefly then reopened without any focus They were the darkest of black, as if ink pots, minute yet to develop orbs. It felt to Daniel that these tiniest dark eyes sucked in all that fell within their range with a gravitational pull, at that moment this included his heart, his complete and utter love which slid over their events horizon into that little flushed hatchling. A love so profoundly intense he could feel it radiate off his body and flow over to that little vulnerable baby.

There was also fear there as an emotion too that competed with that love for the right of way, a fear not only at the look of vulnerability in his fragile new son but also a feeling of vulnerability within himself too, now he had something in this world that he felt he would love until his last breath, it's was an unexplainable sensation that only a new parent could possibly feel.

'We will take this wee guy up to the natal ward and get him settled in. It will maybe take two or three hours then someone will come down and get you so you can come up and meet your son.' This was addressed to Daniel from the nurse.

It went without saying that Lilian's audience with her new son may take another day as she was already exhausted from the procedure.

As Sam was wheeled away Daniel grasped Lilian's hand again and held it tight, she was crying. With his other hand he wiped at her tears.

The waiting to see their new born son was a torture.

Daniel sat beside Lilian's bed in her room.

She was attached to a morphine drip, the opioid's relief in full wing. Just before Lilian dropped off into a deep sleep she was adamant she could hear a fly in the room with her. It was becoming an annoyance for her but Daniel could not hear anything. It was only later that Daniel heard the same sound which she had believed to be a fly as every so often the machine to which the IV drip was connected to would emit a small whirl noise, this must have been the mosquito irritating her before the drowse of the poppy took hold.

Shortly before Lilian had crashed out one of the neonatal nurses dropped by to hand the new parents a polaroid snap of their son. Under the little Popeye beanie, still adorning his head was little preemie Sam. The date was written on the bottom white boarder of the polaroid and Sam's name and weigh, "861 grams" Less than two pounds thought Daniel, that was less than half the weight Daniel was when he was born and how his mum Annie would recall the story of her wee bag of sugar's birth. Now here was Sam, not even the weight of a bag of sugar.

When Lilian had stared at the photo, tears appeared again as she realised how small he was.

Words of comfort from Daniel felt inadequate, both being said and as received by his wife. It was almost a blessing when the ambiguous flea came onto the scene in Lilian's imagination, it gave her something else to think about under the medicating morphine before her eyes finally closed shop.

Despite all their marital problems, arguments and exchanges, at this moment Daniel could only feel a love for his wife, at that precise time he could not have loved her more. He felt filled with gratitude and dared to dream that the little bundle she'd brought into the world would bond them together and change their lives for the better, such false optimism, the cognitive bias of a new father looking over his exhausted wife who had just delivered life.

Daniel had still not told his mother and his in-laws about this new development. From his last call almost four hours ago they would still be holding the belief that Lilian and himself were awaiting the inevitable still birth to happen, awaiting death when now there was actual life but he knew the precariousness of where this new life sat. He did not want to call them just yet, explain how just a few hours ago they were awaiting a dead foetus but then now say they have a life, a grandchild, but then only to tell them to hold the line and awaiting further announcements. There still could be a death, the pale rider had not quite set off into the sunset yet. He needed to see his son first, as if his sight would confirm all.

He did not have to wait much longer.

A midwife tapped on the door before entering and informed Daniel, the only awake occupant of the room as Lilian was gently snoring, that neonatal had phoned down. Sam (He felt slightly strange hearing that name said, as if it were a validation of a life he helped create, which of course it was) had now settled in and Daniel could now go up and meet his son whenever he was ready.

Once the nurse relayed her message and left Daniel, he leaned over to the sleeping Lilian and kissed her on the cheek as gently as pollen carried by the wind creating not a stir.

He said to her sleeping form 'I am now going up to meet our son. I will tell Sam that you give him your very best and that you will be up to see him soon'

He was admitted into the neonatal ward by pressing a buzzer then announcing himself when prompted by a voice through the small metal box next to the door. 'Sam's dad come to see Sam.' The declaration flushing him with such instant gratification..."Sam's dad!"

The nurse who buzzed in his entrance met him by the door then asked him to wash his hands with soap and warm water following the instructions above the sink which covered all angles of this new ritual he would be following over the coming months prior and on conclusion of each and every visit.

The nurse, Sophia as she introduced herself, then guided Daniel to the incubator which contained his new son. It was right at the top of the ward next to the nurses station, it was explained to him that this was due to Sam needing the most attention.

Daniel was then also told in a solemn voice then that Sam was what they termed as extremely premature. He was born at twenty eight weeks with approximately twenty five weeks growth.

The little neonate was on a ventilator, it was very concerning to see but it was common for premature babies Sophia would explain, as their tiny lungs haven't developed at the stage to be able to take in enough oxygen by themselves. The lungs need a substance called surfactant which is required to keep the air sacs open but Sam is still too premature to have this developed yet so needs a little help with his breathing.

Sophia then stepped across to Sam's incubator were Daniel followed with careful tread as if in a shop full of china. He then peered through the glass as if he was about to inspect an exotic reptilian species within a pet shop.

There was little Sam, laying on his back on to of an opened nappy, the smallest one they had yet still it would not fit him Sophia explained.

His right arm was attached to a tiny padded splint, this was to secure a PICC line which was inserted into his arm for intravenous fluids to be given. A feeding tube was in his nostril and a thin urinary catheter in through his urethra and up into his bladder.

Looking so red and exposed lying there on the heated pad within the glass incubator, a vulnerable little figure.

He still wore the little blue woollen beanie on his head to minimise heat loss.

His skin appeared tightly stretched over his little torso, not the tiniest gram of fat was to be seen. He was smooth and shiny with tracing paper skin looking so fragile, little blue veins appearing through its transparency.

The ventilator looked larger than Daniel had imagined it. The loomed upon a stand at the top of the incubator, it's thick blue tube like an anaconda entering through the portal at the top of the glass tank then tapered off at Sam's mouth where there, at the mouth section, it was held in place on his tiny face with what looked like a thick foam sticking plaster. The plaster on that little face seemed like a grawlix covering up a cuss emitting from the mouth of a comic strip character.

With every breath that the ventilator forced into his lungs Daniel would watch the teeny chest expand like a small red wine stained balloon then it would collapse once the breath was to expel. In, then out, the worlds smallest bellows.

Oxygen saturation and heart beat were all being measured on a screen above the incubator, just like the other 7 which accompanied their incubated babies in the room, it looking like some sort of weird and wonderful hatchery.

Sophia asked Daniel if he would like to touch his son. A wave of uneasiness surged through Daniel at this suggestion.

'Don't be scared to touch him, he won't break!' Sophia said seeing the look of apprehension develop across his features.

'Just put one hand on the top of his head and stroke his arm with your other hand. Watch, I will show you how it's done.' Sophia opened both small port like windows on the incubator and placed both arms in. One hand cupped the top of the wool hat which Sam's head was contained in and with the other hand she caressed his left arm gently. Daniel watched with great interest.

She removed her arms careful then told him 'Your turn.'

With great care and attentiveness Daniel entered both his arms through the portholes.

With one hand he clad the top of where Sam's head was its the wooly hat with his palm then with his other hand he started delicately stroking Sam's arm similar to the nurses motions. The baby's skin felt soft and warm to his touch.

Sam's arm flinched, Daniel froze his caressing touch. The father's hand paused, then the little pink hand reached up and grabbed Daniel's finger holding it in his tiny grasp. Daniel's heart melted.

'Awww look at that.' Sophia said, 'He's shaking your hand! Say hello to Daddy Sam.'

Daniel was just mesmerised, the pressure of the teensy finger's clasp was almost imperceptible to Daniel but in his heart it held so firm, no touch he'd ever felt before meant so much.

This was his son holding him, gripping on to his finger. Daniel spoke his first words to his son that very moment, 'Hello Sam, I'm your daddy'.

Something changed in Daniel then and his life was never to be the same again.

4

Annie was the widow of the late Samuel, she was the mother of late James and her remaining son Daniel. She was also the loving grandmother of Sam, a lineage of descendants which were to be obliterated cruelly from her mind during the evolutionary timescale of her dementia.

At age eighty-four her life could not be considered as an abbreviated one now that she was in her final canto. When, soon, once after her final curtain was to be dropped, people would state with compassionate pathos that she had a good innings, as if a long life was the sign of great achievement measured like units on a dial. As a statement this was maybe true of some but the testament of her life spoke out of much more.

She had served her time and had experienced the fruit from most branches of the tree of life. The twines of her later years had sagged, weighed down by the death of her beloved husband Samuel and the resulting loneliness this had brought with it as she cloistered herself at home with her remembrances and photographs as a shrine to the past. But then she found a second wind once her grandchild was born.

With the blessed event of Sam's birth, although premature with precarious beginnings as it were for the little suckling, Annie felt she had purpose again and was determined to prove her worth like an old war horse armed with life's wisdom and experience, brought out for one last hurrah.

When the newly delivered Sam was plucked from his mother Lilian's belly he had been immediately whisked away from the operating room, cast off within a glass tank on top of a trolly wheeled out by a nurse for his short journey to the neonatal for the more specialised attention which he required.

After Daniel had first visited the neonatal ward to see his son close up for the first time, even touching him and receiving the tiny grasping hand around his finger, during when his then post-caesarean carved wife asleep in the arms of a god whose name was used to coin the titles of the opium based pain killers which at that moment drifted through her veins, Daniel used this time to phone the newly crowned grandparents about their new little premature grandchild, break the news that what was expected to be a still birth had now turned into an actual live birth via an emergency Caesarian and that they were new grandparents, at least for the moment.

Firstly connecting his call to his distant, both in miles and connection, in-laws who lived in São Paulo on the opposite side of the Atlantic, he then made the announcement to his mum, Annie.

During the dialog over the phone he heard his mother's voice take a matriarchal tone which he had not heard for many a year as she issued instructions commandingly for him to come and collect her in his car as she was getting her coat on, planning to come and see her new born grandchild with her own eyes.

Then in her mid-seventies, although her mind was still firing on all cylinders, her body was already infirm with arthritis, her joints gnarly and swollen.

Where her knees were already buckled from the corrosion of the osteoarthritis there was also the added stress from the extra weight she had accumulated from the years of stagnancy being closed off from the world like an anchorite since the death of her beloved Samuel, but still determined she was that she should be there to bare witness to her only grandchild.

Daniel had told her with a quiver in his voice over the telephone that the doctors advised the odds were stacked against Sam surviving through the night.

He was extremely premature the doctors had enunciated. Being a product of preeclampsia had resulted in a birth weight of less than two pounds, the equivalent of twenty- five weeks growth, snatched out the scalpel slit womb during the twenty-eighth week in a rush before the placenta gave up its hold on the uterine wall.

Annie knew that the situation she would attend may not be one for felicitations, still too early for such jubilation. Then if not to be present to meet her freshly extracted preterm grandchild, it would be to comfort her only remaining child and his wife in what would be their grief.

Annie had been born in the year Nineteen thirty, a time when Ramsay MacDonald served as Prime Minister and George the Fifth was on the throne.

She was the only child of Agnes and William Campbell.

Agnes, or Nessie as her kith and kin would fondly call Annie's mother worked in the local draperies in their hometown of Stirling.

As a preadolescent Annie would join her mammy on her return from school to help dress the pair of tailor's dummies in the shop's window and sweep up the offcuts of fabric from behind the cutting table, the larger pieces of which she would often collect to sew into the collection of rag dolls she owned which lined the walls of her bedroom back at home.

Annie's father, William Campbell had a more ruddy complexion than the blanched almond tones of his wife Agnes, which she herself had passed down to Annie. Willie liked a dram but it was his only vice and he preferred to partake within his home than with the rest of the lads down the welfare club after work.

His "wee libation for a long life" was after dinner each night whilst catching up with the news on the radio and it never interfered with the quality time he spent with Agnes and Annie.

He had the respectable employment of working as the head engineer for the local coal colliery. There most of his time was spent above the ground rather than beneath it much to the relief of Agnes but she still puzzled over the days he returned home with soot stained black hands which only a scrubbing of olive oil and sugar would eventually restore back to flesh tone. 'Still like to get my hands dirty my love.' he would say 'and not always polish the seat with my arse.'

Willie wore a gold pocket Sportsman watch with the chain on display dipping in a loop at the side of his waistcoat.

The watch face itself would only see sunlight twice during his working day, once in the afternoon when he poached it out from within his pocket flipping the lid open wondering if Annie would be wandering home from her school yet and again with almost supernaturally precision exactly 10 minutes from the horn which would blast signalling the end of another days shift.

The watch was not as much of a status symbol but to be more of part of his attire as was the the white linen shirts he wore under the waistcoat, billowing cotton upper arms with sleeves rolled up displaying meaty freckled forearms coursed with red hair, almost displayed as a badge that would proclaim that the owner had not always been behind a desk and could get stuck in the best of them.

In the opposite pocket to which the head of his Sportsman's watch had been bedded was a small pocket sized bible, a possession given to him from his own father. Willie had carried that small book of scriptures during his time in the trenches of the Somme, a time which he'd rather not recount in his mind and certainly not talk about to either Agnes or Annie, 'times best forgotten' he would only say.

After leaving school at 15 Annie told her parents that instead of following Agnes's footsteps and working at the drapers, a position that was to be hers should she desire, she declared that she wanted to take up nursing, perhaps the attentive needlework with thread on the rag dolls was going to be put to a more practical roll and there was no denying Annie had a tender caring nature which Agnes's friends would comment upon when they came around for tea and cake as a young Annie would sit close to her mammy tending to rips and evisceration of her dollies after Spring, their Springer Spaniel had got his teeth into them, a common occurrence attested to by the mismatched patches woven into many of the dolls.

Agnes loved to have her friends around the house for afternoon tea and was always the most graceful host.

After church on a Sunday morning Willie usually would potter out the back garden or in the shed and outhouse twiddling with this or that, messing around with "that damned jalopy of his" as Agnes called his car, but it did give her some peace and quiet to do some baking before having her familiars around to sample her wares. Victoria Sponge was her speciality.

The rationing would all too soon take it toil on her recipes if it were not for the little soon to be cooperative arranged with her tea party guests who each would bring some sugar and butter with them to replenish Agnes's stock which she would depleted for that afternoon's baked delight. It would be a good deal as they'd leave with a couple of fresh eggs apiece from the hens which the Campbells kept out back.

The good bone china with its blue willowed pattern would be laid out on the table, a heirloom from Agnes' mother, since passed away some years ago shortly after her father.

Agnes was told that Queen Victoria once drunk some Earl Grey from a saucer and cup in the set when her majesty had visited the pottery where Agnes' mother had then worked. Which one of cups and saucers Agnes did not know but there were six set places so the four ladies visiting were sure to partake from the same china which touched the royal lips by the odds of rotation during one of their many visits surely. Unless it was the china cup with a chip in its rim which Agnes, ever the considerate host, would keep to herself. Although every time when the local parish minister would come to visit and discuss church business with her Willie, who was an Elder of the church, he was always served, with a little fanfare, the exact cup Queen Victoria puckered up to!

'Strange that, ain't it Nessie?' Willie would often teasingly ask afterwards 'Does a divine light shine through our kitchen window before you serve him Nessie so you can discern which exact cup and saucer did the monarch drink from?...and if that's the case could another miracle be too much to pray for that a wee measure of the Grouse of great fame should find its way into my own cuppa during the times when himself the good Rev comes around?' Agnes would illicit a suppressed giggle when Willie would jive her with such good natured fun.

Agnes would reply in kind 'if I am to find that a nip of whisky touched the porcelain of my good china then it will no be the work of the good Lord but the mischief of the cloven footed one at play and it's likely to be afterward a baking tray with the imprint of your head on it Willie Campbell! Mysterious ways indeed!'

Such good humoured teasing was common is their marriage and loved flowed in aces setting an example which imprinted upon a young Annie and became a blueprint to what she wanted later in life with her own marriage to Samuel.

Annie's house was a short drive from the hospital. Daniel had arrived at the curb directly outside within less than twenty minutes and found his mother dressed in a long buttoned down woollen coat seated on a migrated dining room chair deployed a few steps back from the open front door looking out to the road, both hands clutching a handbag on her knees as if awaiting a bus.

Upon seeing the car pull up Annie unsteadily raised herself and started to lumber out the door pulling it closed behind her without so much as a backward glance to tug at the handle ensuring the catch had caught the lock securing it.

Daniel got out and opened the passenger door of the car taking

Annie by the arm as he helped his mother into the waiting carriage.

There was a determination to Annie which Daniel had not witnessed before in his mother, at least not for a long time.

She'd always had a calmness, a sereneness he felt that surrounded her since his father's death, an acceptance, as if she was patiently awaiting her own passage of time to wind down but now she had an urgency about her, a focus.

Just before driving away he handed her the polaroid picture the nurse had gave him of his newly born son lying on his back on a small heated pad in an incubator, looking like a tiny pink doll wearing his little blue knitted wool cap, wires and tubes radiating from his small form like a discarded marionette doll.

The only thing more distressing on the polaroid image than the thick blue tube of the ventilator with its connection held in place by the white tape as it sprouted from that diminutive mouth was the writing on the white bottom boarder of the polaroid in blue biro which simply stated the date then "Sam Sinclair 861 grams." That metric measure of live weight dragged heavier on the heart than the units it had read.

As he pulled away from the curb Daniel noticed Annie trace the image with her finger as if inspecting the grain of a wood whispering gently 'Hello wee one.', but then he redirected his eyes to the road in front with an uneasiness that if he were to look to his mother's profile in the passenger seat again there would be tears running down her cheek.

He did not say anything in reply to the words he had overheard as his own voice would betray the presence of the wet beads which were forming in his own eye ducts that very moment.

5

Daniel had been first made aware of his mother's comatose state when he had received the phone call whilst at his work. It was from Shelly, the nurse in charge of the Argyll Ward which was within the complex of the nursing home where Annie was a resident.

As soon as Daniel saw that it was the nursing home calling him from the display on his mobile he stood up from his work desk in the office and briskly walked to the quieter oasis at the back of the open work areas away from the disturbance of clicking keyboards and phone chatter.

'Hi Daniel, it's Shelly here from Carron Village, it's about Mum, she is not doing too great, she is not conscious this morning. We've had the Doctor come take a look at her and he thinks she will not be waking up.'

Daniel had always thought it amusing how the nurses at the nursing home referred to his mother as "Mum" when they discussed Annie with him, it sounded she was their mother too, as if it were a sister he was talking to about their mother. He could understand the kindness that such a familiarity was meant to convey, a charity of consideration suggesting that the subject in question was more than just a ward for the nurses to care for.

'How long does she have?' Daniel asked instantly regretting the question as it left his lips, it sounded so clichéd, a rubber stamped reply to being told that his mother was going to die.

'I'm sorry Daniel but there is no way we can tell. Annie may have a few hours or she may hang on for some days.'

Daniel felt grateful that Shelly replied using Annie that time instead of Mum such was the banality of thoughts going through his head whilst processing this information.

'I understand, thank you. I will be there within the next hour for so.'

As brief as that the message was relayed, received and acknowledged.

Daniel had held his now silent phone down by his side. Turning he looked along the field of the open plan office.

Everyone was working away wrapped in their own tasks, embroiled in their work.

He lifted his phone to look at the time, it was not yet midday. He had hours before his working day was due to end.

A weirdness occurred in his thoughts to which he was conscious of even as it was being considered, a desperation for a return to normality after the news which he'd just received. He thought about his work and finishing his shift before leaving. As if he could just walk back to his desk, back amongst his colleagues and carry on as if he never received the call, then switch back to the situation after he finished to then head off towards the nursing home and tend his dying mother.

The only difference to other visits being that she would be unconscious when he arrived and not sitting there by her bed where she would talk, if he was lucky, reservedly to the stranger that her son was to her now. A stranger not from absence as he visited her almost everyday, but now an alien to her caused by the data dumping of her mind.

Such thoughts of staying on in the office soon dissolved as an option, He knew only too well that he would suffer such a guilt if he were not there and she were to pass away, her soul leaving her body as he was sitting at his desk working the system to resolve telecom faults of anonymous clients.

Walking back down towards his desk he stopped by his manager and explained the situation.

'Of course!' was his manager's reply.

'Just log out and leave Daniel. Keep me updated on how everything is. If you need more time off it's not a problem, we will get you some cover, anything just call me.'

Daniel was grateful of such simpleness to breeze out of the office without fuss or premature condolences.

He briefly said to the others in the team around his desk that he was going to take the afternoon off and had OK'd it with the manager.

No sympathies needed to be shed as no questions were asked,

everyone were too tied up with their work to let out more than a "no worries!" or a "catch you tomorrow." as Daniel did not elaborate where he was going, he just logged out of the PC which he had been stationed at, grabbed his coat from behind the chair and muttered a "see you the 'morrow.'" as he departed for the stairs then out to his parked car.

Daniel had been working for the telecoms company for over 20 years and driving the same motorway from the Edinburgh office were he was based, to his home in Falkirk, it was almost by autopilot.

Being a Thursday, still early in the afternoon the traffic flowed without delay and he made Falkirk within just over half an hour driving within the speed limits, but his head had been racing.

Would this be it? Was it possible that she would not wake up? He found it hard to believe that Annie would die yet he had saw how she was deteriorating almost incrementally on each of his recent daily visits after work but still he somehow always thought his mother as being perpetual in his life.

He was no stranger to losing loved ones having laid his dad and brother to rest, and presently his son had been absent for the last 2 years from his life. Such was the absenteeism which had been forced upon him it felt to be a suffering which he could only describe as a type of mourning, yet it could never be considered under the same banner as a death such was the optimism of his hope to see his child again, a certitude that there must be some fairness, a justice to be had but this had been waning all the more as time passed.

He tried to think of the last words he would have said to his mother just yesterday when he departed after visiting her in her room. Something so simple as "see you tomorrow mum.", not the final epilogue he would have liked to have left but such emotional valedictions like in movies rarely happen in real life.

Annie did look more run down than her usual form yesterday, perhaps "run down" was the wrong description and instead "unfocused" would have been more accurate.

On the Wednesday evening, the night before when he'd last visited his mum, Annie was in bed, sitting upright with her back propped by the pillows. She was running her fingers along the top of the bedsheet which came up just above her waist. As if inspecting the stitching, folding the top of the sheet outward for making an edge of a couple of centimetres then working along the ridge repeating the movement back again once having crossed so far with a look of childlike concentration on her face.

Then she would stop and silently entertain herself by tracing her fingers down the boundary edge of the sheet. She would only smile when Daniel talked to her, she was totally immersed in her work.

Daniel no longer held any shock visiting Annie and seeing such behaviour. There were good days and bad but the bad days had started to outshine the good these past months.

In the beginning when Annie first was moved to the nursing home she displayed more cognition, an awareness of her surroundings. She accepted this was to be her new home and would often be sitting in the resident's lounge of the Argyll ward. Daniel would find her there on his daily visits after his work. Annie sitting on one of the straight backed lounge chairs with a blanket over her knees, cup of tea on the folding table in front.

She would be focused on the TV whilst exchanging comments with the occupier of the neighbouring chair.

Annie appeared to have carved out her very own spot in the semi-circle of eight chairs facing the screen and appeared social to both the ladies which sat neighbouring either side of her who also greeted Daniel during his visits.

Daniel kept his visits short during these early days, just a brief appearance to exchange some pleasantries with his mother who appeared as pleased as punch to see him, during then he also would give some clipped greetings to the other occupants that sat around her.

When Daniel would enter the ward on the first floor, through the secured door of the wing, the lounge would be immediately on his right and a quick glance would tell him if Annie was stationed on her usual piece of turf or if the seat was bare and then if so he would continue along the corridor to her room to find her there.

As the weeks passed it was getting more and more common to find her in the solitude of her room rather than with the company she could find in the lounge.

After a couple of months she predominantly was to be found in her room watching her smaller TV from the chair by her bed.

Annie, when still with slivers of her mind intact, would often ask him when Sam would be coming with him to visit? or She would ask 'is Sam not with you today?' Such questions told Daniel that his mother had forgotten that Lilian had since restricted his access to his son to absolute zero.

To avoid any distress to Annie he would simply answer 'he is busy with school work today but I will bring him tomorrow.' When tomorrow came Annie would have had forgotten asking before and her son's previous answer so would make the same inquiry again so the loop continued.

As time passed Annie stopped asking about Sam. Seemingly he was to be another character of her life scrubbed from her wasting mind, but then other questions were posed which stirred sadness within him at her condition.

She would ask 'Is your dad still alive?' to which Daniel would answer 'No Mum, Dad died almost 20 years ago.'

Annie would nod accepting the answer but Daniel could see the hurt in her eyes, the pain of a confirmation she had thought may be the case but needed confirmed.

Other questions raised would be her asking if her own parents were still alive. This particular line of inquiry stung Daniel even more as he'd never met his grandparents, both had passed on before he was born.

The worst was yet to come which was when Annie stopped recognising Daniel as her son and then for some reason thought him to be 'here's that guy from the council again' which she would announce to any nurses present when Daniel would make his entrance into her room.

'That's your son Annie!' the nurses would attempt to clear up for her, 'he's here to visit you.'

But this never sunk in, Annie never again recognised her son and at some point during this time Daniel felt a part of his mother die when the recognition given to a mother by a son was no longer reciprocal.

There was a silver lining that appeared one in a while when "that guy from the council," came to visit his mother. Annie would appear to be looking out clothes. Opening and closing drawer although not extracting any contents.

She would say to Daniel 'oh! It's you again. Well you can't stay long as I have a man who is coming to pick me up on his motorbike, he is taking me out to Dobbie's dance hall.'

Daniel immediately would perk up hearing this and recognising this as one of her "blessed moments" knowing she was reliving the courting days of when she first met his dad Samuel. He would then play along.

'When is he arriving Annie? Did he say a time?'

'Anytime now' she would reply 'and I told him to turn off the bike and push it up the drive as Daddy doesn't like the noise as it scares the chickens.'

'Is this a first date?'

'No, we went out last week and walked up Alva Glen with Spring.'

Daniel had knew that Spring was her spaniel's name when she was a young girl. 'I hope he was the Gentleman when he was up there all alone with you' Daniel said teasingly enjoying the moment.

He could have swore a blush rose to his mother's cheeks and the years dropped from her face.

'Of course he did, he always behaves!' Annie giggled like a young girl.

'Does he go fast with you on the back of that bike?' Daniel would continue the palaver with a smile knowing fine well what Annie would say next.

'It's got a sidecar attached, and he brings a blanket so it's all very snug.'

Daniel would continue the dialog as long as he could until Annie appeared to get tired, then she would sit on the chair by the bed, within seconds her chin would drop and she would nod off, tired out from the action and then the age would creep back on her face again.

Maybe in her dreams the story continued, the courtship and romance. Perhaps Alzheimer's took pity on its victims every now and again, gave a replay of a happy moment past during it's break from stealing everything.

On another occasion during visiting Annie as she lay in her bed she forthwith announced that she was 'having kittens!'

Daniel thought she was using the idiom that she was upset about something but when asking what the problem was Annie went on to tell him that she needed to find a box. She told him she had been looking after a cat she had found hiding in her father's garage only to discover that it was pregnant and about to give birth to a litter which explained Annie's urgency to find a box and keep the kittens which were about to be born together.

The mind is a strange machine and such was the behaviour of Annie's thoughts during the latter stages of her dementia.

This time upon his arrival at the nursing home, for what was about to be Daniel's final days with his mum, he was met by Shelly at the entrance of the ward who took him into her office first to explain the current situation.

'The doctor has been in to see Annie this morning and believes she will not regain consciousness.' She reiterate all which was said from the call earlier. 'She is comfortable so is not suffering in anyway but we do have a palliative care box locked away here in the office and can administer some morphine if Annie looks to be in any distress.'

It was a strange reality for Daniel to hear such words being said. "Palliative Care!","Distress!"

'If you need anything just ask any of the staff and they will get a nurse' continued Shelly.

Daniel took the briefing calmly although there was a numbness setting upon him.

Before arriving at the nursing home he first stopped at home to pick up a book which went unread for his duration there, a few toiletries all he stuck in a carrier bag and the charger for his mobile. Then another pitstop at the minimart which sat off the road directly across from the nursing home. There he bought some snacks and a newspaper, a large broadsheet, The Herald or The Times, he was not even sure which one he picked up, only that there was a mighty load of reading material within it.

Now that he was in the Argyll ward and fully informed of the situation he opened the door to his mother's room and stepped inside.

One of the nurses, Daniel could not remember her name, was sitting at the bedside of Annie. She pulled face back from Annie as he entered the room. He understood immediately that the close proximity was to check if Annie was still breathing.

'Hello Daniel.' she said, sympathy already etched on her features and within her tone.

Daniel done a quick take of the figure lying on the bed, at first he could not believe how much she had seemed to have aged since he'd saw her just the night before. One of her eyes were open and Daniel almost stumbled over the thought that she was awake.

'How's Annie doing Dianne?' came a voice from behind which almost startled him as he did not hear Shelly follow him into the room, yet he could not remember closing the door either, or even the steps he must have took after entering into the room. There was a certain surreality of the moment which he did not expect.

'Annie is still with us, she is breathing very shallow just now but every now and again she gives a wee start.' Dianne answered looking at Daniel with tenderness whilst answering Shelly.

'Mum's left eye has stayed open but she won't see anything Daniel, it's just like she is asleep, she is not aware of what is happening around her.'

'She may have taken a little seizure before she went out.' explained Shelly about Annie eye being open.

'But she is not feeling any pain' Dianne piped in to reassure, 'every now and again she is moving and letting out a wee grunt and sigh just like she is having a dream but she is not suffering.'

No Pain, No Suffering, Daniel locked onto these words, clung to them desperately as a drowning man would cleave drifting debris.

'As I said in the office, if she appears to be in any pain or if she goes into any convulsions just give any of the nurses or staff a shout and we will give her a little something to calm her down.'

'There are some oral swabs at the side of her bed there on the table...' Shelly explained as Dianne picked up one of the small orange sponges attached to a stick like a small lolly, dipping it in a clear plastic cup containing water next to where it had lay.

'Just give the sponge end a soak in the water and moisten Mum's lips every so often.'

As Shelly finished the sentence Dianne, doing her part of the double act, gently pressed the sponge onto Annie's lips whilst holding the slim white stick.

Daniel had thanked both nurses when they had since departed almost an hour ago and he'd then been left alone in the room with his mum.

It was getting later in the afternoon but the curtains were already shut not allowing any natural light in. The ceiling light was off leaving just the bedside lamp and the illumination from the open door of the ensuite to illuminate the room which gave it a tenebrous atmosphere.

Noises penetrated in from outside in the corridor beyond the closed door. Voices of staff, guests and visitors, the sound of a trolly being wheeled along and the rattle of crockery. The outside world felt a million miles away at that moment as Daniel felt encapsulated in a hermetically sealed room, just his mother and him whilst a pungent odour thickened the warm ventilated air.

He was seated at the side of a bed where Annie lay, the same seat that had been occupied before by the nursing assistant Dianne.

Annie's position where she lay inhumed on the bed had not

changed. There had been one episode so far since Daniel had been alone with his mum. A moment when she squirmed on the bed with a slight jerking motion accompanied by soft whimpering but thankfully brief. Through its passage Daniel held his mother's hand as he rocked up from the seat telling her that it was alright, that he was there beside her. There had been no visible signs to attest that she heard him but she was soon calm and silent again.

Daniel then had released her hand gently watching her face for the onset of any further irritation but there appeared none to follow, just that same phthisical cast with that one open eye destitute of vision.

He walked slowly with a loitering amble along the centre of the room towards the door then back again repeating the circuit a couple of time before returning to the side of the bed as if such motion could keep the sadness at bay, but it would not. He sat back down on the chair, his hand relaxing over Annie's hand keeping contact with it.

6

It had been over two years ago since Lilian first received the Initial Writ, served upon her at her doorstep by a formal looking man who introduced himself as a Sheriff's Officer whilst displaying an ID badge.

It did not come as a total surprise. Daniel had before then been threatening for a while that he would take her to court over his access to Sam unless she relented and allowed him to see his son.

She had since blocked his number from her phone and ignored his pleading text messages and begging emails.

Let the bastard suffer, he is not paying enough towards Sam she would think, but actually in reality what was more to the point, he not paying enough to her! 'Good-for-nothing shit!' she would say out loud often followed by 'Vão se foder ...fuck you!'

Daniel was paying for his son, but his crime, in her book, was that he no longer laying the cash onto her palm as he once had done, an ever increasing payment with more than was fair as often excess was extorted with her coercive threat of withholding Sam from him at the last minute when he'd arrive to collect him with prearranged plans.

Daniel, tired of the blackmail had decided to signed up with the Child Support Agency which, ran by the government, would act as an intermediary by debiting a predetermined percentage of his earned wage from his account each month then pay it directly into her bank account. Daniel's hope was that this clear cut method would be a settled matter, Lilian would get the amount of money officially deemed for her. No more shouting accusingly that he was making more money than he declared and that he was denying his son his proper maintenance share.

He hoped this would stop Lilian attempting to milk him for more when he arrived to collect Sam during when he would hand her the money each week.

Daniel always would be happily disburse extra on Sam directly by getting him clothes and toys whilst he was in his company instead of handing more to Lilian when she demanded that Sam needed new shoes or school blazer, although he never saw Sam wear the requisite apparel when he was to collect him from school or had him staying over.

This was Daniel's aspiration to make the payments more official through the CSA but Lilian was infuriated that the amount she started receiving was a lot less that what she prescribed him to tender into her forever grabbing hands.

The money now had been discounted even more as the CSA took into consideration the overnight stays which Sam had with his Father, she was furious, how dare he make them suffer she raged!

With the wage Daniel earned and further complimented by all the overtime he worked, the amount Lilian received was a hefty sum that in itself many would be happy with as a wage but not her, this was a deduction from her assumption of what she regarded she deserved. It was less than before when even then she would complain and clamour constantly for more or else penalise him by withdrawing Sam's contact.

Well, she had decided then, incentivised by the workings of the system which was open to the manipulation of the nefariously immoral, no more contact with his son for that bastard! Then she would be compensate more by the CSA who would collect extra money from him once she reduced the child's overnight stays with his father to nil! This would also give her the satisfaction of knowing he would suffer not seeing his son! 'Vão se foder Daniel!'

Daniel's relationship with his wife since their separation had grown to something which was beyond strained, in actuality if the "beyond" in this case could be measured in distance it would be in units of light years and "strained" could be described as the same tensity of that on the Titan Atlas's vertebras from holding up the Heavens such was the gulf of affection between them, such was the trivialisation of the description in their case of being "beyond strained".

Daniel often wondered if there had ever been a genuinely real affection between them. Years later clearing his head from emotions, as much as one could, he analysed his own feelings and felt it was possible he was more enamoured with the idea of marriage that he was in love with Lilian who he was espoused with. He was entranced by what he saw as the fairy tale of his parents marriage and desperately wanted similar.

For Lilian's part there would be no honeyed mythos to yearn for subconsciously or otherwise from what she witnessed from her own parents matrimony existence. Her own Mãe and Pai, Fatima and Mario argued fiercely and very frequent like the proverbial cat and dog.

Often, when it turned physical clouts were launched from her mother's clenched fists and if her father were to leave avoiding what was to be dished then soon her mother would find an excuse to vent out her frustrations on Lilian.

Hot temperaments flared more from the womenfolk side of the family, a trait which the migrating Lilian was to continue with her marriage to Daniel.

Marriage had also been an escape plan for Lilian, an escape from under the strict control of her mother driving her to want for a better life outside her native South America.

Europe or the States had been her preference, and meeting a Gringo and marrying him would be her vessel out.

Then at twenty six feeling even more the desperate pressure within her to wed and move out from her parents home, but the thought of marrying a local man did not appeal to her, she wanted more in life, opportunities again which had since closed to her in Brazil.

Lilian had been born in a large city called Osasco in the state of São Paulo and had spent all her life in Brazil before moving to the UK to stay in Scotland with Daniel.

She always aspired to more than what she had been dealt in life. Her parents were not considered poor for a Brazilian family, they would be regarded as middle class by occidental tenets.

The family lived in their own house, had a car and a respectable income in a country which had many cycles of difficulty with its economy over the previous decades.

Lilian's Mother, Fatima, worked as a chemist in a government run laboratory. Working in any government run position in Brazil on either end of the ladder was much desired due to the job security it provided in a country which was always on the edge of recessions mostly due to corruption in high office which had an effect on the confidence for much needed outside investment.

Her father Mario worked as a project manager on construction sites and, as the building trade was always hit first with the slightest whisper of a downturn, his earning ability was never dependable as a project could be put on ice at any moment due to a link in the chain struggling with costs, then his yield would be paused too and with no welfare to fall back on during such moments. So this instability and also the dry spells between projects would have to be relied upon by Fatima's earnings to pull in the slack.

Lilian had went to university to study. To begin with she had always dreamed about becoming a Doctor but found this flight of fancy was soon out of her academic proficiency. The markings she required to branch off into her second year she could not obtained so instead she dropped her sights by sliding down the medial caduceus to nursing, another noble profession with a job security but not as eminent, should she have succeeded, as a doctor's prefix would be on her moniker.

Almost at the end of her second year of studying at São Paulo's USP it came to her attention that the Civil Police were recruiting from the university student ranks for assistants to work within their forensic department as an autopsy assistant. It would entail working in the police mortuary with a group of other technicians assisting doctors by examining the bodies of demised crime victims. Lilian was not in the least squeamish about such things, in actual fact she very much had a curiosity of the inner workings of the physical body.

She was always right at the front and centre when the white sheet was drawn back whilst the Professor would instruct the class with practical lessons in anatomy using the teaching aid of one of the USP's cadavers to dissect. Federal law was soon to come into effect which would regulate the destination of legally unclaimed cadavers for educational and research purposes but before this happened Lilian had had a good innings of mining into the University's cache of formaldehyde penetrated dead tissues and sinews often being asked by the instructor to take the wheel by cutting into the meat to produce cold dead organs like pearls from the shell whilst he narrated he procedure to the class. Some students at the back feeling weak at the knees from the beheld glistening sights but Lilian just relished the work.

This was the sort of training artificial anatomical models or crisped plastinated pieces could never simulate and software development was still distant for that to be considered but soon the University would need to rely upon pathology materials from only donated sources which would reduce such opportunities so Lilian was determined to capitalise from every opportunity and the Professor applauded her assiduousness and skill with the scalpel, trephine and shears so he had no hesitation to be her referee on her application for the Polícia Civil as a forensic autopsy assistant.

The endorsement of an esteemed teaching professor of a renowned university on her submission turned the key and Lilian was successful with her application and got the post. She then quit the University and started her new training at Academia da Polícia Civil. Although she would be working in the police mortuary and not out and about, everyone who had employed with the Civil Police had to complete a basic police training course as she would, then upon completion, be part of the Scientific Technical Police of the State of São Paulo.

Once fully trained there was rarely a quiet moment working at police mortuary as the intake of cadavers was a constant train due to the homicide rate in São Paulo. Also the catchment area for the mortuary included many favelas where mortality from gangs and police shooting was myriad but Lilian took satisfaction in her work. She fitted in with her colleagues and soon found the adage that an necropsy was done with the head and not the heart was true, but the work was getting of a repetitive nature and it was not what she wanted to complete her life, she still felt destined for more.

Lilian still wanted to move from Brazil, get out from her parents house and try her life in another country. Using the family computer at home she discovered online dating and composed a personal ad placing it in the relevant category but the replies were disappointing, the usual masculine responses with some not even attempting to conceal their true intents to meet up.

She filtered down a search further afield narrowing it down to the United Kingdom foraging for an age group slightly older, professional and for someone looking for marriage.

The search was fruitful in volume, the pixelated photos of men gradually solidified from the then double digit kilobits per second transfer speed.

Plenty caught her eye so she then set about composing her introduction making a point that she would be willing to move if she found "the right one."

Her written introduction was then copied and pasted onto the message box of numerous profiles, small amendments to her composed paste, altered slightly to individual addressees to provide names or handles on her first line of greetings as not to seem too generic. The net was cast, the pots set onto the seabed. She would then leave it until the next day to check if any interest was caught but she was still concerned that the distance may put many off.

As Lilian in Brazil scoured the online personals in search of her escape, across the Atlantic in Scotland was Daniel.

He was approaching his thirtieth birthday then and coming home from his work to an empty apartment.

With his quiet nature he found the dating scene challenging. Far easier to break the ice using online dating than the more traditional methods of that time. So when a twenty-six years old mulatto woman from such an exotic country as Brazil had replied to his personals ad it piqued his curiosity and despite the distance parameters which he'd considered when he first wrote his profile, he got hooked and hoped that love, which is said to conquer all, would triumph over the logistics of the situation.

After a few months of messaging each other, then complimented with weekend phone calls, he bought his tickets and flew across to São Paulo for a ten days visit during which he was invited to stay in the spare bedroom of Lillian's family's home.

Daniel had not left the UK since he was twelve flying out to Canada which was with his parents so this was a big deal for him.

He arrived at São Paulo Guarulhos International Airport, which was situated in the municipality of Guarulhos, still over an hours drive from where Lilian lived with her family.

They'd arranged for her to met him in the arrivals area but there was no sign of her when he first arrived pulling his tilted suitcase behind him.

The arrivals area had been crowded. Leaflets promoting close by hotels written in English were being handed out and multiple times he was approached by taxi drivers touting for a fare.

He stepped over to the glass walls of the terminal and saw an alien world outside.

Rows of yellow cabs lined up long the road and at intervals tall landscaped carnauba palm trees stood along the airport boulevard with a searing sun above adding to the feeling of the distance he now felt being so far from the rain speckled airport of Edinburgh from where he had departed from just the day before.

He had touched down in Guarulhos early just as dawn was breaking shortly after six am which his time-adjusted wrist watch told him.

The flight was comfortable enough, he had an isle seat and once the lights dimmed somewhere over the Atlantic he did manage to close his eyes for a bit and get a little sleep although the excitement would not allow any quality rest even despite a couple of inflight movies with which, he had hoped, would take the edge of his adrenaline and settle him.

About over hour before landing the main lights came on and the flight started waking up and coming alive.

Queues started to form waiting to access the small onboard toilets and kids started darting up and down the aisles exercising and stretching their fledgling legs.

The Brazilian kids, all looking the picture of health, were loud and boisterous during the flight. Many of the young boys appeared to have similar haircuts, most of their head having been shaven leaving a small section on the front untouched, obviously idolising the Turma da Monica style sported by their hero Ronaldo who assisted in winning Brazil their fifth world cup just the month previous.

A simple breakfast was soon served onboard comprising of pastries and coffee, then the resulting trash was quickly collected, seats uprighted and window blinds opened with the seatbelt sign lighting up in preparation of landing.

Going through immigration had been a daunting first experience having handed over his passport and the immigration card which he had to fill out only to be directed twice to the back of the queue for reasons he could not understand until one of the airline staff approached him and helpfully made him aware that the card also had a reverse side, if only the immigration officer in the kiosk was as helpful but then Daniel supposed at this time in the morning patience with a half-witted gringo due to sleep deprivation was not high on their "give a guy a break" list.

Daniel eventually did met Lilian in the arrivals area of the airport when she turned up late, something that Daniel was soon to learn as being "Brazil time!"

She was with her father Mario who had driven her through to the airport to collect him.

They immediately embraced finally securing a tangible tactile connection after months of the virtual from a distance.

Daniel found her dusky looks alluringly attractive and her dark eyes seductively enchanting but what drew him into her web the most was how she talked about that she wanted to start a family and Daniel, who always dreamed of having kids was then sold on her completely.

On his last day in Brazil before flying back home he secured their future together by purchasing an engagement ring then announcing to her family their plans and made a vow promising to start the required visa paperwork process as soon as he had returned to the UK and saying he would be returning to Brazil within six months to collect her and bring her back to Scotland with him.

In half that proposed, time three months later he had returned, fiancee visa in his procession and a date booked at the local church for their wedding.

As arranged they returned to Scotland together, the church was booked for five days after their return.

The church wedding was a small affair with only a small number attending. Lilian's sister came in from São Paulo the day before to represent her side of the family as she would be her maid of honour. Daniel had his best man and his mother in attendance.

The deed was finalised as they exchanged both rings and promises in front of the alter, standing close to the baptismal font which later that same year would receive a visit from their yet to be conceived child.

Daniel had left Lilian almost five years from since when they'd swapped wedding vows. Not only due to her infidelity, which eventually was later exposed after much squabbling conflicts, but also on account of her increasing temper to which Daniel, and often Sam, would be on the receiving end of.

Their marriage had never be smooth from the start. Within weeks of the nuptials having been concluded the mask Lilian appeared to had masqueraded in with the acts of tenderness and decency she had shown during their very brief courtship started to gradually slip, and proved just to have been an act, an act which she could not sustain once the drudgery of the day to day routine set in and the glittery novelty of her brave new world wore off, then her true self emerged.

Not long after the delivery of their son and her recuperation of her caesarian she started going out at the weekend to nightclubs with one of her friends, a older promiscuous Brazilian woman that lived near the city in Edinburgh who she'd met chatting on expat online communities.

Often after these nights out she would not return home from Edinburgh until the next afternoon citing that she had stayed her friend's apartment as not to rush catching the late train home.

When Daniel would asked her questions which would require more elaboration, then it would kick off an argument to which she would get increasing fierce to the point where she would soon start to get physical by smacking blows upon Daniel taking her courage from the fact she found that he would not retaliate or counter, just over up from her strikes like a punch bag to her fury.

A young Sam was often to witness this happening. He would stand shakily watching his mom rain down clouts upon his dad who would try to defend whilst also attempting to calm her down with words also compel his son to go to his bedroom when he saw Sam rooted to the spot watching the one sided fracas.

Then her adultery became so obvious it could no longer be ignored.

No man ever want's to discover that he had been cheated upon by his woman and would often prefer to hide the obvious conclusions behind a veil of knowing ignorance as a welcomed self-delusion and Daniel was no exception.

Every man believes he would be able to detect infidelities conducted against him by his own partner or wife. Many play the thought out scenario of a discovery within their own imagination almost like a fantasy if they don't expect it, or if it's been a case of once bitten twice shy it may be a churning cognitive process ongoing to remove or preempt concerns and doubts.

Often when the imaginative performance is acted out upon the internal stage of the mind where it's a theatrical production with almost a pantomime amount of ham overacting.

Imagine this, the protagonist is sitting on a well upholstered Chesterfield chair within the living area, just left of stage, footlights subdued setting the atmosphere of a cuckolded husband sitting with the lights out awaiting the return of his cheating wife to confront her.

Attention stage right as the whistling floozy first announces her return with a audible key scraping the barrel of the lock before she enters closing the door behind, still blissfully unaware of her husband awaiting and the confrontation which is ahead.

Lights illuminate the stage timed with her touching of the light switch on the wall.

An audible gasp escapes her lips, 'Awwww, Alex! I thought you'd still be out at the five-asides!' exclaims Josephine, a slight flush rising to her cheeks seeing her husband seated there in the darkness awaiting her return.

'Why are you sitting there with the lights out?' she says, composure quickly regained.

Alex, dressed is a smokers jacket wearing Persian slippers calmly removes his cherry wood churchwarden styled pipe laying it gently beside the glass of whisky within his reach at the side table, perhaps too much Arthur Conan Doyle influence of this imaginary script but onwards we go… 'I have been thinking' replies Alex calmly getting to his feet, 'and the dark is the perfect medium to think thoughts in.'

'Thinking what?' Josephine replies in a slight chuckling tone to misdirect the fluster she is starting to feel.

'Thinking why you would say you were working late at the office as when I called the reception I was informed that you had a half day!', The accusation is out, a cut and thrust, there is no going back now, the cards are on the table, lets see what the accused has to say for herself.

Sharp intake of breath from the audience in anticipation of her response.

Josephine gasps too, 'eh, oh eh dear I was, eh.' she fights for time mentally exploring her encyclopaedia of lies and excuses volume one to ten. 'I was doing some shopping, I wanted to buy you a gift so I was not wanting to tell you so it would be a surprise!' it's a hopeful Hail Mary pass born out of desperation, even a stern look acted across her face as if to challenge her husband's suspicion as a "how could you possibly" event but then Alex delivers his dynamite blow.

'Very strange then is it not that I find a charge against your credit card for the Holiday Inn!' …whoop, dial back, how would Alex find a charge so soon and would the bloke not have paid for their afternoon's love nest?

Rewrite required…but this would be the fantasy of a man's cleverness in confronting his duplicate wife, logic need not come into play.

The point is that men have a belief in themselves that they will see through the act of a cheating spouse until it happens to them. They think they will not stumble along blindly believing their wife is working late as she screws and fornicates with another man.

They like to think that if it were to happen to them they would discover the crime with Hercule Poirot like efficiency. That the confronted adulteress upon realising the gig is up would then throw herself down upon her husband's feet asking for his forgiveness and mercy.

Sometimes the imagery is more graphic, the husband returning home early and catching his wife banging his best friend in their bed. During that invention the protagonist usually flexes his muscles by socking some blows aimed at his (ex) best friend's face before dragging him nakedly from the bed by his ankles and then pulling him outside to the elements all whilst his soon to be ex-wife is pleading and apologising between the heart wrenching tears of regret.

In reality the realisation and the confrontations rarely match the fiction of page, stage and screen.

In the real world, as this was the stage of Lilian's adultery, the guilty would proceed more cautious and cover their tracks better yet the signs would soon build up to a point where they could no longer be wilfully unheeded for the sake of harmony.

Daniel and Lilian's relationship had been struggling when she told Daniel that she needed some time alone to think and reflect. She was going to travel down by train to a quiet location in the Lake District on a Friday, for the weekend to be by herself so she could contemplate on their marriage clearing her mind of all distractions and recharge her batteries then return on the Sunday evening.

Daniel would have to stay at home looking after their baby Sam as she went on this, somewhat short, journey of self-discovery.

Daniel even drove her to the railway station, carried her bag and waved her off whilst he held their babe in his arms. Waved her off unbeknownst to him that she was away to have a tryst with a lover she had arranged to meet using an internet dating site, ironically the same site on she'd first encountered Daniel.

When she returned she even brought with her a souvenir mug as a gift for Daniel. An earthenware mug, a capacity to contain ten fluid ounces with a painted Lake Windermere wrapped around it.

A mug for a mug Daniel would reflect upon later, which held ten fluid ounces, the same capacity of a heart, a heart which Daniel had given only for her to break it.

Returning she also brought back with her a bottle of Spumante sparking wine and a box of chocolate. When asked she answered that she had got them also as a gift for Daniel.

Alarm bells should have went off then but such is the mind trying to obscure the obvious to spare the heart of pain.

Neither Lilian or Daniel liked sparkling wine, but on his hindsight and her later admission forged to cause him suffering, these items had been gifts to her from the patronage of her lover, too cheap to buy champaign the Spumante had been his choice, an accessory to fornication in a three star hotel and Daniel was too 'fodidamente retardado' to realise.

Eventually the overwhelming hints tapered only towards all the signs that she was involved in an affair beyond that of the overnighters gathered from her weekend clubbing adventures, which a dewy naive Daniel had already suspected but again attempted to protect his own heart by to convince himself that this was was more likely to be his over thinking.

Deep within Daniel with the luxury of hindsight as a light he knew she'd been seeing someone else all this time although he'd fought against acknowledging this truth as being aware of the complexities it would bring into a what was already becoming a sham of a marriage, a doomed union which he still desperately clung to for the sake of their child and with a delusory hope that things could improve with a chance to salvage a future of happiness. There would be not a chance of that!

7

The morning following his first night's watch by his mother's bedside, and the exhaustion of his desperate last prayers of hope now since depleted that she may regain consciousness, Daniel had came to the decision that the time had come to contact his son by sending a text message to Lilian.

Not that he would have the slightest hope of any reconciliation to be born out of pity as to be reunited with his son. He was too experienced on the receiving end of that game to harbour such naivety, he knew very well there would not be any possibility of that. Yet he held some fresh hope that there could be a temporary truce to allow a grandchild to say his farewells to his grandmother, who had, like Daniel, not seen hide nor hair of her beloved little Sam for two years.

He kept the message simple and to the point, politeness to a tyrant whose grasp of power came about by shunning a father from his child. *Please can you tell Sam that his Granny is about to pass away. He may want to say his goodbyes but will have to be soon as she does not have much time left.*

Daniel studied the draft ensuring the tone could not be mistaken for anything else, which it could not be, before pressing send after which he quickly placed the mobile phone on the bedside cabinet as if it were red hot.

There it was on it's altar beside the photo frames to seduce his attention, tightening in it's tenterhooks as he so wished for it to vibrate and chime.

It's small screen stared upwards, another single eye for his attention to fall upon in the hope to see a sign of life, an illuminate which would be as bright as a beacon to him as it would indicate a returned message, hopefully to read what he so desired a short digital dispatch to confirm Sam would come. Then perhaps to see his boy, even in passing and however short, just to exchange the briefest of a reassuring smile, was that too much a hope to fumble for as a light in the darkest of times.

The reply came about 30 minutes later, an anti-climactic briefest of replies simply stating *Told him*.

He stared at the screen which now he held in his hand, did he really expect more?

He still felt as if the wind had been taken out of his sails yet did it really fall short of his expectations when he considered it?

Just as he was discarding the phone the dimmed screen lit up again as it chimed and vibrated in his hand as did his heart in his chest. Another follow on message, *Where is she?*

Daniel immediately responded typing in the address and room number. Awaiting again with newly regenerated hope for a confirmation that Sam would come. Daniel continued to stare at the screen which displayed the reply some minutes later.

Sam says he will come but does not want you there, he does not want to see you there and he will only come if Steve comes with us too

The reply had its desired effect of the narrative Lilian was arming herself with, the impression that the child was afraid of his dad and also to remark suggestively that her partner was a replacement father figure for Sam. A icy double barrelled blast to Daniel's chest when he'd thought the emotional pain could not get any more but was proven wrong.

He returned the only reply he could under the circumstances which was *OK, message me just before you arrive and I will leave.*

That ensuing second day was proving to be a continuation of the day before as Daniel remained faithfully by the side of his mother's bed.

His phone sat next to him by the table with much potency as he awaited Lilian announcing that they were on their way so he could undertake his side of her proviso which he had agreed upon to make himself scarce during his son's visit to see his dying grandmother.

He rocked his body in the chair to spread the tension in an attempt to find a comfort which could not be found. His bones complained at the shuffle he made in the chair.

During the first night he had tried to position his chair as close to the bed as he possibly could get.

He trialed every possible configuration allowing him to hold his mum's hand without too much a gulf between them.

He didn't think that she could feel him holding her hand as her fingers did not curl around his, but the comfort was as much for his sake as could be hers, it was almost a desperation on his part to have as much contact as possible during her final moments.

The safety rails of her bed were down so he could not to stretch his legs under the bed. The best geometry to position his seated self as close as possible he found was to have the chair parallel so that the wood frame of its arm rest was touching the side of her bed and his face positioned about two feet away from her pillow raised head. It was an awkward position for him, uncomfortable, certainly not ergonomic but it was the most practical he could get if he want to reach across whilst seated to hold her hand without contorting his body at even more uncomfortable angles.

Feng Shui it would never be as none of the furniture in the room could harmonise with the surrounding environment. Nursing homes seem to furnish their domains with charitably donated castoffs, furniture and fixtures more for the practicalities for the infirm rather than to compliment the décor.

On a table by the side of a now redundant television was a plastic water jug with a closed green lid sitting on a tray There were also two plastic drinking vessels, one was the conventional tumbler and the other looked like an oversized child's easy grip mug with its protruding side handles and large spout on top of its press down lid. A conscious Annie would use that sealed drinking cup for all her liquids, tea, milky coffee or just plain water.

Also on the tray were a number of oral swabs which were to be used to wet Annie's parched lips as was demonstrated the day before by the nurse. They were small pink sponges on white plastic stems, they looked like lollipops and reminded Daniel of the chewy Swizzle Drumstick lollies his mum use to buy him when they walked home together after she'd collect him from school as a child.

Picking up one of the swabs by its stem he dipped in into the tumbler of water. Once the sponge was saturated he moved back to Annie and touched her lips gently with charged soft pink end. Rivulets of water ran down into her mouth like tears. The tip of her tongue dashed her lips like a lizard seeking out moisture, he was careful the tender expressions of the thin legs of running water did not cause her to choke.

It was unsettling to watch the movement of her lick, as if this was a marionette action governed by invisible string manipulated by a puppeteer to mock in a grim parody.

Second day in the Big Brother Household Daniel jokingly thought to himself which did nothing to lessen the tension, a forced humour which was to add no mirth to the situation.

She was holding out longer than expected.

Earlier that morning one of the nurses mentioned, whilst in the room, that in her own experience sometimes a loved one would wait until they are alone before passing on. She explained that it was as if their consciousness still operates even after their bodies ceased showing the signs of life, so they'd wait, hang on before finally passing away until the family member on the vigil had left the room, even for a short period such as nipping out for a coffee. As if awaiting a lull in live traffic before crossing over into death's embrace.

But Daniel just could not bring himself to prove this theory. He was absent when his father died and also of course when his brother perished on a burning oil rig platform. He felt it would distress him too much if he were not there with his mother when her last breath turned to air, the guilt would be a too heavy a burden on his shoulder to carry.

Was it the thoughts of cultural references that drove that fear? Memories of his younger self watching a fictional Ebenezer Scrooge learn that he would die alone if he followed his current trajectory as in a vision provided by the Ghost of Christmas Yet to Come? The thought of a bleak monochrome scene which could be only projected in the mind curtesy of a silent pointing reaper like figure insinuating the gloomy Alastair Sim's demise would go unattended at his deathbed.

The Japanese even had a word for it, Kodokushi, which meant a lonely death, an unaccompanied death.

The thought of Annie being alone during this time troubled him powerfully, he felt a duty to be there, escort his mother to the furthest point he could as she crossed that bridge from existence to expiration.

Due to this he also had an irrational fear that he may fall asleep in the chair, not being aware when she exhaled a breath which would not be followed on by its twin, that then, if that were to happen he would not have that connected sense of touch which he hoped would help comfort her during her passing moments and that would feel like dereliction of his duty as the loving son he believed himself to be.

A sense of propriety also drove this, a decorum of behaviour he felt he had to follow yet there were no other witnesses in the room to testify or judge.

There was also the thought that being there by his mother's side to comfort her when she passed away would somewhat gild the grief which surely would wash over him like a emotional tsunami once she was gone.

His Father, Samuel, had died about twenty years before Annie was admitted to the nursing home. Lung cancer, the damage caused by cigarettes and cigars laid claim to another victim. Samuel had started smoking whilst in the Army, a common initiation to the vice as most of the troops serving were given tobacco in their rations kits during the war and being quartered so far from home there was also the combat stress and boredom to address.

Cigarettes would often dangled ubiquitously from the lips of battle-weary soldiers so it was as a prized part of the rations as was chocolate and other edibles such as beans, cheese and the steak and kidney pudding which the guys would heat on a portable stove sitting around in a circle.

The tins of bully beef and spam were not as popular and Samuel use to joke years later that he could stock up a warehouse with all the tins of spam buried in the North African desert.

The phone chimed off the table forcing a surprised jolt in Daniel.

He lifted it to view the message. It was Lilian.

Be there at 6. DON'T YOU BE THERE!!.

Daniel replied with a short confirmation that be would comply as instructed.

8

Since after the final break up of their marriage the only time Lilian and Daniel were to be again in the same room together was within the Family Court.

Daniel started an action in the court over 2 years ago when Lilian first denied him access to his son.

He was not entitled to legal aid as his earning exceeded the threshold but upon researching and his visits to the library he decided to represent himself, after all, what would be the point in exhausting his savings and remortgaging his house to cover the thousands a lawyer would demand from his multiple court dates and then be depleted of funds which could otherwise be used to treat his son to the luxuries he wanted for him if successful. He also knew that with Lilian any battle he engaged in to have contact with his son then she would turn into a war of attrition and he was correct in assuming this.

The family court does not award expenses to the victor in cases concerning child contact. It unreasonable claims that as both parties only wants the best for the child at so neither should be penalised if they were to not be successful with their claim. Yet still Lilian would not be out of pocket a penny with her funded defence and Daniel would still be out thousands through lodging motions, writs and Bar Reporter's fees which as a pursuer it would be his responsibility to cover having first raised the action.

Daniel had made it clear within his Pleas In Law when he drafted his Initial Writ, that he requested to court to see fit as to grant him access to see his child.

Daniel then, upon drafting the Writ had no contact with Sam (who was then seven), for nearly six months since Lillian discovered that she could no longer blackmail him with threats of keeping their child away unless he paid her the ever increasing sums of money which she demanded.

Of course Lilian's Legal-Aid lawyer could not give that as a defence as to why Lillian was denying the father access to their son so she used the more common-or-garden defence claiming it was because Daniel had been an abusive husband and when the child, when in his care, would not be properly looked after.

The Sheriff on the bench sighed whilst hearing this. It was the usual story to which he wished he'd had a coin for every time he heard.

The road to resolution was always the same in such cases so the Sheriff immediately gave his ruling that The Pursuer, Mr Sinclair should be given contact with the child on the Saturday of each week from 10am in the morning, then to return him by 6pm that same evening to his mother's door.

The Sheriff then ordered for a Bar Reporter to be appointed who would investigate the accusations made on both sides and also observe the child in the company of his father before asking some questions of the child himself.

Once the report was completed and handed to the Sheriff another Child Welfare Hearing would be convened to decide if overnight visits would be appropriate hinging on the findings of the report.

"This is my ruling!", bish-bash-bosh, "All arise, Court to be adjourned awaiting completion of the Bar Report.

Daniel had been happy with this preliminary result. He did not expect overnighters with his son to be granted immediately but he felt that the Sheriff had saw through Lilian's fabricated defence as to why he should not be allowed any contact with his son, he also had faith that the Bar Report would be favourable for Sam to have overnights with his him. He knew himself to be a good father and looked after Sam very well when he'd been in his care.

Daniel was right to be optimist, at least in those early days.

The Bar Report was compiled by Rachel Cummings who had returned within its findings a recommendation that the The Pursuer to be given overnight contact with The Child.

Daniel, from the research he had done, knew the most likely outcome would be that he would get every second weekend so on his Initial Writ had also added to his pleading that he should be granted an additional overnight contact with the child every Wednesday of each week as to collect Sam from his School on the in the afternoon then return him to the school gates the next morning in time for his first class.

Daniel had explained that his work was flexible with his time allowing this to be possible, and also, remembering the "Golden Rule for Child Contact', he asked this of the court, not because it suited him, no, but as it would be in the best interests of the child as Daniel, on the Wednesday immediately upon collecting Sam from school would take the child swimming, an activity which was prescribed by experts as good for a child with dyspraxia, which Sam had.

Not only would the child benefit from more time with his father, he would also be taken to a positive activity which would help with his development.

Daniel's plea for this extra overnight contact was also was in harmony with what the child had told the Bar Reporter which was that he would be happy to see more of his father.

So once the court reconvened the presiding Sheriff signed off on a contact order stating that Mr Sinclair The Pursuer was to have every second weekend with the child from 6pm of the Friday returning him on the Sunday evening by the same time, also to be given every Wednesday overnight returning the child by the Thursday morning to his school.

The Sherif then put the case into a "Sisted" state, which was legal terminology stating that he had paused all further proceedings. The Sheriff did hope that this would be the last he would see of both parties in front of his bench and thus reaching a expeditious resolution (best part of a year being expeditious in family law terms).

The Sheriff's optimism was misplaced as he forgot the old saying that "Hell has no fury like a woman scorned" and Lilian had left court that day very much scorned.

Daniel of course was delighted with the outcome, his son would be staying with him overnight four nights every two weeks, he could accept this. Good result he thought. Perhaps not great as School holidays were still never agreed but he had contact with his son and not only at the weekends!

He was a father again, a completeness to contain the desire he always felt but this ballon of elation was soon to pop as he reached into his pocket to retrieve his phone after leaving the court building and about to enter his car.

Glancing over the screen for any messages pending since he had been in court and there was Lilian the harbinger of grief fuelled by spite.

The message simply read **Mothers decide what's best for children not judges.**

Lilian had been already furious Daniel had been granted access to Sam during the day from the first court hearing so when it was deemed the next month that he should get overnight access too she was ballistic with anger, she had already calculated the reduction this would mean to the benefits she was being paid out from the government.

The day before Sam had been due top meet with the Bar Reporter at Daniel's house, she thought she had prepared the boy for what she anticipated would be the questions Cummings would ask of him.

'When you get asked tell the reporter that you have seen Daniel hit your mommy!', the boy nodded his head in the affirmative to indicate he understood.

'Also make it very clear to Mrs Cummings that you want nothing to do with Daniel, that he treats you badly and only wants you so he can make mommy suffer!' Again Sam nodded to this and repeated the answers which she had expected of him when she asked him to tell her what he intended to say.

Upon her seeing the completed Bar Report during that second hearing it was abundantly clear that Sam had not stuck to their plan, he actually went off on the opposite direction and declared that he wanted not only to see Daniel but also that he would be happy to see more of him!

Lilian had waited with a pent up wrath for Sam's return from School that day then pulled him up as soon as he stepped into the house.

Sam went pale as his mother slammed him against the wall demanding why he had went against their agreed script when he had talked with the Bar Reporter.

'Don't you understand how much I care for you?'

'Can't you see that Daniel just wants to use you to hurt mommy?'

'Daniel doesn't love you, he only wants to get at mommy!'

Lilian spat these statements out at a trembling Sam whilst tugging forcefully at one of his ears as if this would sink the words into his head. It terrified him so much he could feel a trickle of warmth down his leg.

Lilian went on to breach the order which proved not to be worth the paper which it was written on as not forceable by the police nor did the Sheriff seem willing or able to punish Lilian for transgressing the will of the court apart from merely giving her a ticking off during her next showing, the reasoning was that to punish the mother would have a knock on effect on the child.

Lilian would not send Sam out to Daniel's car when he pulled up outside awaiting for her to send their son out for his court appointed contact weekend.

She kept him out of school every Wednesday so Daniel could not collect him, she seemed unconcerned of the effect this was having on his schooling despite the calls from Sam's teachers telling her so. His education was already suffering due to lack of concentration in class due to the disruptions at home caused by his mother's constant harassment of the child to stick to the script that it was the boy's own decision to not see Daniel.

She started using the excuse that Sam was afraid of his father and did not want to go out to him when Daniel was to come collect the boy, that Sam was terrified to attend school on the Wednesdays as he feared Daniel would come to collect him after his class.

The court process ground as slow as ever when getting around to Daniel's request for the court to "unsist" the case and then to get another hearing with the Sheriff, the result of which, once that came happened, was for the Bar Reporter, the same one as before, Rachel Cummings, to be assigned again to compile yet again another Bar Report to find out what the child was saying.

The length of time it would take to get to that point allowed Lilian her needed duration to installed the fear into the boy so that he began to say he no longer wanted to have any contact with his father.

The child would not budge or elaborate as to why! Lilian's talons of terror were sunk deeply into his flesh.

Over the next days, weeks then months she continued to work on the child with the strategy of an alienator attempting to fill his head with unjustified negativity regarding his father and threats to what would happen if he never followed what she told him to say, what she justified as was for his own good.

No Sheriff or court in the land would forcefully order a child to meet with his father if that child was adamant he did not want to due to what was said to be the dreadful fear at the possibility of having contact.

Lilian also continued her narrative that it was her son's choice and she, being the good mother would do everything to stand by his decision.

9

During the course of the second night of Daniel being by his mother's side, Lilian and Steve set off from Glasgow towards Falkirk with Sam.

Once they were within a few miles of the nursing home Lilian sent Daniel a text message advising *Will be there in 10 mins. Make sure you are not there.*

His reply was almost instant *OK, I will go away now. Please message me once you leave so I can return.*

Lillian read out the received reply aloud to Steve and then she turned around to face Sam who was sitting in the back of the car.

'Don't worry Sam, he won't be there and Steve will be with us.'

Sam never answered, he had been quiet since learning from his mom earlier that day about his granny's fading condition.

She had broke the news to him with a clinical dispassion void of humanity. Sam had kept his face composed without emotion.

She had then went on to say that she would be taking him to say goodbye to his gran but he needn't worry about Daniel causing him any trouble as Steve would be coming along too with the purpose to watch their backs.

Sam did not even ponder over the ridiculousness of the statement about Steve watching their back or the ludicrous insinuation that his dad was of any danger to him.

Sam's thoughts were directed to his granny that moment and a feeling of grieving remorse that he had not be able to talk with her for these past two years.

Steve had reached the car park of the nursing home slowing his car down to a crawl then he drove as if on patrol around the scant scattering of parked cars before pulling up to a halt parking in one of the bays.

'No sign of him' Steve announced, 'I will come in with you. If he is there we will just walk straight back out to the car!'

It was just after 6pm so the main reception doors were closed and it took a few minutes before they were buzzed in after announcing themselves on the intercom by the door.

After enquiring directions from the first staff member she saw, Lilian then lead Sam up the stairs to the Argyll ward with Steve trailing at the rear.

Another door, another intercom. Once buzzed in she asked the nurse, who was to lead them to the door of Annie's room if the old woman was by herself which was then confirmed by her being told that Annie's son had left about ten minutes earlier.

They reached the door of her room, Lilian and Sam entered.

Steve said he would wait outside in the corridor just by the door, he did feel a bit like an intruder on the scene but never mentioned that.

There was terrible underlying smell which clung to his nostrils when he first entered the ward but it was gradually dissipating, partially replaced with more general odours such as the canned scent of the spring meadows air freshener as was recently sprayed but still unable completely mask the underlying smell of what he considered to be "old people's smell", a cocktail of urine, musky mothballs, sweat and puke with a dash of Dettol disinfectant to his nose.

His olfactory senses were partially correct with that of the disinfectant. His is neurones lit up a memories of hurled upchuck by fellow kids from a classroom years ago, the resulting vomited mess usually being cleaned up with Dettol and green paper towels as often was the case hence the vomit sensory link but he was wrong about the rest of the bouquet.

It was the nonenal tang in the air that was the cause of the mistaken identity of other scent sources which ran through Steve's head

The smell was caused by the chemical changes which happen on the skin when people get older, it's exacerbated by the decreased natural antioxidant protection in the matured skins of the aged. The odour is hard to guise and cruelly mistake for something more unhygienic radiating forth from the elderly.

Steve never knew this of course so just concluded the worst. He could not be judged too harshly on such a wrong conclusion, most people believe the same. Yet to presume that behind the door which was connected to warrens of corridors within the nursing home there would be residing old wrinkled relics dressed in urine dampened pyjamas was an ignorance.

To a degree this may be true of some of the less reputable establishments in the past but certainly not there in the Argyll Ward or any of the other wards within the nursing home complex of buildings in which he now stood. Yet still often when the first time visitor to a nursing home enters for the first time, they have this preconceived image in mind and have already formed an opinion about it before they have had any experience.

Much can manipulated by what we have heard or been told but never experienced. Much like his preconception about Sam's father being an abusive man who Sam was afraid of. He had never met the man but also never questioned the hearsay delivered from Lilian.

A swell of grief washed over Sam as he looked down at his granny and engulfed him with such an flourishing anguish his breath felt as if it froze in his chest, he did not expect this scene when his Mum told him that Granny was going to pass away, he'd thought she would just look as if she was asleep, napping as she often did when he nipped into her room upstairs during the times he stayed with Dad.

He would often quietly creep up the stairs and in to see her, 'Quiet like a mouse!' Dad use to say to him, 'don't disturb your gran if she is sleeping. She is old and needs her rest.' Sam would then stalk up the stairs like a ninja to her bedroom as if it were a game, treading on the outer edges of the steps as not to elicit a creak from the wooden stairs. Softly, softly, catchee monkey steps. He would then, almost silently open her door and glide through the opening, not daring to breath, a grin on his face in anticipation that if she lay wake she would quickly pivot her head around where it lay on the pillow and shrilly revel 'I see you Sam Sinclair, sneaking in here!' whilst reaching up her arm with hand pretending to be claw as if to grab him like the wolf with Red Riding Hood.

"Who's that tripping over my bridge?" she would sometimes call out in her best attempt of a Troll's voice to a Billy Goat Gracious Sam.

"I'm going to gobble you up!" reaching out to tickle Sam at the very last moment which he would at that point burst out the breath he was holding in and scream with giggles and then a roar of fainted surprise as if his master plan, like a Gretel catching off guard the Witch, had been foiled. Then he would bend over to get the mandatory peck on his cheek concluded so he could tell then Granny about how his day was or often how is prior week was since he last time he saw her. On the occasions when she was truly asleep he would approach her bed and look upon her sleeping form closely as if to study. Watching the flare of her nose as she snored on her back. If her arm lay unsheathed out of the sheets while she dozed he would stroke the arthritis gnarled knuckles and joints of her hand, ever so lightly with the tips of his fingers with the gossamer discreetness of a wisp, an action which would have caused him extreme embarrassment if witnessed by another living soul but such was his affection for this old lady, an intimacy he would cringe to show without the usual tomfoolery to merge it within during time they spent together.

In his granny Sam also found a surrogate for the matronly love and attention he so desired but found in scant supply from Lilian.

Sam was everything to Annie and she attested this fact with every moment she spent with him.

Never did she say a loud word against him, in his granny's company Sam was cosseted with kindness and love always, and he felt this when in her presence, a contrast from the storm clouds above always threatening to erupt which gathered overhead when in the company of his mother.

Sam heard his mother from behind tell him to say his final goodbye. He remained standing there looking upon the shrivel figure on the bed with a rasp starting in his throat. He recognised this old lady as his granny but at the same time he saw a stranger laid out on the bed. A stranger wearing a ill fitting body costume of his granny and who could not fill it out. The cheeks and jowls which were once so quick to ripen with smiles were now attenuated into boney frames with darkly blotched parchment stretched over them.

Worst of all was the open eye gaping up towards the ceiling, the other closed within its deep cavern.

The open eye drew his attention like water flushing into a vortex, he stared at it's blank stare.

He recalled when once Dad took him to visit Kelvingrove Museum in Glasgow, he remembered walking around the gallery rooms bored with what seemed like endless hoards of homogeneous oil painted scenes of countrysides and doddery old lords posed sombre but then next room contained paintings of a more recent contemporary Glasgow, of the tenements and the people who dwelled within.

One particular water colour canvas captured Sam's attention

enthralling him on the spot to stand and stare at each painted detail. The small panel beside it informed it was "Windows In the West by Avril Paton"

It depicted a snowy tenement block standing in a street in Glasgow. The setting was early evening in the painting and most of the little rooms were illuminated within the windows on the tenement apartments. If you looked close you could see figures and goings on through the windows within the rooms. Sam stood and stared like a voyeur, examining the scene behind each window which were not shrouded by curtains or darkness. He scrutinised imagining clockwork life behind each finely done pane.

With that same studious application he now focused on his Granny's face, into the cloudy artic blue of her fixed open eye. She could not be numb to what is around her, she could not be asleep or unconscious to never to awaken, no, this was not how things happen, not how people die.

He felt the intensifying heartache explode into a sudden panic as if the reality of the situation slid into place, his heart raced, the room around him seemed to contract in towards him compressing then expanding, dilating as he breathed out with the mushrooming hysteria, the berth of the room stretching and squeezing in time with his rapidly increasing respirations like the bellows of an accordion. Bulging, contracting.

The unease in Lilian grew as she watched Sam standing there in front of her. It was a mistake coming here, she should have not mentioned anything to Sam until Annie had died, it would have been better, she did not want a martyrs death impression to bud in Sam's mind regarding his remembrance of his gran and a grievance against her, his mother for restricting his access to her especially over these finally days.

Annie was her mother-in-law and as such was a proxy of Daniel in her mind, an enemy dowager by birthright alone.

'Come on Sam, let's let Granny rest.' Lilian cooed gently with what she thought was the right amount of compassionate tone hoping to break her son's trance.

The child appeared to ignore her, she thought for a moment that he was actually standing there catatonic and she was about to repeat herself in hope to break the spell but before she could call out again Sam broke forward, falling towards the bed like a toppled vase in fast forward motion spraying himself across it snatching his gran's wizened hand from where it lay.

"Wake up Granny, wake up, wake up!" he screeched pounding her hand which he held onto into the paillasse surface between her body and the edge of the bed.

'Wake up...Look Look Look!' he screamed to her face but to no avail, as Annie's single eye'd stare remained unfocused and unresponsive.

Lilian was shocked at Sam, she felt a disgust and her first instinct was not to comfort her child but to to grab him by the upper arms and pull him back from the bed violently with an excess of force which she did not mean under such circumstances so quickly deescalated with release once she shot the boy back from the bed jerking him against her, but immediately Sam leaped forwards again like a recoil.

'I want Granny!' Sam bawled out crouching by the bed and taking Annie's hand again.

Lilian had the sensation of being a trespasser, an encroacher upon the the scene there witnessing Sam's emotional outburst towards the paralytic form of his granny.

For the moment she felt she had lost control of the child, that all the presstitutes she has been pressing on him to cement him in her corner were being cast off like silken veils at that moment, this scared her immensely.

Steve had heard the commotion from outside the door and stepped in. The scene that was presented to his view was that of Sam bent at the side of the bed with his head against the old woman's hand letting out mournful pleas and sobs. Lilian stood behind him looking angry but also indecisive.

Steve felt the discomfort of an interloper who wandered in on a private stage show but the chivalrous course of action he felt was to comfort the obviously distressed child, in fact he felt it to be the only humane action but something which the mother seemed incapable of doing for reasons unknown.

He knelt by Sam and tenderly placed his hand on the boys heaving shoulder, he felt tissue thin and so very vulnerable. 'It's OK Sam, she is not suffering.' the words felt inadequate but he felt he had to voice something out as there were no words of comfort forthcoming from the mother.

Steve felt the little body of the child beneath his palm heave with anguished sobs, yet his mother would not step forward to aid in her child's comfort. He looked behind him up towards his partner's face as if to question why but he saw only a barely suppressed rage in her expressions.   This disturbed him even more than the scene he just newly walked into. 'Trip, trap, trip, trap' Steve could just make out quietly being recited by Sam through his sobs, 'Trip, trap, trip, trap across the bridge Granny.'

10

Shortly just after the dawning of the third day, Nadia, one of the nurses, visited Annie's room before the ending her nightshift and the subsequent handover to the day staff who were due to start soon.

On a tray, which she brought in with her, was some toast and milky white coffee for Daniel, an unrequested hospitality that she had done on the previous break of day due to her kindly nature. Despite Daniel neither being asked or commissioning this early morning fare he made an appearance of welcomed thankfulness.

Once Nadia left the room he would drink the coffee and wrap the untouched toast in some toilet paper then bury it under some crumpled newspaper in the waste bin as he also done that previous mornings. The coffee served a functionary purpose but the food he neither could face nor did his body craved its nourishment yet he never wanted to leave the toast on the plate untouched, he felt that his would seem like a rudeness in the face of such an act of kindness.

Nadia asked how he was holding up. After Daniel's usual practiced prevarication of declaring his wellness Nadia went to the foot of the bed and lift the layers covering Annie's feet for an observation as to the progression of the cyanosis.

Nadia, replacing the bedsheets at the end of the bed, then reached across the bed parting the curtains to allow some newly birthed natural daylight into the room before then switching off the low consumption artificial light as she left the room.

The natural luminance from the dawn's rays castigated Annie's face in a way Daniel was not prepared for. Even without medical training or death's experience he could see that her time was close. Dark dusky splurges of discolouration marked her face as the circulation started to prioritise the vital organs over the external presentation tissues that people so pride themselves and measure beauty upon.

As he sat back down on the chair. He then lifted the semi-closed claw of her left hand and placed once again the uncurling fingers over his.

The purplish marks hoarded over the parchment thin skin of her hand. Daniel could feel a lump in his throat, a sensation of emotions whilst looking at her hand, his mother's loving hand now reduced to a scraggy discoloured bird like bony talon.

The thin blue veins under the emaciation of the back of her hand reminded him of the venations on the tissue of a leaf, now such was the display of the ravishment of her progressing deteriorating condition.

These were once the hands he'd found comfort in as a child when they stroked his tearful face, the same hands he once held crossing a road or was to tug upon like a bell-pull when he needing attention, now diminished into what would pass as a ghoulish prop.

Daniel leaned over and kissed the back of her hand. "Aww mom" the groaned escaped from his heart scrunching up his eyes as if in pain.

Daniel thought back on his father's hands as a way to rerouting his current dark thoughts. It was strange that his attempts in the past to remember his dad's face in an animated way was difficult, there was a blur to any vivid recall, a mist, yet he could still picture his flexing hands clearly and their dexterous movements when he watched them at work with the wood he carpentered with.

They were big hands, seemingly at odds with the stature of the man himself.

Samuel was slight in build, lean with sinewy arms with these big callused paws on the end of them. His work after the war was with wood as he had trained as a joiner, and his pastime was also woodwork, either in his workshop or in the garden on fair weathered days sawing, hammering and chiselling. Sometimes he would labour within the house putting up new shelfs or rehanging a door, not that there was a lack of shelving or anything wrong with the original setting of the door within its frame, only he had to keep busy. As a result the garden was full of homemade wooden trellises, log arches and benches.

Daniel could also remember how these strong hands would pick him up as a child with affectionate benevolence and lift him up carrying him around satisfying his requests for a callycoad ride. Around the house or down the stairs upon rising at the weekends they would lift then heft him about.

He could remember the comforting cinnamon warmth smell of Old Spice aftershave and shaving soap that would diffuse from the old man's scruff when Daniel pressed his face in closer to his neck to secure himself tighter against his father's back whilst being carried.

Annie was fifthteen years her husband's junior having met each other after the war, both being widowers. Annie had been married only a short time with her first husband Bill before he was diagnosed as having Hodgkin's then passing away soon after they wed making her a window which drove her back to stay with her parents.

Samuel's first wife, Elizabeth passed away a few years after he'd returned from the war, she had a cerebral haemorrhage which took her life leaving Samuel as a single parent to their one child who they had called James and was aged two.

Samuel had met Elizabeth in London when he had moved down to from Scotland looking for work before the outbreak of the war. Shortly after they were married and the war did brake out Sam was drafted to serve.

Their house, which was in Welwyn Gardens, had been razed to the ground by a Luftwaffe raid the year before the war ended. Samuel had been serving in Italy at that time and luckily Elizabeth had been spared as she had been evacuated by the sirens into the depths of the underground when the bombing raid took place.

Upon returning to Blighty they were to spend their last few years together in rented accommodations before Elizabeth passed away after which Samuel had decided to move back up to Scotland on his BSA motorbike with his son strapped into its sidecar holding tight to a green Dunhill's Pontefract Cakes tin in his lap which contained all their worldly possessions. A tin Daniel still had at home.

When back in Scotland he stayed with his older spinster sister Edith who was still living there then having had moved to their departed parents house.

She would watch after James, who was now called Jimmy, when Samuel went off to work with his new employer Ogilvie construction were he would work as a joiner fitting up new houses in the boom which took place during the post war years.

Annie was introduced by mutual friends to Samuel as they were both single widows.

Annie was a bit reluctant at first considering the age different and that Samuel already had a child but she decided to go along with it and agreed to meet him.

Samuel would come and collect Annie in his BSA motorbike and sidecar then off they would go to Dobbie's dance hall to have some fun. They soon proved to be as inseparable from the start as they were to be all through their married life.

Within the same year they were introduced to each other the bonds of matrimony were sealed and Annie would consider Samuel's son Jimmy as her own and raised him as such with the boy calling her his mum.

They were happy. Samuel working as a carpenter at a local builders yard and Annie then working as a nurse.

Annie's parents were retired and always available to look after Jimmy who they doted on.

It was to be over another twenty years before Daniel was to arrive on the scene, an unexpected and unplanned surprise but one which would be most welcomed by all three.

There was some concerns considering Annie's age but all turned out fine.

Daniel was born just early on Maia's month weighing in slight at just over four pounds, a light but health enough little screaming red faced boy. 'My wee bag of sugar!' Annie proclaimed to visitors when looking upon him and he was just that, a sweet little baby with a smile that would soak into you and parents who would love him and spoil their "wee bag of sugar" with such love and attention.

Jimmy, who had turned twenty-five when Daniel was born loved his new brother and took to Daniel as Annie had to him these years before.

There was a gulf of an age difference between Samuel and his son. When Daniel was born Samuel was within his last year of his "fifty somethings", this was much to the amusement and mirth of his younger work colleagues who'd tease that Sam had 'plenty lead in the old pencil yet!' but Samuel would just laughed it off as good natured as it was meant to be.

Jimmy had worked in the oil production industry for some years and had decided to work closer to home changing to the oil platforms of the North Sea over the Islamic cultured sandy planes when Daniel was still in his pre-teen years.

A few years later after he'd made the decision to work off the Aberdeen coast, fate would have it that this would be his, and another 166 poor souls last vestiges on life upon the platform of Piper Alpha in 1988 when disaster was to strike.

Jimmy, was forty-one years old and would not age another day when he was blasted off into the North Sea contained within the rig's living quarters when the explosions shook the platform.

His father Samuel aged after the death of his first born, both physically and mentally.

Annie suffered the torment too but looking after her husband kept her going during this tough time.

Daniel was sixteen years old at the time of his brother tragic death so still had the resilience of youth to somewhat regulate the extent of his grief, friends rallied around him giving him attention which he coveted under the circumstances.

His difference in age with Jimmy did part them slightly from the usual unity of brothers, the pain he experienced was served up more by watching the decline in his father.

On many occasions Samuel would get confused and call Daniel by this deceased brother's name, Jimmy. Daniel did not correct him but the pain he felt was intense like a knife in his chest.

The peak of Samuel's suffering was prolonged as his son's body was not recovered for almost three months, until in October of that same year when part of the accommodations module was hoisted from the sea bed.

A fresh wave of grief was to sweep through the victims' families as with the reclaimed deceased oil workers bodies there were to be another round of funerals, the actual belated funerals now there were bodies to be buried or cremated. Fresh tears to be added to the count shed at the memorials done both at the oil town of Aberdeen and later for individuals at their home turfs.

Headlines announced in bold font "Piper Alpha Accommodation Block Recovery" or variations of such plastered the newspapers accompanied with photos of the module rising like a great biblical leviathan hoisted from the waves dripping foaming salty water and containing a sadness within even a Gustave Doré mind could never imagine.

Dredged up from the deep the accommodations block was a huge communal coffin which was taken ashore for a team of forensic police to start a grim search inside for the bodies.

Once opened it gave up its sad treasure of eighty-seven water bloated mortal remains.   eighty-seven Fathers, Sons, Uncles and Brothers, each and every one a catalyst to cause a relapse to the grieving process of their loved ones which were already on its third month step.

Friends of Jimmy, many of whom were fellow oil workers who luckily had been rostered off that fatefully night in July, approached his family after the funeral offering their condolences.

Fond if perhaps somewhat anecdotal tales of Jim were offered up by his mates with their tales of adventures whilst working in the Middle East, many were told during the meal after the cremation, it raised some smiles and comical rolling eyes when it was mentioned about Jimmy being the instigator of creating a partnership of fellow Scots building a small home distillery producing some home brew to bypass the strict Islamic laws, and of the cavalier attitude they all had, hardworking young roughnecks who enjoyed a drink in a dry foreign land, portrayed them as Lawrence of Arabia like figures but fighting off a drought of sobriety rather than the blood thirsty Turks, a band of brothers united by their sweat and now united in grief of friends missed.

Daniel listened intently, a sixteen year old kid basking in the camaraderie earned by his older brother amongst these men, the smiles raised on his parents faces which were so rare of recent.

 It was to be another ten years before Samuel was to breath his last and that smile did not reappear much during his remaining decade much to Daniel's regret.

That third afternoon in the nursing home slowly drifted into early evening as Daniel carefully tended his mother by sopping the small orange oral sponge in the water then, holding it by it's lollypop stem, gently pressing it against her top lip allowing the water to trickle thread thinly down upon her lower lip causing a gathering tongue tip to appear which would still protrude at the sensation of moisture like a hermit crab poking out of its shell.

He was drained, both physically and mentally. This would be his third night at her bedside, he wished dearly that she would give up her silent fight and succumb to what must ineluctably happen.

He leaned across her bed and reunited the ends of the curtains together as murk was gathering outside.

Daniel was glad there was no more natural lighting to enter through the window, he much preferred the dimness of only the lamp in the room casting just enough candescence through the assembling shadows as not to accentuate the discoloured blotching marks on his mother's face, stains which continued to gather like dark vultures over carrion.

Annie's bouts of bleating flails still continued every so often causing her son to press up close by her side to give comfort and support as if it could be her time, yet still she hung on as if with determination.

There was not the slightest sound emanating from her to denote breathing. The swell and wane of her chest had to be scrupulously surveyed to validate her continued existence such was the calm of her pulmonary ocean and imperceivable bellow rise of any intake of air.

Daniel felt a certain irrational guilt at prolonging any suffering that may be existing somewhere deep within her husk during these purgatorial last days by the scant hydration he provided with the small sponge against her darkening lips yet to cease would feel mercilessly inhumane considering how her tongue readily searched for the sparse trickles yet Daniel wondered if she'd still be here if he had discontinued it's administration from the first day.

He's also though how effortless it would be just to place his hand on her chest, not even to push down just the heft of his appendage would, he thought, be enough to deny another intake of breath.

He torturously played this thought of action around in his head. To hold her hand, kissing her cheek whilst deploying his other hand to rest upon her chest. A laying of hands to commute another sort of blessing, a mercy surely delivered but could he play at being a god which he never believed in? No, he knew, he could not. At least not such a direct act, although he was aware that he was already participating in a passive euthanasia as the water through the little sponge which he delivered would not be enough to sustain a bird, this thought tugged violently enough against his heart so he could only imagine how his guilt would be with a more direct course of action.

"Bis Pueri Senes" was a latin proverb roughly meaning once a man and twice a child. Daniel could vouch for the truth in this having witnessed the later stages of his mother's almost completion of the full circle. The tottering unsteadiness of Annie's gait progressively got worse over time. This was foreseeable with the ageing process. The arthritis and excess weight she carried from inactivity contributed greatly to her deteriorating mobility but it can only be expect for the litheness to diminish as the body is on the wain, "old age brings more than the pension" Annie use to be fond of saying and very true it was. Annie only accepted the need for a zimmer frame a couple years before finally moving out the house into the nursing home for help transmitting herself around. Hand rails were, before this point, screwed into the walls at various points on the trails Annie would use around the house.

During her last stay in the hospital brought on by a fall, also proving to have been her last stay in her house, Annie appeared to regress even more quickly.

Daniel had tried to look after his mother at home. His work was very kind to him and gave him hybrid working where he would only have to attend the office a couple of days a week and work from home on others.

He did have the support of a carer who would arrive every morning to shower Annie and help her with more intimates.

On the days Daniel had to drive into the office the carer would allow herself access using the key safe which was around by the back door.

Daniel's attempt to care for this mother at home was commendable but as her mobility and dementia grew worse eventually he knew she needed professional around the clock care.

The final admission came when Daniel returned from a quick trip out to the local shops and could hear a moaning coming from Annie's room. He rushed up stairs to check out what was happening and found her lying on the floor repeatedly calling out for her 'Daddy!', a childlike regressive mental state that really scare Daniel to witness.

She was damp underneath due to having not made the destination of her travel which was the bathroom and she seemed to, at first not recognise her son as he approached her fallen form on the floor.

Unable to determine if Annie had broke anything due to her tumble Daniel phoned for an ambulance then sat with his mum calming her bleating and comforted her as she seemed to slowly dawn as to where she was again and that this was her son beside her.

Once the paramedics arrived their examination found no bones broken, but due to her still, although now less than before, confused state the crew decided the best place for her was back into hospital for evaluation.

Annie never did return home, from the hospital she was eventually moved to a nursing home where she was to spend her last days.

11

On the morning of the fourth day Daniel's waiting was about to come to an end.

A gurgle noise erupted from Annie on the bed. Daniel perched forward on the chair, holding her hand and using his other to stroke it whilst soothing that all would be alright.

Once again Annie seemed to settle back into her sentient state. Daniel sat back in the seat with his heart heavy.

The curtains open at the start of another day having dawned. He could see the tops of trees from his first floor window view, they swayed back in forth with the breeze blowing outside, it was a calming effect, he tuned his breaths to that windblown canopy of the rustling green back and forth movement, the tree's mechanism to dissipate the wind's energy exerted upon it.

Daniel copied their method in an attempt to dispel the tenseness he felt, sitting upright he rocked his body in the chair in time to the trees, and it was working, he could feel a relaxation as the anxiousness started to drain from his body.

The start of a whimpering cry soon started from Annie's lips again ending his waltz of distraction and brought him back to reality as he cast his gaze back down to his mother redirecting it from the escape of the window. Her groans intensified as if she was in torment.

Daniel could sense a difference already to the many previous stumbles before.

He raised himself from his seated position on the edge of the chair still holding and caressing her hand, now leaning in he bent his lips close to her ear assuring her that it was alright for her to go now. 'Thank you so very much mom, I love you, Sam loves you, thank you for everything you have done for me, Dad is waiting for you!' His words came out as rapid gasps, words determined to be said but no sign of being heard by the recipient as the wave of her distress was building up like a mounting tsunami.

Stroking the side of her head now as gently as he could, he repeated his mantra of love and thanks as if they were incantations desperate to be spilt from his lips, desperate to soothe and ease her passing.

This was the moment, the inevitable ending he was waiting for, dreading yet yearning as not to perpetuate any further suffering.

The previous sporadic turbulent episodes were just dress rehearsals to this event as the fear driven panic seemed to animate Annie who swept her head from side to side the pillow. Daniel's mollifying words escalated in tempo and tone as if to keep pace until the crescendo, the waxing and waning of her lamented complaints like a kettle reaching boiling point, then a stumbling down with the turbulence easing off as finally the death rattle sounded to heralded her passing, her fight ended with the terminating bleat of a murmurous sob fading as if the final expiration of a hymn, the last wheeze of a life into the air, her one agape eye having never shown any of the recognition Daniel so hoped to witness. No cognisance to be witnessed of a descending angel reaching down a hand to soar her heavenwards or a familiar face of a previous departed soul who had stepped over the threshold to help her towards the proverbial light.

Daniel watched, his attention forensically focused to inspect for the slightest sign of the tiniest volt of life still in Annie, hoping this was it, no more curtain calls, no more suffering if she was indeed suffering, certainly he was, but still he was uncertain to call it, to confirm to himself his mother was now at peace. He peered as if trying to ascertain if the pilot light was still alit within a boiler, there was no sign of animation however slight to be seen.

He hurdled tightly in towards her once the acceptance of the her death registered true in his mind. An altered Pietà in reverse, a son looking upon his dead mother whilst cradling her.

His eyes remained dry, tears would surely come later, perhaps once it registered more and he had time to reflect, surely then the grief would come more intensely but for now there was a surrealism, a feeling of disconnection, almost a relief was washing over him that she was now at peace.

Her left eye remained open in death still staring out of the shell. Daniel gently pressed the tips of his fingers down over the flap of her eye lid, as he saw done in the movies, the thought of which projected silently in a swift montage of film noir clips in his mind as he attempted so but the canopy of skin would not obey post mortem and returned to its open position as if in a last act of defiance, a stubbornness of the flesh determines to get it's last word in.

He stroked back some stray whorled white strands of hair from her forehead then caressed the side of her face saying 'goodbye mom, I love you.' which immediately after leaving his lips felt like a cliché before his spoken words died on the air.

Lowering himself back into the chair his emotions remained in check. Chest feeling like a hollow drum, dry eyed and composed which felt disappointing within himself. Part of him felt like he should be sobbing with warm salty tears streaming down his cheeks in rivers but he was stoic and this apathetic feeling was a shame which pricked his conscience almost with a self-disgust.

Her rage against the dying of the light almost felt like a bantam weight performance now viewed in the rear view mirror of his perception of the recent concluding events. Her last wrestle with the inevitable almost felt to Daniel like an anti-climax but did he really expect consciousness to return for farewells at the departure gate? The absurdity of such thoughts. Did he really expect more of a quickening or some totem of divinity to be shone illuminating from the scagliola sky?

The minute hand of the clock upon the wall had only travelled a quarter of its fixed orbit when Daniel hoisted himself out of the chair deciding it was time to announce his mother's passing to the nursing staff.

He walked steadily to the door, exited and walked down the corridor to where he saw one of the nurses, a young girl who'd often opened the security door allowing his entry to this part of the nursing home where Anne was billeted exchanging the briefest of pleasantries before rushing back to re-attend whatever duties she left to get the door.

'I think that's my mum passed away now.', the words were relayed clearly as if making a statement, served as actual fact, no blubbering and no lump in his throat only internal irrational thoughts which ran through his circuitry of his mind things that his lack of tears would draw judgement against him.

The nurse's face morphed from its readiness for morning salutations to serious confirming acknowledgment then sympathetic condolence like a chameleon acting to its environment, not shading to colours but contorting and knotting to conform with what ever etiquette the situation would required. "I will get someone to come and check!" she replied and started off with a rush towards the direction of the office.

Returning back to the room Daniel stood by the bed, a short wait and there was a knock at the door before Nadia entered in the company of the young nurse who had fetched her.

It was somewhat comforting to see Nadia attending his mother this final time, he had thought the older nurse may have finished her nightshift by now since dawn had already broken some hours before. Nadia bend at the side of the bed gently taking hold of Annie's wrist checking for any signs of life.

Confirmation was soon returned. "She has passed on now." said Nadia whilst delicately replacing Annie's hand on the bed. Daniel felt the younger nurses hand on the back of his shoulder giving comfort, he actually wished he could produce tears especially at this moment feeling it would be the right result, perhaps even expected from him but nothing came. "Would you like to wait with your mum until someone from Purves comes?" Nadia asked.

Purves was the funeral directors who Daniel agreed previously as to who should deal once this inevitable moment arrived.

Daniel answered "no thank you, I think I'd rather just go home.", he felt exhausted, the days and nights on the hard chair were taking their toll, "to get a bit sleep!" he added as if to explain himself.

"Certain. You get away home and get some rest. Purves will contact you later to discuss what will happen next, if you need anything just give us a call." she replied.

Daniel nodded and expressed his thanks, he was sincere at the kindness shown but desperate to get out the room, leave the building and get home, start the grieving process in the privacy behind the closed doors of his home.

Before departing the nursing home he collected a few items from Annie's room, the framed photos was the obvious choice of selection but his Mother's white and pink toiletry bag seemed an odd pick but whilst in her ensuite collecting his own toothbrush he popped it in his carrier bag too Her little comb he also collected, her long hairs still entwined within it's teeth.

There was a feeling of checking out of a hotel room, he had to temper his urge to look around the room to see if there was anything left behind. No charging cables in sockets, rolled off sock under the bed, passport on a chair, only the carcass of his mum with her soul since departed lying on the bed awaiting uplift.

He crossed over to the bed and gazed down once more to her face with its oracle eye still gaping as at odds with the death of the vessel it was planted upon.

He reached and touched her hand, saying nothing but feeling everything.

He stroked her hand as he held it, a tenderness that the receiver could no longer appreciate.

A "relevance of Yorick" moment came over him. How we remember that death is the great equaliser and comes to us all. This hand he stroked, this unresponsive hand was once a soft hand, scented with primrose, moisturised surface layers, the same hand that would pulled him up when he fell as a child, rubbed balm into his gazed knees, lotion into his sunburnt skin. Now there it rested, indifferent flesh.

Death is a twofold process, its the cessation of bodily functions and the consciousness, but, at least to all observers, Annie had already lost her consciousness but the prior had to catch up with the latter to fully cross the Rubicon.

It's said that being dead is indistinguishable from being unborn, or even comparative to a dreamless sleep so therefore should hold no terrors.

What seems frightening is the prospect of dying, Daniel did not sense any fear of this when talking with his mother when her mind was more sincere.

He suspected he feared his mother's death more than what she did herself. We, the living never experience being dead, we only experience losing someone to death, perhaps too much a subjective perspective to provide comfort but nevertheless something to reflect upon.

He could feel an emotion rising, flickering like the filament of a light bulb, glowing intensity before burning out, he thought for a moment tears were about to come but then nothing, the feelings were intense but the head was still too numb to express the them yet.

* * *

Outside felt like a different world, it was early, Sunday morning and the birds were chirping and the air tasted fresh as he set off on his short walk home from the nursing home.

He never felt like someone who just witnessed the death of a beloved mother, he wondered if this was normal. How should I be feeling he thought to himself, why wont the tears come?

There was a guilt, a self-condemnation which he reproached himself with using these thoughts.

Daniel felt somewhat detached from the situation, severed from the reality of the loss of such a leading player in the acts of his life, surely this should be hitting him more?

Cars drove up and down the road beside the pavement which he was walking along , did he really think the world would notice the death of the woman that gave him life?

He dipped his hand into his pocket and lifted out his phone, immediately his heart rate increased and breathing changed with the thought of sending a message to Lilian as for her to inform their son that his granny was no longer there.

Hi, Please tell Sam that his Granny passed away peacefully this morning he typed then reread the words, as was his habit before hitting send, he did not expect an swift reply so replaced the phone in his trouser pocket as he carried on walking.

Within a few minutes he felt a vibration against his leg indicating a message was received on his phone, upon. Looking at its screen he could see it from Lilian, an acknowledgment more than a reply simply stating **Told him**.

No mercy though pity would allow him to even have the slightest hope of a contact with Sam. Could I have expected anything different from that cold creature he thought with a brief flare of anger billowing up through him.

He slowed his pace and on his phone typed **I will send you the details about the funeral once I have them**.

There was still no reply to this message once Daniel arrived home, it remained unanswered, he expected nothing else, an expectation of none partly drawn from the previous received message. "Told him", two short words which radiated a frost which he knew from the sender, there would be no amnesty given even to allow a child to grieve for his gran which would under the circumstance at least allowed Daniel some comfort of seeing Sam albeit during solemnities, a gilt to the pain of the grief.

12

Lilian entered Sam's bedroom and told him in her matter-of-factly manner that his granny had died that morning.

She did have some apprehension about making the announcement to Sam after his spectacle at the nursing home a couple of days before, a drama which still angered her but he appeared to accept the news in his stride. He just looked up from where he was kneeling on the carpet with his blocks and toys, nodded in accepted acknowledgment to what she had just told him answering OK then returning to his play.

Is he really that resilient thought Lilian?

She expected more of a response, dreading any calamity that may start up from the boy from the information she was to part but never expected this, for him to receive the news that his gran had died then hardly lose a beat upon hearing it.

It was a feeling of relief that washed over her as she stood watching the child continue to play unheeded.

Any show of emotion which he may have demonstrate for that cursed paternal side would feel like a deduction from her own and a betrayal of sorts but here he was, told that his Daniel's mother was no more and taking the news as if she had just make an announcement that his dinner would be served in another hour.

Perhaps his bedside display at the nursing home when visiting Annie was just release of a buildup of tension he must be feeling because of that bastard Daniel does not let them free to have their own life.

Her relief more due to the impression Sam did not care about someone from Daniel's side passing away than believing that her son was not suffering anguish and distress through the grief of bereavement, that would be too altruistic on her part, a testament to nurturing maternal affection which she did not have. Any love she carried for Sam was overridden by the loathing of his father. Although she would never admit it, even to herself, she would sacrifice her only son on the altar of the forsaken offspring if it meant it would add impetus to Daniel's suffering as such was the vengeance she wanted served upon her ex.

If you cut away half the roots of the bush it would wither and she was already hacking away half of Sam's foundations in her attempts to punish his father, she knew that the child suffered due to her chosen course of action but she would never face this fact and would, if considered it, believe it to be short term pain for a long term gain for Sam.

She'd always attempt to justify her actions to friends that Daniel did not care for his son, to him the child was only a way to get to her, a tool, a bludgeon he would use to beat her with knowing her affections for her son.

How ironic was this, attempting to legitimise her own actions by implying that it would be the motive of another if she gave him the chance, allowed him her son to be used as ammunition. Such contemptuousness makes blind the perpetrator who forces estrangement of a child onto a devoted parent without virtuous rationale.

She continued to stand by the door studying the child for any delayed response. Did he fully understand what she had just told him?

'Sam, did you hear me? Your granny has passed away this morning!' she repeated. The words "your granny" stung her lips as they parting from them as she hated to acknowledge any connection of kin the child had to that side.

Sam paused his actions with his toy and looked up at his mother.

'Yes, mom' he acknowledged 'Granny is dead, I heard what you said' he continued to stare up at her awaiting further words.

'How does that make you feel Sam?' asked Lilian, she tried to soften her tone.

'Sad?' Sam answers in the air of a question but then quickly followed on 'I feel sad because she was someone who was once a nice old lady who'd use to read me stories when I was little.'

Lilian continued to look down on the boy, examining his face for sincerity. Is this truly his reaction for is he just telling me what I want

98

to hear? she thought.

'She was old!' Sam started up again explaining as he felt prompted for more clarity by his mother's stare

'Old people die to make room for the new people.' he continued, 'Miss Henderson told us so in class.'

Lilian digested his answer watching his face but did not see anything different as to question the genuineness of his words. Such the candidness of children she thought.

'Will you be wanting to go to her funeral?' she asked, anticipating a invite which she would most certainly be refusing on behalf of herself and her son.

'I don't think so.' he replied, 'everyone will have sad faces and Dad will be trying to look all caring about me in front of everyone.'

This answer gratified Lilian but still hearing him say the word "Dad" instead of "Daniel" annoyed her somewhat, that title still implied of an attachment which was a crease she was wanted desperately to iron out of the child's mind.

'You are right Sam, I don't think it would be a good idea if we went!' she said as if the decision was the boy's.

'Daniel would just be a pain trying to act all loving and nice in front of all his friends there, you know what he is like, trying to act like the good father, trying to hurt mommy!' she watched his face as she said this, another drip of poison administered.

There was no sign of dissension on his face but still she wondered if these were the answers he gave as he knew it's what was expected of him, giving utterances for her approval. After the his act at the nursing home she had been irked at his show of emotions, and Steve seemed a bit perturbed at her too which annoyed her immensely.

This old bitch chose her time to kick the bucket well, she would not be allowing Daniel to gain any pity points from Sam over this episode. She felt she had regained some ground back over now with Sam's reaction, and his answers which pleased her.

Even if Sam had wanted to go to the funeral she would find some excuse for him not to attend. At least with his own answer which he gave her she could spin it, especially to Steve. She could say that the choice is Sam's and as caring considerate mother she will be respecting this and aware of how Daniel, even on such a solemn occasion as his own mother's funeral, would attempt to use it to his own advantage trying to gain traction with Sam in aid to hurt her the child's mother. Yes, she could put this to her advantage.

* * *

The bedroom door closed as Lilian departed from Sam's room after delivering the news and being satisfied at the boy's answers to her questions.

Sam continued to push the little red car around the play matt on which he knelt, propelling it along the lanes printed onto the fabric to emulate roads and crossings. He was in autopilot, zigzagging between lanes and snaking along the mat pressing down on tiny tin roof of the toy hard causing it's four little plastic wheels to plough shallow furrows into the twill of the weaved fibre.

He still wore the mask drained of animation, the indifference he displayed for his mum just a few moments earlier was still there, although the neutrality of state had been effort to hold up but now he could feel a twitch in the corners of his eyes to match the lurching within his chest.

He would not, he could not give in to the torments of grief which were now swashing like uprush waves against his little heart.

He was already too familiar with his mom's annoyance should he give into the tormenting pain of the intense sadness he felt.

He'd lost the battle once already when he saw his granny lying on the bed there in that room within the nursing home. The anguish he felt there that evening took over any control he fought so hard to contain. Afterwards he could feel mom's infuriated disapproval radiate from her like heat from a fire. He was grateful for Steve's presence then as he felt with him being there her rage was held more in check but he had to be more careful now, he could not display any remorse again.

He felt a tear run its salty path down his cheek. He quickly wiped it away and sucked in a breath of air hoping no more would appear, mom could return at any moment to check, perhaps she is still outside his door listening for any sobs which would betray him.

Did he hear her footsteps recede down the hall? He could not be sure, he had to play it safe, maintain his composure. He could give into a measure of grief later whilst tucked up in bed pressing his face into the pillow but for now he needed self-control, like that guy with the pointy ears on Star Trek, he needed to be emotionless.

Another warm tear sprung from his eye and dripped like a solitary raindrop onto the mat before he could wipe it from its journey down his face.

He rubbed the wet Mark it produced on the mat just as another fell then another.

There was no blubbering or snivelling, he felt totally in control but these tears continued to drip as if they were revolting against his command, a mutiny of his body.

He did not rub his eyes, they'd have to stop soon and he did not want any red eyed indication to show that they had made a unwelcome appearance, if mom was to see him.

They, the tears, were now streaming in rivets down his face, refusing to obey his orders to cease and desist. If his mom were to open his door and see these shedding tears he would be busted, his facade of not caring would be done for.

His tears did eventually stop and he was left with a desiccated feeling around the eyes and within the heart.

His subterfuge of heartache went under the radar when he was called out his room later to have dinner with his mom and Steve. Nothing more was mentioned about his granny that evening, Sam was thankful for this.

Overnight for the next few evening whilst tucked and left in bed Sam would squeeze his face into the pillow when the lights were off to muffle any agonising sobs which would bubble up with the tears and memories.

He allowed his grief to trickle like sands of dirt down the trouser leg of a POW then to get stamped into the yard by a foot as he paced.

He accepted she was gone, she was already gone when he visited her in the nursing home, she was gone when his mom determined him not to have any more contact with his dad, she was no longer part of his life from then.

Only the sting of her absence remained like an echo in the room with Sam.

On the second evening, pyjama clad and after lights out he carefully stealthily climbed out of bed and went across to his "memory box' within the larger Lego box casing and quietly removed a photo within which he had of his granny and him.

It had been taken by his dad a few weeks before the contact stopped. One of granny's "better days" when his dad took them both out to eat in a restaurant.

There was Sam pictured from across the table sitting next to his gran. Sam looking at the camera with a small sign of embarrassment and Gran looking in the direction of Sam with only love on her face.

Sam stroked the image of her with his finger down her cheek, gentle as if it were her sleeping flesh.

He felt his heart strum a cord and fresh tears develop.

'I love you granny!', his breath told the photo, 'I am so very sorry!' he undeservedly said although he was not clear himself what he was apologising for, perhaps for her passing, or not being there to say these words to her from his own mouth.

Her absence weighted heavily on his little heart as did his father's, a burden of pain unjustly suffered by such a young soul.

13

The bottle clunked against the laminated surface of the floor as Daniel knocked it over whilst, his view blinkered by the wing of the sofa's upholstery, clawed over the side of the armchair trying to grab its neck to refill his glass.

He shot out his slouched position gyrating around the sofa's edge with his hand on its arm like a fulcrum for balance, then bending to straightened the bottle surveying the decanted puddle of ten year old malt whisky before hurrying through to the kitchen trailing an array of curses with him.

He returned with a tea towel laying it almost ceremoniously over the small pool and its formed rivulets, scrunching then mopping the residue dregs, soaking it up within its fibres.

He held the green glass bottle up to the ceiling light angling he head to check the level of liquid within. 'All good!' he declared satisfactory to himself. The bottle was already half empty before being bowled over by his searching hand, or half full as the optimist would state but this Sunday afternoon Daniel was neither an optimist or pessimist, none trumped the other on the road he now was navigating down in hope to seek solace in oblivion.

He splashed another liberal measure of the whisky into his glass toasting Slàinte to the dust motes riding the struts of fading sunlight peeking through the closed vertical blinds of the front window then settled back down with his drink in hand.

He sipped his straight liquor swirling it around his tongue before allowing it to trickle down his throat savouring the peaty taste and feeling the warm traction inside his craw.

It was to be the scenic route to oblivion and Daniel was enjoying the ride, drinking for equilibrium to balance the grief which was coursing through his heart. Glass in hand as his compass he raised it to his lips again.

The tears were still running late with no approximate time of arrival as yet, the stone birds had already nested heavily in his chest, he could feel their weigh but still his eyes remained a barren desert.

Although it was still only a couple of hours into the post meridian he was well into his solo soiree.

The blinds on the front window were drawn, not as any symbolism of a home in mourning only as he preferred artificial light at this moment instead of the glass filtered sunlight streaming in.

The polythene carrier bag sat on the seat beside him, deposited there upon arrival and unopened since as no urgency to explore the contents within.

Upon arriving home Daniel went straight upstairs intending to lay on the bed a while, which was especially inviting after the three nights he'd spent twisted on that chair attempting to jury-rig some comfort. He'd stopped at the door of his Son's now vacant bedroom opening the it then entering.

He sat on the low slung child's bed kicking off his shoes, laces still knotted. There he laid seeking sanctuary within Toy Story themed bright bedsheets which were all shades of grey as the curtains were shut.

The structure groaned with the unexpected weight of adult bulk.

He had to curl like a a Peruvian Pachacamac mummy to fit within its confines otherwise his lower limbs would hang over the end positioned more as a welcomed guest of Procrustes than an uninvited Goldilocks.

His position would not appear to be the most comfortable to an observer but there was a soothing to be had for Daniel to be there upon his son's bed within Sam's bedroom, almost a therapeutic serenity which serviced his exhaustion well.

He closed his eyes surrendering to his fatigue and within a few seconds he slept in that foetal position.

He was out for a couple of hours, blessed dreamless sleep.

He came too in more of a gallop than shades then sat upright at the side of the bed planting his feet on the floor.

Sam's bedroom had been repainted since his son's departure. Revised from a jungle green to a gentle purple and the walls were with posters of Marvel and DC Superheroes.

Two Sam-less Christmastides had passed since his son last was under his father's roof, but prior to each Daniel would go out and buy toys and books for him.

A Nintendo Gameboy, its outer box untampered sat on a shelf, other boxes with Lego branding bookending one side of it with a pile of annuals on the other, many with a date since expired on their brightly coloured spines.

Nerf gun, plastic dinosaur and various other bootie to delight a child where stacked again the wall.

They were Daniel's candle in the window for his absent son, a yellow ribbon around the "ole oak tree".

The room was like a shrine to his boy. Memories lived like manitou souls in the old toys, with hope wished from the new on the altar.

He raised himself from the bed, nothing to rush for.

He slowly climbed the stairs down, his palm scuffing down the smooth pine of the banister rail, and once down there he found himself in front of the drinks cabinet.

To hell with all, he though, the sun is well and truly over the yardarm and I carry the excuse of the bereaved.

The glass door was thus opened and the bottle of cask strength Laphroaig removed, the cork stopper popped.

An here was Daniel now, couch locked as he sipped more whisky from the glass. The glass was Edinburgh crystal, part of a set of 4 which came with a decanter, a wedding present from his best man, presented to him when he still believed in happy endings, now a vessel to contain his anaesthetising medicine to aid the shuffling of more recent thoughts to the back of the pack.

He had started collecting bottles of single malt whisky a few years ago, investing in a new bottle every couple of months and now he had a modest collection displayed in the glass fronted cabinet so this evening of wrack and ruin would be with a quality malt and not some gut rot but no comfort was forthcoming with that thought, alcohol had only to serve an anaesthetising purpose that afternoon rolling into evening, so it made no difference which corner of the country it was distilled in or age of the cask, only that it would blunt the edges which here horned from the sorrow of the last few days, he embraced the burn as it ran down his gullet.

"To La Frog!" he toasted the vault of emptiness around him parodying the name of that particular single malt and wishing for the somniferous effect of the alcohol to bite him quick before any memories could barge up under his defences.

There was a rap at the front door startling Daniel from his melancholy. He was tempted to ignore it, but with his car in the drive it was as much a signal that he was at home as a flag up the flagpole and although the blinds where drawn and it was still in the last dregs of daylight out there in the world, the light from within could still be detected from out so there would be no hiding, it would be an unconvincing act on his part not to answer its calling.

He got slightly unsteadily to his feet and marshalled himself to the door where he could see a blurred shape though the frosted glass square laid within it.

He turned the key and pulled the door open.

It was Dale his friend, a confidant from work to whom he had confided the situations of his mother's state and the affairs of not seeing his son.

Despite Daniel's initial reluctance to receive a visitor he felt an appreciative happiness seeing his friend standing there even with his somber air.

Dale was the other person Daniel sent a Text message to during his ambulatory march home from the nursing home that morning.

Hi Mate, the dispatched text had read then went on to announce **My mum died this morning, please can you tell HR I wont be coming into work tomorrow as I will need a few days off to make arrangements cheers.**

The resulting reply consisted of condolences and an affirmative to the request, and now here was the recipient on the dispatchers doorstep, a pilgrimage undertaken by a friend due to concern.

With the door open and both parties facing each other on the threshold Daniel felt a twinge of awkwardness which was not breached nor diminished by the intoxicating doses of whisky he had consumed. At work banter flowed freely between the pair but here was a undertaking of a propriety but as yet Daniel was not feeling like the grieving son unable to present sackcloth and ashes.

Dale extended his hand which Daniel docked with his, shaking it with the formal firmness that the circumstance of the encounter merited.

'I'm sorry to hear about your mum Mate!" Dale condoled, "thought I'd pop around to see how you are" He handed Daniel a white envelop as he said this, the sympathy card in the tradition of condolence, Daniel accepted with thanks.

The phrase "Pop Around" was a play down of the distance Dale had came on this Sunday afternoon thought Daniel without realising that the afternoon had already dripped into early evening as the setting sun was give witness to.

Dale lived a good distance away from the town Daniel aboded in so it was small feat to sacrifice an late afternoon with family at short notice and travel in from the other side of Edinburgh to see someone under such bleak conditions, this touched Daniel a lot and bedded into his head more the gravity of the past events and an appreciation of such friendship.

"Thanks Pal, I appreciate it. Come on in.", Daniel was attentive when talking, carefully articulating his words as not to sound emotional from grief or effected by the drink but warily also not to sound cold.

But he needn't have worried about the appearance of his tone, the pitch was of equitable delivery, neither bubbling or too crisp, the alcohol did not add to any slurring either.

Acting the clown, the geezer and consummate professional were familiar comfy shoes for men to slip into when meeting up but overemotional bubbling sentiment was still deficit from the traditionally masculine repertoire. Daniel was no different. During a normal working day in the office the passing of the daily toil would be lubricated with jocularity, a verbal swordplay of ripostes.

Working in a telecom engineering office environment gaiety was never in short supply as the work got done sitting at their desks driving a keyboard and steering a computer mouse resolving software issues in exchanges around the country without leaving the seat.

Daniel first meet Dale about 16 years ago, as a newcomer to the team. Promoted to an office role instead of climbing up poles and going down holes in all seasons Dale, with his equable temperament and pitching in during all hands to pumps moments was a hail fellow and well met by his new colleagues.

Daniel and Dale especially got on once it came apparent they both shared the same tastes in music and started going to gigs together. Daniel always felt at ease in Dale's company, there was never any airs and graces between them. Dale was his confidant when Daniel separated from his wife and knew her hostilities over their son and the proceeding court action for contact.

During the disintegrate of Annie's health Daniel found it

therapeutic talking it over with Dale during lunch breaks and the odd social event they attended when the booze flowed.

Dale had always supported Daniel during his woes with a patient ear and good advice, this moment was to be no exception.

Dale accepted Daniel's offer of a mug coffee, it somewhat clashed with the glass of whisky Daniel was drawing upwards to his lips but Dale knew alcohol and driving would not be a good mix.

Usually when at a party and one were to drinks a soft drink and the others down intoxicant there is usually a slight knock of the disharmonizing cords settling into the gathering, like a priest with a confessor but it was never the case with these friends, bones had been laid bare before when Daniel opened up to Dale about separating from Lilian then about her revengeful retribution by withholding contact with his son.

It was not a secret in the office that Daniel had split from his wife and being denied access to his only son but the intricacies of the matter he would share with Dale which only strengthened their already staunch friendship.

'It was just after 8 this morning when she passed away. I was right there at her bedside, peaceful enough and thankfully no need for any palliative measures, she did not appear to be in any discomfort.' Daniel sincerely hoped this was true when he spoke the words, her thrashing and moans were as if on an unconscious level he so dearly hoped.

'I came straight home after she passed away and had some shut eye upstairs in my bed, I never waited for the undertaker but was told by the nurse that they will be in contact with me to arrange a viewing and the funeral.'

To his relief his pitch and tone was matter of fact, no bubbling or breaking, the resolute stiff upper lip was engaged and maintained.

'That's good mate!' Dale replied, 'it's the best way to go!'. Daniel nodded his head to show acknowledgment of this statement.

It was not a case of courage in the face of pain that Daniel was determined not to show emotions for he knew Dale would understand and empathise, but there was a vulnerability in grieving emotions and he wanted to keep a tight rein on his.

Daniel realised he had not yet opened the card yet which Dale handed to him on his arrival. He picked the envelope up and opened it thanking Dale as he did so with the broader Scotch 'och yer needna have bothered mate!'

The card inside was a a tartan thistle on a matted white background with the words "with heart felt sympathy" bannered underneath. Inside were the words "thinking of you on this most difficult of days" signed Ann and Dale. The gesture touched Daniel.

'Really kind mate. And please thank your wife too, very kind thoughts.'

Dale brushed the gracias aside and asked 'how you holding up mate?'

Daniel just shrugged and replied 'I don't think it's really hit me yet, I don't know what I should be feeling if I'm honest.' as he finished speaking he dipped another swig of the whisky.

The talk was getting more sparse the more alcohol Daniel was to consume but Dale remained rightly knowing that his company was needed for a little bit longer.

Dale saw the plastic carrier bag on the seat next to Daniel, it was bulged with contents.

'Is that something you should stick in the fridge mate?' he asked, realising Daniel was quite out of sorts due to the mixture of whisky and the grief he believed that his friend was attempting to hold in and keep a latch on.

'That bag Dale is a sack full of memories!' Daniel answered cryptically.

'Right!' Dale just replied, not expecting any elaboration.

Daniel reached over his hand into the bag and pulled out the first item his hand was to touch. It was a small wooden comb. Daniel held it up to his face for closer scrutiny. He noticed the long grey hairs snared around its thin wood tines. That little wood rake proved to be the catalyst needed as then the tears came.

14

In the Iliad Homer recounts the obsequies of both Patroclus and Hector each with their own funeral rites. The former covered with a white rob, his body anointed with oils while Achilles all night long weeps mourning his pederastic lover whilst scraping up dust from the ground to pour upon his own head surrounded by his Myrmidons also grieving whereas the latter, Hector, the tamer of horses was placed on a funeral pyre which was nine days in the making before being lit, after which wine was in great quantity of supply was consumed by the Trojans as the bones were collected, wrapped in purple cloth before being placed in an urn then buried.

Churchill's state funeral in 1965 was broadcasted live around the world by the BBC. His body lay in state at Westminster Hall for three full days, his casket on a black velvet-draped catafalque. It had a Union flag draped over it, while a black silk cushion placed on top held Churchill's insignia as a Knight of the Garter. His cortege went from Westminster Hall to St Paul's and then back along the river from Tower Hill to the Festival Hall, before departing by train from Waterloo for Bladon.

When Daniel's brother Jimmy died on Piper Alpha his parents and him attended three funerals, the first was held in a local church, a strange affair without a coffin front and centre. The second was a memorial in the city of Aberdeen which was held for all of the victims and then finally, once the sea gave up its dead and his body was excavated from the risen accommodation module there was another funeral held, this time with his corpus delicti encased in a casket. During each stage tears were shed openly.

Samuel's committal almost ten years later played out to a packed house with standing room only in the aisles. The old favourite Highland Cathedral was played over the sound system as the box rolled on its track through the curtains for the pit crew behind the scenes to burn later.

Annie's ceremony was a very much quieter and a less attended affair. Daniel just choose the most basic of coffins and a merely functional floral tribute which would sit on top of the box during its transit in the hearse from pallor to crematorium. A "Scented Wreath" which the recipient would never smell. It's circular shape intended to symbolise eternal life but to a nonbeliever like Daniel it was just a window dressing, only chosen as it appeared to be the done thing, a testimony of love and respect shown by the mourner. As if some white lilies, roses and carnations attached to a foam frame can signify how much this son loved his mother and would express, even in the smallest means, how the past years were! Insensate organic matter placed a top a box containing dead organic matter, each destined for its final place, one to be ashes the other to be compost.

There was a numbness, a certain stupefaction about the whole undertaking, it felt almost mechanical, going with the flow. During the past five days all was happening as if he was in an autopilot mode. Since Dale's departure on the evening of Annie's death that past Sunday the days lacked their definition. Monday came and went, normally the start of the working week just felt like any other of non-description with Daniel pottering around the house, segmenting it into parts by the meals he had, breakfast, lunch, dinner then supper before bed.

On the Tuesday he had attended Purves the Undertakers. He discussed the details of his mother's funeral. Basic coffin choice from the brochure handed to him as he was seated in their office opposite a very solemn gentleman.

His consideration of choice was purely based on cost, it was just an empty box to contain another empty box, that being Annie's body, a shell departed of its contents.

Veneered MDF filled his requirements in the coffin selection, he glanced at the others available, wicker coffins, willow coffins, coffins made from bamboo, seagrass or even banana leaves.

'Unfortunately we don't have the Seagrass or Banana leaf weaved caskets available at this time.' the funeral director helpfully spoke out as he watched Daniel's eyes glance over the pages. Hungry salesman on commission he thought, the contemporary Charon, now earning five percent instead of one obol and ferries the bodies in a long, glass-sided estate vehicle.

The Cavendish, The Cambridge, The Canterbury...Banana Eco Coffin, Subtly elegant, this 100% natural coffin is made from the leaves of the banana plant after fruiting. Charming description he thought, after fruiting to carry a fruiting body. It looked like an oblong Christmas hamper.

He handed the glossy brochure back across the desk, open and his finger on The Cavendish, A veneered oak coffin with matching solid oak combination moulds, traditional embossed side panels and half round beading to the lid, Veneered MDF it was to be then, its just firewood at the end of the day, he would have accepted the cardboard box which it had came in if that were possible.

It was not about thrift, if he thought for an instance that a highly polished casket featuring images of the Last Supper by Leonardo da Vinci "The Corpus Christi" or a Pure white casket with a high gloss finish, matching bar handles mirrored supports fitted with crepe interior and sunburst pattern in the inside of the lid "The Stourton" would be any difference to the comfort or dignity of a traveler within he would not have hesitated but to Daniel this was just transport for disposal and any excess would just we allowing the vultures to cash in on misery.

Daniel had already paid top whack with his love and emotions towards his dear mother.

'The Cavendish, that's a beautiful casket!' the undertaker confirmed Daniel's choice taking note of it on the pad at his side. Daniel somewhat felt like the client of a sommelier who had just approved of his choice of wine.

'Would you like a have a look at the engraved name plates that we can provide to place on the lid of your chosen casket?'

Greatly appreciated Charon but think I'll just stick with the basic package, cabin bag only, no inflight meals, drinks or scratch cards but Daniel, more politely than his thoughts answered 'No thanks' but he did accept the next brochure which was floral tributes and picked out the "Scented Wreath'

Now it was Friday, the morning of the funeral and Daniel had showered, got dressed into his black suit, had a brief panic when he could not find his black tie but then eventually found it concealed in his sock drawer buried among balled up socks.

He'd never made and announcement about the day's event to anyone who may have cared, the cremation of his mother's empty shell was just to be such, any respects to be paid would be the memories anyone held of her in their own heads during better times when Annie's mind was complete and she had a life.

As far as Daniel was aware the only people who knew about the day's upcoming burning was the funeral crew and the church minister who'd never even met his Annie as since joining the local parish long after his mother had stopped attending Church since her husband's death, her last visit being nearly a decade ago when her grandchild was baptised. As a non-believer himself he just considered the minister to be another clog in the clockwork necessity to complete the business of disposal, a mercenary for hire.

Some of Daniel's work colleagues knew of course having heard from Dale since his Sunday visit and as they since enquired about Daniel's absence in the office.

His manager Alistair and Dale said they would attend the funeral to support Daniel, he was touched at their concern yet felt he did not need any support, his mum had died in shades over the years and on this day he was just disposing of her empty vessel. That would seem like a cold outlook but that's how he felt.

There was something meaningful to him that day however and that was the possibility that the son he had not laid his eyes on for the past two years may be attending.

He had sent Lilian by text the date, time and location of his son's grandmother's funeral but received no reply, although this was not surprising, but did hold some hope he'd may see Sam in attendance.

Daniel stood by the inside of his front door fully dressed awaiting the arrival of his friends who, by prior agreement said they would drive him to the crematorium that morning where the hearse would be awaiting them at 10:30 with his mother's coffin charged in the back.

A thought ran though Daniel's mind about his mother, about how ten years ago she would be awaiting for him, her son, to collect her in the car to drive her to the hospital to see her first sighting of her grandchild, waiting as he was waiting now.

He heard a car pull up outside and door closed, he stepped out. His two friends had arrived. Dale arrived with Alistair, handshakes were exchanged with the stiff solemness that comes with greeting the bereaved.

Daniel filed into the back of the car and they headed off on the short drive towards the crematorium.

It was a strange being in the company of friends and the atmosphere being so sedated he thought . Being seated alone in the back of the car had a chauffeured feel about it. The talk was small and mostly about the weather which as currently raining.

Daniel silently stared out of the window by his side, watched the rivulets of rain water stream horizontally from the slipstream of the car then the leading tears peel off into the wind.

He just wanted the day to be over, the forthcoming event to be completed yet he carried a ball of excitement in his belly, an anticipation that he may see his son in attendance.

Soon they arrived at the crematorium and the black hearse was there, parked outside with the coffin as seen through the aquarium windows at its rear.

From his window in the car Daniel scanned the small sparse assembly which stood protected from the rain under the canopy of the entrance searching for the scaled down figure of a child.

He recognised the faces, the minister, one of the church elders who lived across the road from what was once Annie's house and another familiar face he knew, Nadia the nurse from the nursing home, but no Sam he was crestfallen to notice.

The car was parked. Following the actions of his companions he stepped out.

They all smoothed down their black suits as if synchronised then walked across the gravel towards the entrance of the building.

The gathering shuffled upon Daniel's arrival.

His hand was shaken and words of condolences were delivered.

The minster went inside to take up his position and Daniel was ushered in to take his seat up the front row, a row which only he sat along.

The other pair who he had arrived with sat immediately behind him. Daniel felt a supportive hand on his shoulder but never turned his head to see which one of the pair had placed it.

The music started when someone out of sight pressed the play button the CD behind the scenes as the coffin containing what was once his mother was carried in and placed up front upon the raised catafalque platform.

The minister then gave the eulogy of a lady he'd never known since he'd came to the parish, then shortly after that he said his words, as an out of sight switch was thrown, music started up again and everyone stood as the minister commanded as the coffin slowly moved forward as if by magic on platform where it had been laid and entered the curtained off tunnel which lay ahead opened to accepted the offering.

That was it, job done was the thought that passed through Daniel's numbed head as he exited the crematorium receiving more handshakes with words of condolences from the attendees.

The book which was once his mother's existence could be finally closed as the epilogue was now completed.

15

"Let my heart be wise; it is the god's best gift' once said Euripides, a tragedian of ancient Athens. Old Wife's Tales and proverbs also had his back with their many "look before you leap" variations. Then there was "haste leads to waste, prevention is better than the cure" doing the rounds of advice too.

The klaxons are bright red on the walls of everyone's consciousness to be noticed especially those "once bitten" but still a Pavlov's dogs like response happens when that glockenspiel scale beats in our hearts again. The brain salivates its oxytocin and the Dantesque "abandon all hope" sign above the path about to be taken is ignored.

It had been almost two years since his mother, Annie had gone. An epoch also measured by not having contact with his son Sam now counted four years, four long years for the absence of a loved one is measured by the heart and the days, weeks, months and years passed slower can on any calendar.

Both their absences felt such a large presence in his life but he had to live now, to continuously mourn his mother and live the cycles of hope then disappointment over his son was too hard on his mind and heart. Grieving has no set rules for either.

We go into an ice age when someone important to us dies. The ice takes time to thaw and once it does we have a new landscape to navigate across, a new life without that loved person. This was no exception with the death of Annie only except the frost of that oncoming ice age settled on the ground slower, when her memory started to fade was when the first snowflakes floated down from the heavens.

His mother, he lost her in shades, the expulsion of her final breath that morning a year since in the nursing home felt, on reflection as just being the eraser crumbs being blown off the paper, the final step of the gradual expunging of his much loved mum due to her dementia. Praise given to the human psychology that we can forget the suffering is a blessing, as to replay its raw qualities in the mind would be an unbearable anguish.

Annie now took her place in Daniel's memories only, another gap in what once was a familiar array of people in his life now in its halls of remembrance.

His lamentation for his son would continue however but his optimism in the family court system was at an end, the longer it persisted the more favourable the prospects were for the manipulator which was the child's mother.

It had felt like a futile struggle to continue when Sam was resisting, yet at first he refused to give up, to stop felt tantamount to Daniel as giving up on his son but the realisation that he was getting no where and would get no where was soon apparent and a joint motion was to be signed with Lilian's lawyer as not proceed further with his action for contact with Sam.

Losing his mother and extinguishing the last embers of hope of seeing his child again was as excruciation to bare but he was determined the pain he had felt would not debilitate his life. He thought of the glamorised words of Nietzsche "What does not kill us makes us stronger" but these were words written by a man who was the decaying from a terminal syphilis which would metastasised into paraplegia and dementia, not exactly an encouraging example but still Daniel was determines not to just sit back and mourn.

He was back on the dating scene as his self-proclaimed social status would corroborate to if asked. *Single to Dating* then the *In a Relationship* were frequently interchangeable, the brief *In a Relationship* distinction lasting for six months before breaking up with mutual consent.

So back into the fray of Online Dating he went and not to be deterred at this method was also how he met Lilian.

Tinder was apparently the way to go as he'd been told by some of the apprentices in the office. It was a notorious "hookup" app and expectations amongst colleagues were still not positive that love could be found through such a medium but it was a god send to Daniel as the traditional methods of "live" social interaction to choose a possible partner filled him with dread, at least he could break the ice first by exchanging messages over the internet rather than interrupted snippets of conversations in a night club or probing questions with the guise of casualness over a table in a restaurant from a mutual friend induced arranged meeting.

He was astonished that the more timorous of the heart had be able to populate before the invention of the internet or the ones which had, the ones who could with reliance upon Dutch courage never all died due to cirrhosis of the liver as he thought back of the copious intoxication to the state of dipsomania when hunting with the packs during his youth.

He pinned his photo online and chose another couple which he thought he looked passible in. The blurb description he completed on the dating site he hoped would make it clear be was looking for something long term, it was important there was no mistaking that, he was serious about a relationship and if he was to present himself into the world of what some believed was a cyber meat market he did not want to advertise to the wrong buyer.

The workings of Tinder was quite simple once he downloaded it on his smart phone. The app would   display a slideshow of photos, profile photos of the opposite gender, each with a small biography, then he would be prompted to either swipe left if he were not interested or right if, on first sight the person displayed appeal to him. They, the other party, would do the same and if both "swiped right" then it would be a "match" and the channels of online communication opens by giving the option to send and receive messages.

Simple enough operation but it did feel a little cold to Daniel, a bit like online shopping, choose a product then add to basket,   e-commerce for desires.

Some profiles just had a single photo, others had multiple, up to six different photos.

He, like many, was guilty of judging a book by it cover, by only inspecting the small biography attached if the picture caught his eye

Some matches were made, conversations initiated but lots appeared to abruptly end without explanation, ghostings, the most probably cause being the other person had found someone else to meet or to concentrate their energies on, or simply felt there was no spark, the online dating equivalent of turning your back and walking away, except in normal life such behaviour is not so common through politeness, but on the virtue world with it's anonymity and click n'close finality manners were easier to discard.

On the occasions were there was a glimmer of a spark Daniel would exchange phone numbers then level up with voice calls. Hopefully the final step before an actual physical meeting, the ultimate goal of leaving the comfort blankets of cyberspace and phones by progressing to a date, the safety net whisked away, the curtain pulled back to judge if the photos match the online profile and the body language translate as acceptable.

Daniel has progressed on to the date stage five times so far, three of which did not lead past the first dinner notch, although polite enough during and at departures

And then there she was!

The photo was that of a blonde girl, the first of a quintet of images which Daniel would later frequently examine with an amorous heart as if he were a poet rooted to the floor of the Uffizi gazing upon The Birth Of Venus, milking every inch, hungry sucking up the view as if it were opiates of inspiration for the heart.

The cover photo on her dating profile, the one which first piqued his interest, was that of her standing in the sea up to just below her knees. She was wearing a white blouse, the top of which was sloped down on the left bearing a tanned shoulder. She wore sunglasses and was staring off into the distance to her right, a smile on her face. Blonde hair tied in a long braid dropped down the anterior of her exposed shoulder. The hem of her dress finished some inches above her knees, above the shallow waterline her slim thighs were golden.

The scene looked foreign, the sea, a small bay with mountains in the background and a small row boat further back. The fashion in which she was dressed would suggest a warmer climate.

The other photos were also of only her. One with a dog at her feet, a companion as she lounged back on a recliner in what looked to be a garden, these long golden legs again. Daniel could see her eyes were dark brown, they enthralled upon his gaze, captivating his focus. Flaxen blonde hair, darker in some pictures than others but always long and looking inviting for fingers to run through it.

On another photo she posed with her back against a graffitied wall, every inch of which was a vibrant colour yet she flourished out more brightly than her background wearing just the simplest black t-shirt, standing with the ease of a model, arms above her head and hand closed within tousled hair, a necklace of what looked to be shells decorating her neck.

There were another two photos on her profile, one where she stood wearing black legging with a white blouse, a hat on her head smiling at the camera standing in front of what looked to be a trailer containing two horses who peeks inquisitively over the upper openings.

On the other photo again wearing a white blouse opened at the neck and wearing a different hat, this time looking to her left with a smile. A smile she selflessly shared with the world.

Her face was rounded, her cheeks full but not with plumpness from corpulence , no, it was as if designed to accommodate the plethora of her smile. Almost cherubic with it's divinely pure nature, this was a face you would dance like a jester just to see it light up, just to bask within the radiance of its beam.

On each photo her skin was shimmering as if gilt with gold, she shone, actually glistered. The white she wore in three of the photos just accentuate her glow all that more, she discharged the very essence of beauty to his mind.

Beauty was subjective in Daniel's world, to his eye, as the beholder he was drawn to the more exotic. Dark eyes, brown skin, quite the opposite of himself. But many of these features were now more objective attributes in the realms of attractiveness so he knew such a creature would be in much demand by the partner seeking males with their thumbs posed to swipe right and trial out their best patter.

The colour of health was once white, white bread white rice, white flour, like the bridal gown white was once the signature of refinement and purity but that had since changed somewhat in society over the last century. A more contemporary colour of health became brown, brown bread, brown rice, brown flour, a more unrefined heartiness than it's predecessor.

No more cream complexion seeker for the majority, they hunted the golden tan of sun exposure.

Changes in society brought on by the easier access to the French Riviera in the 20s beckoning the playboys and girls to frolic under the sun escaping from the colder clutches of Northern Europe.

The momentum of sun-bronzed carried on through the years and here was Daniel, captivated by this goddess of incitement before him.

The name of this celestial being was in the description within her profile which Daniel started to read after he feasted on her photos.

Maria was this angel's name. He shaped the words in his mouth before breathing them out.

Age: Forty Two, Just a couple years younger than myself he thought. Location: Glasgow, ahhh, the geography bequeaths its blessings.

Status: Single and looking for long Term Relationship, be silent my beating heart.

Education: Pontifical Catholic University of Rio de Janeiro, what the hell?

She was Brazilian! Shit! A spanner in the works! Lilian the ex-wife was, is, Brazilian, his ears still echoed with the Brazilian Portuguese insults she hurled at him and her fierce temper.

After that disaster of a marriage Daniel has said never again, never again to woman but then here he was back on the scene dating and looking for love.

But another Brazilian? Come one Daniel he thought, don't blanket judge the population of a country the size of a continent on the merits, or more accurately the demerits of one person.

This Maria was in Glasgow, its not as it I have to lug myself across the world. What's the harm in trying. Be objective here. Anyway, she probably will not even reply, with these photos she will be inundated with responses.

Ahhh Stuff It… Daniel swiped right.

Maria did reply.

She like the look of the guy's photo. Ignoring it was obviously a selfie, and with a ridiculous blue "Team GB" cap he wore on his main photo she would thumb through his other pics to ensure he was not balding with the cap just as concealment but no, he had a full head of hair and it was red, she liked what she saw.

In one pic he was wearing a Hawaiian shirt, meu deus que cara louco… but the narrative he wrote did appeal to her.

Likes Traveling, Non Smoker, Single and Looking for Long Term Relationship, Proper Gentleman with Old Fashioned Values Looking for His Lady..ahhh she though, a bit cringe but lets see.

She decided to take a chance and swiped right.

It was a "match" the screen flagged up, apparently they liked each other.

Maria decided to gambit an opening and sent him a message online **Olá, Hi How are you?** Nice simple opener she thought as she continued thumb flicking through other mugshots of potential dates appearing on her mobile.

The little square in the corner almost immediately flashed up to indicate a reply, she clicked it open with her fingertip.

Olá, como você está esta noite? I'm Daniel. Opa she thought, hello Daniel. She then responded with a reply.

Você fala português? She inquired asking him if he spoke her language.

Nao, but I have Google Translator :) came the honest reply.

The exchange of of messages continued and gained momentum. The interchange of small talk which was being dealt out between them like playing cards on a table started to morph more into conversations, the topics varied and was diverse, maybe not always with a consensus of opinions but always with respect and politeness.

For Maria it was a freshness to type talk with someone she felt was not trying to redirecting the flow to shallower waters when she started to write about more esoteric topics, he seemed very like minded too and would ask all the "right" questions when she touched on her life.

Daniel was equally engrossed in what she had to say, he was fascinated to learn about her life, her experiences and opinions.

After just over an hour of riveted chatting using the communication channel opened by the dating app they both came to the conclusion that it was not adequate enough for the pace of their discussions and agreed to exchange phone number, a progressive step neither had ever took so decisively and so quickly before.

A Friday night was to be their first actually physically meeting, the much anticipated inaugural date, an agreed rendezvous for an evening's table d'hôte at the Merchant City Restaurant, table booked for two at eight under the name Sinclair, the bearer of the name was to stand outside the restaurant to greet his invitee as she arrived by taxi.

There he stood waiting, jittery with nerves walking and back and forth upon the pavement like a guard on sentry duty, phone in hand for any updates on the anticipated arrival.

Each time that a car headlights would herald its arrival down the darkened side street Daniel would stop his pacing, compose himself awaiting focus of incoming vehicle to identify if it were a taxi. On a few occasions that it were a taxi the butterflies would escalate their flutterings in his guts, only for the cab to pass by the restaurant after which he would feel a mixture of both relief and disappointment before starting his traipse back and forth again trying to burn off some nervous energy.

He'd received a text message ten minutes ago, **Getting in Taxi now, be with you in five.** Five minutes came and went, the zenith of anticipation now extended.

The lights beamed down the road once again, about turned Daniel alertness peaked as it slowed down close to the doors of the restaurant. A black hackney carriage, too dark inside to glance through the front windscreen to see the occupancy of the back seats.

A interior light snapped on to assist the commuter to count their change to pay the fare.

It was a woman, this was her, she had arrived!

Suddenly the air started ringing within Daniel's ears. Calm be calm he repeated to himself in his head like a mantra as he straightened up more and squared off his shoulders.

The back door of the taxi opened and she exited, Maria.

Daniel approached her in four strides smiling.

'Hi, you arrived!' he stated the obvious with a grin.

'Hello!' she beamed out in return with that smile he had studied so intently on her photos.

She moved forward offering her check which he pecked in greeting then repeated on the switch, the fur stole which she wore around her neck tickled his cheek delightfully and the delicate fragrance of her perfume warmed his senses even more.

'Really lovely to meet you!' Daniel said and he shook her hand in a more formal greeting.

'My pleasure!' she returned, 'sorry I am a little late, the roads here were quite busy.'

And so the welcoming salutations and concession played out before both parties entered the restaurant announcing to their host their reservation and were shown to their table once they were decanted out of their winter outer garments to be hung on a nearby coat stand.

Daniel was mindful to be seated only after Maria took her pew at the table, polite manners count especially in first impressions.

Maria ordered a glass of pinot noir when drinks were offered by their waitress who had directed them to their table as they browsed through the menu, Daniel asked for the same, two large glasses.

'So do I look like as in my photo?' Daniel joked, a practiced ice breaker for meeting an internet arranged date.

'You look better!' laughingly retorted Maria, to which Daniel exaggerated a snort.

She rubbed her hands together over the table displaying an attempt of friction for heat, 'It's freezing out there!, I don't know how you people survive in this country!'

'It's our polar bear genetics, we would struggle in hotter climates. Your Brazilian blood will soon acclimatise.'

'I don't think I will ever get used to this cold, I can actually see my breath out there!'

'A wee dram of whisky will soon thicken your blood and solve that problem.' Daniel found himself attempting to deliver that line exaggerating more of a Caledonian inflection than he had intended and silently chided himself for sounding like Mrs Doubtfire.

Maria giggled 'You have a beautiful country but it's so damn cold!'

'We keep it cold on purpose or we would be overran by bikini clad Brazilian!'

She giggled at this.

'Do you have some nice bitches?' Maria enquired.

'Pardon?' Daniel asked, trying to mask his befuddlement at what he just heard.

'Nice bitches, we have lots of good bitches in Rio, is there any here?'

Well there was his ex-wife, she is certainly a bitch but in no way a nice one thought Daniel but answered 'Bitches?'

'Yes!' insisted Maria, 'Close to were I used to live in Rio we have Ipanema but I don't know about here."

Ahhhh the penny dropped. 'Beaches!' he exclaimed to an amused response.

'Sim, Bitches!'

Daniel cackled with laughter, 'sorry, lost in interpretation', he went on the explain which Maria regarded with mock embarrassment such was the scandal of being misunderstood.

The ice was broken, they feel into their roles with comfort. Their wine arrived and any nervous tension drained as the night went on. The conversation flowed easily from both.

It was determined that Daniel was not a fan of the "Bitches" in Scotland due to his fair skin and what was once termed as his "carrot topped head" as a child and the trauma of a terrible suffering of sunburn down in Blackpool with his parents, the outcome which lead to his back being liberally dabbed with calamine lotion saturated balls of cottonwool, a sensation he still recounted to this day with a PTSD he joked.

Maria was a devotee of the sun when she was back home in Brazil, but here in Bonnie Scotland, Daniel assured her, she'd struggle to find a suitable altar to worship her solar deity as the weather there in the northern hemisphere favoured more the blue eyed bred and lighter skinned vitamin D gatherers than the brown eyed and tanned skinned.

16

After their first date on the Friday night, which they'd both deemed to be a success and as such deserved a sequel, to follow on they arranged to rendezvous again the next day.

It had been Daniel's suggestion taking Maria to the Kelvingrove Art Gallery, he'd used the unnecessary excuse that he wanted to show her Salvador Dali's Christ of St John of the Cross which was a permanent resident there. Maria never needed an excuse to want and see Daniel again, she was already hooked on this strange Scotsman and would have accepted another date anywhere to do anything, even if he had proposed picking litter up from the streets.

Daniel collected Maria outside the hotel where she was staying, a temporary abode until she found an apartment to rent for the duration of her contract in Glasgow.

She got into the passenger side of the car, Daniel having held the door open for her with old fashioned civil manners. Daniel walked around the back of the car to the driver's side, stopping first to open the rear door she he could extract a bag on the seat behind where Maria sat, then joining her up front. Seated behind the wheel he handed the bag to her.

'A wee surprise I got you!' Daniel announced as he passed her the plastic bag before buckling up.

Maria, exaggerating caution, peered into the bag before lifting out one of its contents, it was a tin of haggis with a tartan ribbon sellotaped to the top.

She chuckled at the gesture with delight, 'you certainly know what a girl wants.' she laughed.

'I know you don't yet have a fridge so this canned national dish will not go wrong.' Daniel retorted.

The other item in the bag was contained in a small box, as Maria opened the box she was already laughing again, it was a small dumpy battery powered nightlight for babies in the shape of a unicorn.

Maria flicked the small switch with her nail and it lit up casting a soft pink light before turning blue and changing to green then repeating the colour cycle.

'I saw this and knew you just had to have it!' professed Daniel through a wide grin. After all, Unicorns are Scotland's national animal and you need one at the side of your bed to protect you.'

'Until I have you!' Maria teased with a smile, Daniel blushed then started the car as if to change the subject.

Kelvingrove Art Gallery was only a short journey from where Maria was staying. It was a massive baroque styled building built in the early nineteen hundreds and sat adjacent to Kelvingrove Park near the main campus of the University of Glasgow.

After parking the car they walked through the entrance into a grand hall with high vaulted ceilings and organ music playing within as if to greet their arrival. There was a pipe organ recital in the museum everyday at 1pm and they their visit coincided with this time.

Directly across the hall from the entrance large brass organ pipes climbed high upon the wall like polished vines, the spectacle was quite remarkable.

The reason for their visit, or more accurately the excuse Daniel was on the first floor up on the south balcony so up they climbed, Daniel almost bouncing up the steps at her side such was his excitement to guide her around.

During the drive in Daniel tried to blag a knowledge of art which he'd crammed up on using Google that morning before collecting her.

On their first date the night before, he'd learnt she had a passion for art and that her mother back in Brazil was an artist.

Daniel was somewhat a philistine when it came to art, he never knew Impressionism from Surrealism but he knew there was this iconic Salvador Dali painting hanging in Glasgow, so during that evening he hoped to win kudos from this beautiful lady by mentioning it and suggesting he should take her to see it, which she agreed to and here they were now.

The painting had a dimmed viewing room dedicated just for it on the first floor such was it's prestige but then immediately upon reaching the entrance they could see the wall where it should be hanging was bare and a small sign on a pedestal informed that the painting was on loan to a gallery in County Durham for the next six months.

Daniel voiced his disappointed that Maria would not be able to view the work but she tittered in reply that in another six months time when the painting had been returned to Glasgow Daniel could then use the same excuse again to be with her and bring her there on another date, Daniel smiled that she had read him so well by easily seeing through his excuse to be in her company again so soon.

There was a red leather Victorian confidante styled rounded settee along the corridor on the balcony which Maria walked over to then sat down upon so Daniel followed suit. They pivoted in the seat towards each other so they could talk.

'I'm sorry the painting is out on loan, I really wanted you to see it.' Daniel apologised smiling as he carried on with the act.

'Yes, I am so disappointed, I could have been at Ikea instead.' She mocked to which both laughed.

'I can still take you to Ikea, it's not too late, we can dine on Swedish hotdogs in the food hall.'

'No thanks!' she replied, 'but let me take you to the cafe here and treat you to a coffee.'

Daniel gladly accepted her offer, 'Perhaps a piece of cake too?' he added enquiringly whilst looking at her with the feigned parody of an anxious child.

'Only if you are a good boy!' she answered teasingly revealing a bright smile which to Daniel was more valuable than any collection of art he could ever see.

Then another day and another date to be shared, their third date and they were to meet to have a Sunday lunch together.

There was still something Daniel had not told Maria about which was weighing on his mind. She knew he had been previously married and had a son who he had not seen for some years due to the bitterness of his ex but he'd never told Maria that his ex-wife had also been a Brazilian too, the same nationality as she was.

He did not know why the prospect of revealing this to her this would give him such apprehension, Maria already knew that be has visited Brazil twice but he had always been vague with his details as to why, so Maria naturally just thought it was for touristic reasons as many gringos enjoy traveling to South America.

His omission regarding his previous wife's nationality really vexed him and weighted upon his mind. He felt there was something special to be had with Maria and he wanted to be completely open and honest about everything with her so felt that this was an important fact.

As he waited for her at the steps outside her guesthouse he'd came to the decision with his deliberations that he would tell her that day, a prospect that really worried him, he so hoped it would not put a dampener on the lunch he had planned to take her out for.

Would she consider him any less that he could not keep a marriage alive with one of her fellow countrywoman or that there must be good reasons for a Brazilian mother not to allow her child to see his father? Although thinking such thoughts now in the cold light of day seemed illogical, it had been churning in his head keeping him awake at night, but did he really think Maria would be so shallow to believe less of him at such a revelation?

When he told her that he had a son who he has not seen for four years she was very sympathetic, but he felt there was something noble with fighting in court representing himself for access to his child and perhaps won kudos at this fact but how could he really consider himself open and honest if he were to not drilled down presenting her with all the facts, and that being that his ex-wife was Brazilian as was she.

The sound of the guesthouse door closing jumped him out of his troubled thoughts. There was Maria bounding down the steps to meet him, how stunning she looked thought Daniel, and how lucky that he was to be going on another date with this amazing woman, they had a whole afternoon ahead of them and Daniel was buoyant with the delight of that fact.

Daniel had booked a table for lunch in a restaurant called Jabuticaba. It served South American food, a taste of home for Maria which may appeal to her he thought, and it was just a short walk along Sauchiehall Street from her guesthouse so they'd left the car and strolled along filling each other in on happenings since their last meeting, which was not much as they were together at Kelvingrove just the day before.

Once seated in Jabuticaba they ordered from the menu, the famed Brazilian feijoada and some lunchtime cocktails. Daniel choose a caipirinha as he would not be behind the wheel for some time and Maria got a drink called a Batida cachaca which upon arrival looked to have a consistency somewhere between a milkshake and a slushy.

'I've never had feijoada served with fried banana slices before.' Daniel exclaimed with a pretend grimace once the waitress had walked away leaving the steaming hot plates of black bean and pork stew.

Maria laughed, 'it's called plantain and it's very popular in South America. On the farm we usually sprinkle farofa over our feijoada, its a powder made from manioc flour.'

'I love farofa!' replied Daniel, 'but I could never get used to eating sliced oranges which I was sometimes given with my feijoada when I was in Brazil.'

'The oranges are more a Rio thing, it is supposed to help digestion as feijoada is heavy food'

'Aye, that it is. Fairly sticks to the ribs as my auld mother would say about stogie foods.', ' Do you to consider yourself a Carioca or a Paulista?' enquired Daniel referring to if Maria thought of herself more from Rio than São Paulo.

'I was actually born in Campo Grande which is in the state of Mato Grosso do Sul. It is to the west of São Paulo and it boarders with Paraguay. But we moved to Rio when I was 4. I lived in Rio most of my life so I guess I consider myself a Carioca. Have you ever been to Mato Grosso?'

'I think I may have passed through it when I took the bus to Foz do Iguaçu!'

'I don't think the bus would have went as far up from São Paulo to travel through there on a journey to Iguacú, the falls are quite a bit south from where Paraquay boarders with Mato Grosso.' Maria advised him, 'You said you have been to Brazil twice, where else have you visited whilst across there?'

'Just Rio, São Paulo and Foz do Iguacú.' he answered.

'There is much more to Brazil than just São Paulo and Rio de Janeiro you know!' Maria laughed, 'you must really like Brazil. What attracts you? Is it the food or the latino woman?' she punctuate the last word with a coquettish grin as to suggest Daniel's past travel intents and by this upping her flirtatious ante slightly and enjoy the gossamer of crimson she saw raise upon his cheeks.

Daniel swallowed, this was his opening to tell all.

'There is one thing which I never mentioned,' Daniel replied, 'which is that my ex-wife, she was Brazilian!', there!…it was out the bag.

Maria's eyes opened wide as if with surprise, the smile stayed painted on her face which encouraged Daniel to continue.

'I met her in Brazil, in São Paulo, well actually I started writing to her from here, Scotland but then after some months we decided to met and I traveled to Brazil to see her.'

'Wow!' Maria reacted, 'was she from São Paulo?'

'Yes, Osasco. I went across there twice to meet with her, on the second time she returned with me to Scotland and we got married here.'

Maria was silent, eyes still wide open but more in theatrical execution than the initial astonishment, the smile remained.

'A holiday romance that went wrong you could say.' Daniel added to lighten the tension which he felt about the revelation he just released upon her.

'So your son is half Brazilian?' Maria declared with an amused look.

'Just the good half!' Daniel replied with a smile hoping he was reading her reaction true, 'sorry I never mentioned this sooner.' he added, 'I thought maybe you would think less of me if you knew I failed my marriage with a Brazilian.', upon leaving his lips he realised how little sense this made and she seemed to read his mind.

'Of course not, I think I understand now. Brazilian woman can be the worst. They can be like piranhas', 'I am sorry this happened to you!' she said with her face turning more sympathetic.

She'd genuinely meant what she said. Although it did come more of a surprise than a shock that Daniel's previous wife was Brazilian, with some later thought it never surprised her too much as it is said that opposites attracted and Daniel seemed the calm quiet type whereas Brazilian woman where often much more flamboyant and loud as anyone who'd ever seen a group of Brazilian together would surely testify to that fact.

It was their fifth date that sealed their fates as a couple.

Maria had invited him for dinner, a reward earned for advise given over the phone how to operate her heating system in her newly acquired rented apartment, a necessarily with the evening chills but it was a puzzling arrays of dials and buttons for a Carioca more familiar the operations of air conditioning.

By then she'd already had a guest staying over with her for the week, one of her work colleagues cat named George.

Although apple cake was the bait, the angler was more the lure for Daniel, he keenly accepted the offer and arrived as RSVP'd at eight that evening sharp, even sat outside her apartment in his car for ten mins as arrived early. Such punctuality was the British, not so much the Brazilians who would normally consider an invite for eight a show for half an hour later at the earliest but Maria was already as much acclimatised to the British timekeeping as she was to their polite ways but never to their weather.

Daniel was armed with the traditional weapons of a date, flowers and a box of chocolates.

The symbolism of such gifts were not so obvious to him but it were to be pointed out that flowers seduce the bees into their role of fertilisation and the chocolates have phenethylamine compounds which the body produces internally when undergoing sexual infatuation Daniel would have been as embarrassed as if he had arrived with a packet of condoms, tube of flavoured lube in his hands and a kiss me quick hat on his head.

Maria had set the Culloden moor of her chosen battleground. This was their fifth date and so far she saw no other indications from Daniel other than friendship.

She could she a shyness within him, but she wanted also wanted a lover not just a friend, a relationship not just a companion to drive her around as a guest in his country.

Tonight would had decided, no more dubiety. She would leave no questions of her intend on how they should proceed forward and force him to show his hand, all cards on the table.

She knew her limitations in the kitchen, dried pasta would be simple enough and some asparagus, the aphrodisiac of lovers she smiles as she thought this. Some hand picked tunes on the play list to set the evening up, nothing too obvious, at least not at first...no Oysters on a bed of Pomegranate seeds.

Before Daniel's arrival as she prepared some of the food, she felt the cat rub its body against her leg as it past, 'let's see if you are the only body contact I will have received by the end of tonight!' she said to the feline as it slunk off elsewhere.

The main course was pasta with asparagus. She would aim to al dente the conchiglie and the simplicity of it to be drizzled with olive oil and chopped asparagus would make it palatable enough.

Daniel enjoyed the simple enough fare which she had prepared, although the apple cake, not apple pie as she had called it, was less desirable yet when asked by his host Daniel somewhat misrepresented the truth and claimed 'Really nice!' Years of white lie practice to avoid rudeness made the falsehood undetectable on his face when Maria scrutinised it searching for signs of a bluff.

They were standing at the table which divided the kitchen from the living area. The wine was going down the hatch too smoothly, Daniel was conscious he had already drained his second glass, already in exceed of the legal limit's tolerances if stopped by the police on his drive home should he leave at that moment.

Maria lifted the pinot and tilted its neck over his glass to which he placed his hand over. 'No thank you, I'd best not, I need to be careful for driving home.'

'Come on. Some more, drink with me!' she commanded like a disciple of Dionysus.

Such a Siren call would surely have led Odysseus onto the rocks. Daniel looked across the room at the leather sofa. The cat was curled up on it.

'Would it be alright if I were to sleep on the floor for tonight across there?' he asked nodding is head toward the direction of the sofa.

Maria let out a laugh and in a teasing chastising tone said 'as if the cat sleeps on the sofa and you on the floor, you are an idiot! My God what a crazy guy!'

She had a smile on her face as she spoke these words shaking her fist to an unseen deity.

The flush of a blush rose to Daniel's face, the Freudian facial version of an erection, his heart was hamming a tattoo in his chest.

Maria trimly stepped around to Daniel's side of the table gently removing his hand from where it perched on the top of the wine glass and held it to his side looking up at his face throughout .

She reached her face up to his which he leaned forward to meet with hers.

They deeply kissed each other lingeringly. It would be a kiss Daniel would never forget and delightfully, tangibly taste for the years to come.

With her soft velvety lips docked gentle against his there was a warmth and moisture which radiated as if a summer rain pattered on sensitive tissues.

Her lips slightly parted inviting his tongue which he probed with gentle grace savouring its teasing conference with hers.

He placed his hand against the small of her back, skin exposed by the crop of the shirt. A slightness of a quiver being returned to his touch as silky as a butterfly's caress on a petal.

He initiated a conclusion releasing her lower back slowly glazing his hand from palm to fingers as it parted stepping back, his eyes looking into hers.

He took a deep breath through his nose inflating his chest then blowing out exaggeratedly through his mouth.

'Wow!' he simple exclaimed.

'Wow?' she replied his words back as if to ask clarification that this was what he just said.

Daniel shuffled bashfully as if reverting to a child, nervously conscious of the changing dynamics which just occurred.

'I just don't want to take advantage of you!' he proclaimed as if saying out a caution, he never knew why and on reflection later when he replayed this moment many times over it made no sense, just a line like wadding to fill a moment as in the absence of the adequate of anything to fill a vacuum.

Maria latched on to what he just said, still smiling but with a little awkwardness creeping in on the peripherals replied back 'What do you mean? I know what I'm doing!'

'You have just been drinking, I just don't want to take advantage.' Daniel clarified digging his hole deeper and starting to feel a sinking sensation sway over him.

Maria looked at him studiously then, still amusement of her face which Daniel found difficult to read before she said 'I think you should leave!'

There was a pause. Daniel nodded his head, tightened his jaw with a bite then answered 'I am sorry, I don't know why I said that. Yes, I will go.'

He looked serious, there was an awkwardness about the moment which he seemed to grasp right there and then, at that precise moment.

'Can I just kiss you again please?' he asked as he moved towards her not awaiting the answer and pressed his lips on hers again, firmer than before but meeting with no resistance.

His body had mutinied against his earlier failure with words, he kissed with a passion, a hunger. He clasped her entwining his strong arms around her torso like vines around a tree and pulled her tight against him.

They separated and she immediately took control before anymore words could be said.

She held his hand and guided him towards the ajar bedroom door, but upon reaching the door Daniel then took steer and went to the sofa scatting George the cat who at this point was no longer in slumber as curious to where this strange dance he was witness to was heading.

Daniel sat down facing her beckoning with his hands for her to sit straddled facing him. She bent to reach his trouser belt but he shooed her hands away.

'I want to see you first!' he said with a firmness.

She straightened and working on the knot in front of her white blouse at the waist and once undone pulled it over her head. Her breasts sat firm and heavy in her white laced bra.

Daniel unbuttoned his denim shirt, pulling his arms out of it then tossing it to the side to where he sat.

She straddled him and they kissed, now deeper and now furiously than before. Daniel reached behind her back clawing at the hooked fastener of her brassiere releasing it and allowing it to fall then swiping it away.

Her breasts were firm when he planted his face in them, kissing them, savouring before drawing his head back to take in the nipple, accommodating it then rolling the soft bead along his lips, his sensual pleasure being enhanced by the low sighs from her mouth.

He stood up out of the sofa, lifting her with him at first before planting her feet back on the floor. He wrestled his belt open pulling it through the hoops discarding it to the side then, unbuttoning before letting his trousers and shorts fall down as far as the snag of his knees then paddling his feet out of them before kicking them to the side.

She had already been making process on her jeans, they were now off too with her panties curled inside.

Standing facing each other she curled her hand around his swollen manhood and pumped it with her hand as his tongue rummaged within the cavity of her mouth.

Their mouths parted, their faces showing fervour desire in want of the moment. She now guided him to the bedroom leading him by his erect member, there would be no detours this time.

Daniel lay on the cool bedsheets, the lights were dimmed and she had her back to him doing something at the bedside table. He watched her back, its golden cast dappled with the shadows rendered.

135

Music started streaming from a small device, very calm and low, atmospheric. She turned, came gracefully up upon the bed as lithe as a panther and mounted on top of him sitting over his hips. Her head lowered towards his face, he kissed her heavily, his hand behind her head lightly clamping her mouth down onto his as if to gain deeper access with his investigative tongue.

He felt her hand jostle with him below as she channeled him into her wet entrance.

His entirety penetrated into her with a totter of their synchronised hips. She let out a small sigh as she sunk onto him, him into her, a soft audible signature to the pleasure they both shared whilst experiencing each other that night and the rest of the weekend.

17

Maria and Daniel's relationship had developed at a gallop, which had enchantingly exceeding both their hopes and expectations.

During the week, after finishing his work, Daniel would drive from his office in Edinburgh straight to Maria's apartment in Glasgow where he was becoming quite the regular guest.

At the weekends they would travel out to visit new places around Scotland where Daniel acted like the faithful travel guide and informed Maria of the history of the area, often after reading up himself on it the dat before. He felt a new excitement seeing these familiar sights through her eyes.

Castles, stately homes, parks and museums were very much a staple of their weekend trips, and often such days ended with an overnight stay in a hotel or a bed and breakfast. This felt like a honeymoon period for them both and they fell even more deeply in love.

Their behaviours complimented as both were polite, and courteous to each other. Their discussions ranged widely from the most palpable with serpentine wit and shrewd observation to the more complexities of thought requiring serious rumination from them both. They would often disagree with each other but respect for opposite views always remained intact.

Walking around they would hold each other's hands displaying a body language as if they were teenagers strolling together.

Maria had came to Scotland after signing off on a six month contract to work as an events manager in Glasgow. She had previous experience from working at the past Rio Olympics so that endorsement on her resume had opened the door for her coming to Glasgow during the build up to the European Championships which was to be held there. The six months passed very quickly for the love birds and so Maria then, upon completion of her employment, gave up her tenancy of her apartment in Glasgow and moved into Daniel's house in Falkirk.

There was no problems for her staying in Scotland on the immigration front as she so also had a Portuguese passport which she was entitled to due to her family's lineage and although Scotland had recently voted to depart from the EU, holders of European passports who were already in Scotland, as was Maria's case, had what was to be called the right to remain so there she remained much to the pleasure of Daniel's heart.

Maria soon saw that the house in Falkirk was very much in needed of a woman's touch which Daniel, although through bouts of protesting at certain renovations, donations to charity shops and parting with some of his gadget, soon relented to and found that he actually enjoyed the resulting new fresh environment of his, their home.

Gone was the shrine that Daniel had kept maintained which was Sam's bedroom, this was the most painful ghost for him to exorcise, piling out of date annuals and toys, most of which even a current Sam would consider childish if he were to see them now, placing them in the boot of the car and delivering them to the local charity shop as a donation.

Daniel did feel a guilt, almost as if he was giving up on his alienated child but he also started feeling a lightness too.

He'd never realised the weight seeing such item had on his heart when he'd walked into that bedroom each day.

Once all had been dismantle from his son's past bedroom they gave the walls a fresh lick of paint and made the room into an office where Daniel would often work from home when the opportunity arisen and other times Maria would also use the room when she was doing some consultation work for other events which she was working on remotely.

During trimming off the excess emotional weight there were times where memories would unexpectedly wash over Daniel like a tsunami knocking him off his feet, once such occasion was whilst they were gutting the shed at the bottom of the garden.

Maria was pottering around the outside prising open the rusted lids of paint cans which Daniel was decanting from the nether regions right at the inside back of the shed when he whisked away a tarpaulin to reveal what it was covering

He was aware of what was under the tarpaulin in the shed, that was not what had taken him by surprise, the shock was the wave of nostalgia that hit him like a thunderbolts sweeping the legs from under him.

He sat down on a stacked pile of cement bags, impelled by the groundswell of remembrance which ambushed him from the innocently inanimate object that had been shrouded by the tarp.

It was his son's bicycle.

Maria had called Daniel's name, asking him to come and see if the contents of one of the paint canisters which she'd opened outside was worth salvaging but when she never got a reply she went round to the front of the shed and entered.

There he was, seated, head bend forward with his hands balled against his forehead shaking with silent sobs.

'Love?' she enquired but had almost immediately fathomed the reason of his collapse upon seeing the child's bike and the cover which unveiled it hanging off.

'Awww Love!' she said removing the gloves she had been wearing and knelling down at his side gently rubbing the top of his back, 'I know how these memories must hurt you.'.

The bike had a black frame with yellow brake cables and grips, there was the open bat symbol on the chain cover, that of the superhero franchise which it was part of. The size of the bike and its caricature of branding which suggest it was for a much smaller child than the age Sam would be now but it's potency to lacerate with memories was certainly very evident on how it hit Daniel.

'It was his first bike!' he mournfully explained, 'I would take him out to learn him to ride. It's got stabilisers on the back wheels but Sam still struggled to grasp the peddling, maybe partly because of his dyspraxia.'

Daniel's face brightened into a grin through his tears as be recalled something, 'I attempted to demonstrated how to peddle, you know? Press one foot down on the peddle whilst allowing the opposite foot to propel back up with the returning peddle. It seems such an intuitive moment but he could not do it so I sat on the bike to demonstrate and as soon as I plonked my big behind down on the seat both the rear stabilisers folded up off the ground because of my weight.', Daniel smiled through wet eyes at the recollection.

He stood up and pulled the bike further out to show the back wheel and the attached stabilisers which indeed appeared at an awkward angle to the wheel.

'Sam let out such a scandal!' Daniel laughed now, 'he cried out "you broke my bike!', his lips trembled, 'it feels as if it were yesterday!' he let out voice cracking before he crumbled again tears streaming free, 'I miss him Maria, I miss my son'.

'I know you do my love, I know.' Maria would coo softly to him stroking his back.

There were many tripwires around the house which would set Daniel off, not just with nostalgia about Sam but also with his mother, father and even his brother.

Daniel would walk down the same stairs which down his father would carry him when he was a child himself, a "fireman's lift" Samuel would call it when he carried him down these stairs which, then years later, Daniel would do the same with his own son Sam.

It's not ghosts which haunt us, these phantasms and spectres are echos of memories. Loved ones no longer with us or love which has been denied.

It was only with Maria's healing balm of love that Daniel had the strength to fight through the mire of memories and move on to otherwise impossible tasks such as dismantling Sam's trampoline which had been taking up space in the garden, without Maria's support such an action would be otherwise inconceivable for him to do, it would feel like giving up part of his son, giving up on a hope that he may come back soon and use it..

Every object, from the smallest bric-a-brac to more the substantial all had strings of memories attached which pulled at the heart when they were lifted to be removed. Maria's gentle encouragement for him to move on helped untangle and release the knots which bound him so painfully to the past.

Maria told Daniel that in Brazil they had a word for what he was feeling, it was called "Saudade", the closest translation to english would be melancholy yet it was much more than this, more profound. An intense ongoing feeling for the beloved yet absent.

'Melancholy is about missing the person we once were in the past, the way we felt in our life at certain moments.' Maria would explain, 'but when we feel "saudade" it's much more than that, its a feeling for the person we once loved and lost as we still have a tremendous feeling of love for that person.".

It was such sentiments that cascade his heart in waves with such thoughts of how he felt when his since departed family were alive or when he thought about particular moments with his son such as when he attempted to learn to ride that bike but the feeling of saudade was a constant submersion missing these people of his past as the love he felt for them would never dry up.

18

Sam lay on his bed in his room. He knew he'd should be trying to sleep as he had school in the morning but his head was full of churning thoughts.

He'd been thinking more and more about his dad recently, thoughts he would keep concealed in his mind as if it were a iron vault as he knew what would happen if such forbidden sentiments where to be found floating about by his mom such was her intolerability of the very notion that Sam had a father.

Four years now since he'd last saw his dad, four very long years without any contact.

Another of Granny's phrases came back to him, her voice echoed in his head as if she was saying it there and then. 'Donkey years' she would say meaning a very long time. When Sam would visit his gran with his dad she often tell him that she'd missed him and had not saw him in donkey years, an exaggeration as he would have saw her just the previous week but it started becoming a ritual of greeting when he came around to her house.

Sam had misheard her at first thinking that she'd said "donkey ears" and wondered if this was because donkey's ears were very long? When he asked her this she hooted with laughter at his misunderstanding and told him that it was an old docker's term meaning a crank which was called a donkey with what they would use to wind cargo up over the side of the ship. The cranks were very slow and when the loaders shout up asking how long it would take, they were told "donkey's years!"

Granny was very clever, she knew a lot, Sam used to wonder if he would be as smart as her once he was as old.

He missed her very much. If she was here now he would ask her what to do about his dad.

He knew his father had gave up on the court action the year before, forced to throw in the towel much to his mum jubilance when she talked about it with Steve or when Sam overheard her discuss with it with her family over the phone.

She made it sound like a great victory, something to be proud about, and she included Sam in her celebrations claiming that he was a brave boy renouncing Daniel to the court with what he told the Bar Reporter, telling Mrs Cummings his fears of having contact with his father. She would act as if these words which he had told were Sam's own and not what she had instructed him to say!

Sam wore the shame of this deep within him and he was distraught with the idea that his dad may consider this to be true, that Sam was afraid of him or even worse than that, would his dad think Sam had teamed up with his mom and that he now stood against his dad too and never loved him?

He so terribly wanted to reach out to his dad and tell him the truth, let him know how it was living with his mom and how he had to side with her or the problems it would bring him.

He thought long and hard with a deliberation in his mind if he could risk contact with his father without mom getting wind of it and how he could approach dad.

He came up with an idea, there was risk but the suffering of doing nothing was eating him up.

The month before, mom had gave him a mobile phone. It was not a fancy gadget laden with all the apps as some of his friends at school had. He could not download the games he liked and play them upon it but its purpose was to be contactable by mom at all times or for him to let her know if he was going to be late home as he was staying over at Oliver's house on the pretence of doing homework together, but they actually would he there playing games on the console Oliver had in his bedroom connected to a massive tv.

Oliver's mom had separated from his dad he had told him and said it was great! How could it be great Sam had asked him knowing his own sadness of when his dad left mom. Oliver said that he now had two bedrooms as he would go to his Dad's new apartment every second weekend where he had an xbox and when at his mum's house, in his bedroom there he had a playstation, both parents were competing with each other for his love and he though it was great!

So here was Sam lying on his bed, mobile phone in his hand and surrounded by the stillness of the late night. He also had his dad's mobile number on a slip of paper which he had kept in his box, out of sight from his mother, now that piece of paper was there with him as he lay in bed, there folded beside his phone.

That little fillet of parchment inked with numerals burnt his hand as picked it up and held it as if it were uranium, such was his feeling of its power. His indecision now was if he should or should not transfer the digits on the slip of paper to the keypad of the phone, not to make a call, that would be too much a risk at this point, too blatant a risk, although his heart fluttered even more at the very thought that it could be in his capacity to hear his dad's voice and even talk to him, but no, if he were make contact then it would have to be a text message, a signal send under the wire.

The safe option would of course be to scrunch up the slip of paper, rip up into a million pieces then scatter to the winds and his worries would cease about if he should do it, but then still that gnarling in his chest would remain, maybe even worst as then he would always know that he had the chance but never took it so would never know what could have been the possible outcome if he had! What a dilemma! He wondered what his granny's advice would be.

He made his mind up then, he came to the decision and entered the numbers into the phone, he would send a text message to the recipient who he missed and so yearned to have a chance to tell his side of the story to.

Then he considered if this number was still in use by his father. It had been more than 4 years since his dad slipped the number into Sam's pocket after having his son over for the weekend.

If he were to send a text and the response was to be an undelivered status returned then all this troublesome dithering about should he or should he not would have been for nothing.

He decided then to try out the number and at least see if it was still in operation. He typed a one word message then pressed send on the tiny screen.

There was to be no sound, he'd already muted the phone. He watched the status on the small screen under the one word message he'd sent...it morphed from "Sending" to "Delivered" which confirmed to the boy that the number was still in use and as he stared at the small status letterings with intense concentration he watched it change to "Read" certifying the sent message was opened at the other end.

The connection was made!

He lay there on his bed as tense as a bowstring holding the phone to his chest excited at what he had just done. Should he send another message? The one word which he sent would not give the receiver a clue as to the identity of the sender, should he proceed and make this clearer on a subsequent message now that he knew the number was still in operation? "Yes!" the answer came back to his head, "in for a penny, in for a pound.", another one of his granny's old sayings!

Daniel was propped up in bed with his head against the pillows reading a book when he heard a ping emit from his phone denoting the arrival of a text message.

He looked across at Maria who was asleep at his side, she seemed undisturbed yet he silently cursed himself for not muting the phone as not to ruffle her sleep with such an occurrence.

He placed his book still opened face down in his lap as he reached across to side table to where his mobile sat and picking up the device sliding the mute on first then focusing to read the recently delivered message.

The message was one word which simply said **Test**, the number which sent it was not one which he recognised. Although slightly perplexed at the singular word message and it being sent from an unfamiliar source he replaced the phone back facedown on the table and continued with his book.

He found it hard to get his concentration back to the book so decided to call it a night.

Leaning across to his side he switched off the lamp's illumination then turned to join Maria in some slumber. He spooned up to her, she wiggled then murmured a little bit as she, still asleep, adapted to the pressing body behind her snuggling in.

Sleep was not coming easily to Daniel, he could not figure why, he had a flea in his mind which he could not pin his thoughts on to understand why.

He switched positions many times, often moving the pillow to find a cooler spot against his face.

After a short while he reached across to his mobile to check the time then he saw that there was another text message delivered from the same number awaiting his perusal but this time his attention was piqued by its contents, it read...

Hi, I am sorry that I haven't spoken to you in years.

Daniel immediately swung his legs out from the bed and stood up, Maria moaned slightly in her sleep at the quake of his upheaval but still she never woke.

Daniel quietly left the bedroom and padded downstairs to the living room where he turned on the lights and sat on the sofa.

He read then read again the message, digesting and processing every pixel that built up the lettering on the phone's screen.

It was not signed off by a name but Daniel was somehow under no illusions as to who it was from.

His heart, which was already beating at a rate, pelting like thunderous rain against a tin roof as another text appeared on the screen he was staring at it, a bolt of lightening would have not surprised him more.

I've tried to get mum to let me contact you in any way in the past but she wouldn't allow me to. She would always say you don't care about me. Now I have had to do it on my own. I am sorry.

These words removed all doubts to who the sender was, it was his son Sam.

Daniel was shaking, he held he phone with both quivering hands and felt a thrumming along his nerves like the plucked cat gut of a guitar.

This was his son making contact with him, something he'd almost given up on. Believing it to be beyond any hope. Where could this lead to? He composed himself and carefully worded a reply.

Hi Sam, you don't need to say sorry to me. You are my son and I love you always and think about you every day. I am so very happy to receive this message from you.

With a dry mouth Daniel checked through his draught, reviewing it multiple times before hitting the send button, his reply was transmitted forth from his phone with a whoosh sound.

The small grey indicator under the text bubble changed from Sending to Sent then a couple seconds later to Read. He was perched on the tip of his seat staring at the glass screen of the phone waiting for a reply. He did not have to wait long as a reply came soon after.

It's great that you still care about me. Most other dads in this situation would be like "who are you?!?"

A followup message immediately came in... **I am sorry for not going to Granny's funeral, Mum would not allow me to attend.**

Daniel gapped at the messages, of course I still care for you, you are my son he thought, my own flesh and blood who I will always love, how could I ever give up on you, and I know how things must have been for you with your mother! These thoughts ran through Daniel's head like a train but would not, could not, be so blunt, especially at this early stage, considered it would not be good form to criticise his son's mother in any way. He was sure she was filling his son's head with nonsense about him over the years but he refused to play the same game even if although what he could say would be the truth. She was still his mother and as such he had to shield a young Sam from such the realities of what she was.

Instead he wrote **I will always care about you Sam and I am proud that you are my son. It's been a terrible situation for you with being so young and I understand the pressures you must have been under, Granny always knew you loved her and she would understand too.** Despite the simpleness of the dialogue Daniel proofread the words again as if he were a lawyer studying an important contract He could only guess how his son must be at that moment writing to him and presumedly without his mother's knowledge Daniel thought, courageous little man.

This was their first exchange of dialogue for over four years, Daniel wanted to proceed gingerly and not make his son feel under any pressure or stress, especially he did not want him to feel guilty, his son did not deserve to feel guilty, all that had happened was of Lilian's doing, that morally depraved bitch but Daniel bit down his bitterness which had been rising with the thought of her. He would not bad mouth her here to Sam, no, he must concentrate on this chance to reconnect with his son.

Once more he checked over the text that he'd composed before hitting send and again he anxiously awaited a reply.

Sending…, Sent, Read.

I wish I could visit you. came Sam's reply.

When Daniel read this he felt as if his heart was going to rupture. This was what he had been waiting for long enough, what he yearned for and now here it was, his estranged son wanting to meet him.

He tried to contain himself but felt such a exhilarated elation of a tsunami washing over his entire being.

He forced a calm over himself before replying to that six word message which meant the world to him.

Of course you can visit me Sam. You are my son and I will always

love you. My home is your home anytime you want. If it would be easier for you I could meet you somewhere and we could eat out in a restaurant and catch up or if you want to come to the house I can collect you somewhere and bring you here. Never feel any pressure Sam, I am here for you always.

He pressed send and heard the message whiz away. Sending... the status came back then as Sent. Daniel then waited with bated breath as the indicator progressed to Read.

He started to worry if the vibe from his message would come across as too pleading with his son, he had to go softly softy. He chided himself as he examined the message he'd just sent whilst awaiting a reply, *slow down* he said to himself, *early beginnings*.

I better go to my bed now but I will write more tomorrow after school. Good night Dad.

Daniel replied **Good night Sam.** That was the first time he wished his son and good night for over four years and by god it felt good!

He would have much preferred to chat more, all night if it were up to him but he had to allow his son to proceed at his pace.

He sat there in a rapture of euphoria at the exchange which just occurred, he hardly could believe it.

His face felt wet, placing fingers against his cheek he was surprised to find that tears were there. The tears were an emotional release, he had waited so long for contact with his son and here it just happened.

'Why are you down here? Can't you sleep' came the voice from his right as he sat. He swivelled his head and saw Maria standing there having just walked in through the door coming down from upstairs. She was looking groggy from sleep having just woken not to find her man at her side.

She scrunched her eyes to focus when Daniel turned his head to her presence and she saw that he was crying. She marched with concerned alarm across to him placing her hand on his shoulder.

'What's wrong love?' she asked with apprehension in her voice filled with concern for her man.

'Sam has just made contact!' Daniel replied handing her up his phone so she could see the messages exchanged.

Maria came around the sofa and sat down next to him then started reading the messages.

'This is amazing!', she said examining the exchanged missives, 'Are you certain that it's truly him?'

Daniel told her that he was certain, he could feel it, and from what

Sam knew, what he wrote on the texts just seemed right, it could be no one else.

'You are going to meet your son again love after all this time!'

Daniel's tears became a cascade with sobs, Maria turned on the seat towards him and held him tight.

'I can't believe it love, after all this time!' Daniel said with a breaking voice, 'its's happening!'.

Whilst Maria embraced Daniel on the sofa in Falkirk across in the west Sam lay on his bed contemplating what he had just done. He had went against his mum's wishes and had contacted his dad, although the excitement was immense within him he still felt the trickle of fear and worry that his mum may somehow find out, but he was not sorry for his actions, he was glad he had initiated the contact.

His mum had gave him the phone last month so she could contact Sam anytime when he was at school incase she needed to tell him something. It was a simple device but he prized it nonetheless and soon got into the habit of messaging his friends sending memes and funny photos.

It had taken him some weeks to pluck up the courage to contact his dad, he was not only worried about if his mum should find out but also what his dad's response would be.

Sam had an immense feeling of guilt and worried that his dad would resent him somewhat after what he's told the Bar Reporter but after tonights brief exchange of text messages Sam felt that his dad did not hold a grudge, in fact Sam felt very loved and felt he was wanted from the replies he received, a sentiment which was missing in the company of his mum.

Sam had saved his dad's phone number on his contact list as "David" just to be on the safe side if his mother should check the contacts on his phone.

Sam had every intention of meeting his dad but had to think where and plan it smartly. When asking to visit he did not consider how to get to Falkirk, he would need money, time and transport all of which could affect the covertness of his mission.

Dad had suggested meeting him which was great and would certainly solve these problems. Perhaps they could meet in the mall but then Sam worried about if one of his friend's mothers recognised him then told his mom about seeing him sitting eating with a unidentified man, he would need to think carefully about where to meet his dad. He would consider everything carefully tomorrow as he said he would write again after school.

He would also need an excuse to give his mum as to why he would be later coming home if he were to meet his dad. It was of paramount importance to consider all the angles carefully he thought again, but the hardest part was now done, he had made contact after all these passing years and his dad said he would be keen to meet him.

Sam was excited and went to sleep with an optimism that things were about to get better.

19

As Sam's arrived from school he was told by his mum to clean up then get his homework done before his dinner, the usual routine he had to follow when he was to return home and his mom was there stationed upon his arrival.

Steve was already sitting in the living room watching the news on the tv, he'd arrived home earlier that day from his work. Steve shouted Sam over to give him a high five welcome.

Such moments felt awkward to the boy as often his mum's partner would make such gestures as if he and Sam were best friends but when his mum discussed about his dad with her usual venom Steve would just agree then add some of his own barbs in too with generalised defamation despite never having ever met his father.

After his limp slapping gesture of his palm meeting Steve's enthusiastic high five Sam was glad to escape to the bathroom as to wash up before Steve started playing at being a father and asking him about his day.

Whilst he was washing his hands Lillian opened his school bag to remove the books within.

Often Sam's teacher would add a note for his mother's attention, a short communication written in the boy's school jotter to highlight points that Sam should be focusing more on during his homework.

When Lilian was discharging the contents of his school bag the mobile she had bought him slipped out, she picked it up. She'd often discreetly check its contents, look through any exchanged messages he had been trading with his friends, all innocent kid's talk she would normally see yet she'd continue to check, there was always that niggling worry at the back of her mind that he could start a communication with someone prohibited, someone sam was told he should never be in contact with, the name of that person best left unsaid.

Lilian knew that checking her son's phone messages was a breach of trust in her son but she also felt she was protecting him in doing it so this, in her mind, mitigated the intrusion. She still heard the water running in the bathroom, the boy always dillydallied whilst washing his hands and face upon returning home from school, burning up time before having to be coxed to do his homework before dinner.

It was not password protected, she would have never allowed Sam to do that, it was one of the conditions of him having his own mobile. So she got into the contact list immediately and scrolled through it, nothing unusual. That moment she was not expecting anything different from the usual trash talk he exchanged with his friends which she'd checked out the past couple of weeks, her monitoring was getting more lax, just developing into a mother's curiosity now as to what her son had been up to but then she saw an recent exchange of text messages to with contact named David.

She was not aware of any of Sam's friends by the name David so without any hesitation she opened the messages up to investigate further and that was when her worst fears were realised. She read the contents. Sam was in communication with Daniel!

She could actually feel the tremble work up from the floor through her legs into her body as the outrage in her started to boil up like a volcano.

She was still standing there when Sam, shaking his already dried hands, came into the room then froze almost comically when he noticed his phone in his mother's grip, a tightening grip since having surveyed the exchange of messages to his father.

'Bastardo!' Lilian roared out as she raised her face from the screen of the phone and looked at the boy.

Sam stood there increasingly getting paler as the colour drained from his face, he was not sure if his mum's curse was at him or his dad but it was certain that she had discovered the text messages from the night before as he'd read the situation immediately within a nano. Her face was pulsating crimson with anger.

Steve looked up from the sofa wondering what was happening, 'what is it?' he asked looking first to Lilian then to Sam. If she was on the cusp on one of her frequent temper fits because of something Sam had done, or more often these day, something he had not done, then

Steve wanted to be ready to try and jump in to defused it.

'This little shit has been messaging that bastard of a man!', she directed the screen of the mobile towards where Steve sat as if he could make out the words from the distance he was sitting at. White spittle foamed on her lips from the force of the words she said between her clenched teeth.

Steve immediately stood up to approach towards the offered phone in the attempt to get a better understanding.

Sam turned around to go to his bedroom, he could feel the ferocity building up in the air radiating from his mother.

As Sam turned Lilian bolted towards him scattering the mobile from her grip before Steve could reach it. Sam instinctively twisted away and covered his face.

She clouted the boys across the top of his leg, a full force smack with the palm of her hand which caused Sam to emit screams of pain from the severity of the blow which shuddered his whole body from the force.

Sam crumpled to the floor from the beating he was then taking to his legs as Lillian towered above him delivering further brutal slaps, pulling at his arms with one of her hands so as to get access to the areas he desperately attempted to protect when Steve stepped in and pulled her away. With her departing frenzy she let out a kick towards the child too which hit just above his calf.

'Enough!' Steve shouted out.

He had saw Lilian smacking Sam before for misbehaving, he never agreed with it but had to accept it was the punishment a mother deems of her child but such beatings were getting out of hand, he could just not sit there by the sidelines and watch.

'No more Lilian, look at him, you hit him enough!' his voice was loud, much louder than he'd ever spoke up to Lilian before, 'He know's he has done wrong!' Steve added a little gentler trying to switch to diplomacy now that he had her attention, hoping to control the situation in a civil manner.

Sam was cowering on the floor, arms wrapped around his head in anticipation of more blows.

Lilian looked at Steve with a sneer which he had never saw directed at him before, it chilled him instantly. 'Cala a Boca!' she aimed at Steve, 'Não vem para cima de mim!'. She lifted her hand again to strike her son but Steve held her in sway by grabbing her elbow. He did not understand what she'd just said to him but the malevolence with which she spat the words out at him and that look she gave told him that it was nothing but pure venom.

'Lilian, don't hit the boy anymore, look at him!' his words trembled with adrenaline as Steve spoke them, he had never saw Lilian as worked up as this before, she seemed possessed.

'There will be bruises, do you want the school asking questions as to why he is marked then the social work coming to the door?' Steve continued hoping he could at least get through to her with logical sense.

Lilian looked at him, some of her anger draining from her face.

'If they see that you are beating him they will take Sam off you and give him to his dad, is this what you want?' this was a measured statement and seemed to serve it's purpose as Lilian stepped back whilst Sam scurried in reverse then stood up and left at speed towards his bedroom slamming his door behind him.

'Look what he has done!' Lilian said looking at Steve through tears born out of outrage as she bent to pick up the discarded phone, 'he has been messaging that loser of a father, I have told him not to, I warned him! He will take advantage and try and see Sam again, he does not love him, he will just do this to get at me!' "To get at me!" was Lilian's catch-cry like an axiom she would throw down every time she were to mention her ex-husband's behaviour and here she did it now as if trying to justify the unjustifiable which were her actions.

Steve took the phone from her clenched fist, prising gently as she seemed reluctant to handover the evidence until her point was made. Steve looked at the exchange of messages on the still opened screen.

'I don't want that man back in my son's life!' Lilian reenforced.

'Lilian, its natural Sam is curious about his father and so he reached out to him, there has only been a few messages swapped, lets leave it at that, perhaps it was a bad idea giving him a phone, tempting this to happen!'

He is not a father to that child!' Lilian yelled making Steve regret is choice of word worried that the situation was about to escalated again 'And all his friends have them' Lilian screeched pointing at the mobile phone, 'he has been asking for one and I thought it would be good as I could contact him anytime to know where he was but not for the little shit to do this!' The last word was shouted as if to emphasise her point which there already could be no mistaking.

'It's Ok Lilian! We can hang on to his mobile for the time being!' Steve said placatingly, he sensed that the situation could be deescalated again if he watched his choice of words but he was still shocked by Lilian's behaviour and the force she used, 'But you can't hit a child like that, he is small and this is too much, far too much!'

Maria and Daniel stayed at home that evening to eat dinner, his phone was unmuted and never more than an arms distance away as he awaited desperately another message from Sam.

Now and then he would pick up the phone and look upon the screen as if expecting a text may have snuck in avoiding the tripwire to flag up it's arrival with an alert but nothing as yet.

'Looking at it won't make it happen any quicker love,' said Maria with a smile, 'it's still early, he will probably wait until everyone is in bed, when he messaged you last night it was almost midnight.'

'I know love.' Daniel responded, noting to himself that his tone was a little harsh such was his tenseness. He added more gently whilst reaching across the table where they sat at to hold her hand in his, 'I'm just anxious my love, his contact came out of the blue last night, I was not expecting it and there he was, a drop into my inbox! I am still shaking thinking about it!'

'Awww!' Maria coo'd stroking his cheek with her other hand, 'don't be so tense love. He now knows how to contact you so just be patient.'

Looking her in the eyes Daniel smiled, he was so lucky to have her support and he knew this very well.

After dinner they moved to the sofa where they sat together watching the tv. Daniel could not concentrate on anything. The hours passed but still nothing.

'Go up to bed love, I'll let you know soon as I hear anything.' Daniel told her.

'I'm fine!' Maria replied, 'I will just stay here, keep you company if you don't mind!'

Of course Daniel did not mind, this woman had helped him so very much to confront the demons that once tormented him from the angst of his loss, both of his son and his mother. She had turned the Dragons which slithered and squirmed inside of him into Butterflies, which could only pitter-patter around his heart now instead of the past rendering and tearing by the agitating turmoil of hydras.

He held her hand giving it a soft squeeze, he felt as if there was an electric current running through his body such was the jitter of his nerves.

Another hour passed when Daniel decided he had to try and initiate a reply from his son.

He reached for his mobile whilst telling Maria that he would send his son a message, to prime a reply he hoped. Her advice was to hold back, be patience and let Sam drive the pace but Daniel was too itching for contact to be reestablished as soon as possible.

Hi Sam, it's me, just hoping all is well :) it was a short simple text which he hoped would start an exchange with his son again. The indicators ran along their procession from Sending to Sent then to Read but it was another nervous hour before the reply sounded to cue Daniel who grabbed the phone from the arm of the sofa next to him as quick as a gunslinger going for his pistol.

Maria, who was dozing next to him, startled but gained her senses back within the blink of an eye then asked Daniel what did the message say as his eyes were scrolling down it.

I committed a mistake here. I was very angry and upset when I wrote to you. I had an argument with my mum and wanted to get away from the house. This are back to normal now. I see you and I have nothing in common, actually we don't even know each other. I don't want to communicate with you. I don't know where my head was. Do not pass on these messages to anyone.

Daniel handed the phone to Maria, his heart felt heavy again with disappointment but he contained the tears which he could feel queuing up behind the windows of his soul awaiting to be shed.

Maria saw the hurt wash over his eyes and knew the reply was not good even before she was to read it.

'I'm sorry love!' Maria said handing him back his phone.

Daniel held the phone then typed a reply, **That's ok Sam, if you don't want to communicate anymore that is your decision and I am sorry but if that is what your want then I will respect it. I will always be your dad, I will always love and care for you and will be here if you ever want to reach out again.** He sent the message but after a few seconds a "Sent Message Failure" note was returned with a small red exclamation Mark at the side of the message he had attempted to send advising the message had not been delivered.

He pressed send again but a few seconds later got the same response. His number had been blocked on his son's mobile phone.

After sending the message to Daniel, Lilian removed the sim card from its slot within the mobile phone with a hair pin then arched the ends over causing the chip to snap up like two tiny gold tectonic plates. With her fingers she peeled one half off its white plastic backing then added all the pieces to her open hand before ceremoniously serving it into the dust pail from a height.

'Hopefully he's now got the message after that!' she addressed to Steve who was at her side. Her face was a face of achievement as if she had accomplished something bold and brave noticed Steve.

'This is a bad business!' he replied, 'nothing good will come of this, perhaps he will realise the reply was not written by Sam.'

'It does not matter anyway, this channel of communication has now been cut, and Sam will not be getting another phone anytime soon!' she smirked a cold reptilian smile which concerned her partner.

Sam was already in his bed some hours earlier, Steve had tucked him in. As Sam dressed in his pyjamas Steve noticed the bruises on his upper thighs from Lilian's administered slapping yesterday. The angry red marks had since matured to a deep bluish brown indicating even more the force which had been used to inspire such a motif on the child's epidermis.

He felt a knot in his throat after just viewing the resultant of what he had previously witnessed as being done by the hands of his partner.

He loved Lilian but was getting more concerned with her rages and how she would unleash it upon Sam, he certainly hoped it would never be directed at him, but it was bad enough that a small child should be the target.

Although he had stopped Lilian's beating upon Sam he still held a feeling of complicity which he could not shake off. He had observed her hit Sam many times before, not with as much ferocity as he saw yesterday but still some pretty solid blows which flinched Steve when he watched.

He had tried to excuse what she did by telling himself that as a mother she had every right how she thought fit to install discipline in her child, although he may not necessarily agree with her methods he did believed once that he should respect them, and he always took her side if Sam complained but yesterday was too much as the markings on the lad's skin would testify.

'Make the skin sing!' she'd once told Steve. "Fazer a pele cantar" she would then go on to explain how her mother would do it to her as a lesson when she misbehaved as a child as if that was a justification, as if it had somehow kept Lilian on the straight path and would do the same with Sam .

Making the skin "sing", to his interpretation was a slap, an open palmed sting of the surface flesh quickly retracted but not the blows with which she had beaten Sam with yesterday.

To see how the child cowered as she stood above him hammering down such heavy handed blows, it played deeply upon his conscience.

On a few occasions she'd mention about the beatings which her mother released upon her when Lilian was a child and how it meant she had to stay at home a few days after as not to attend her school for fear they would notice the markings, this did concern Steve when she told him this, a mother's love is one thing but a mother's abuse! Well that is something else.

He'd heard how violence can be like a cycle, the abused becoming the abuser and he was reflecting upon how Lilian was now getting more physical with her son, he also recalled the confidential intimate communications they'd use to share with each other when she'd tell him about her mother beating up upon her dad, would that be also part of the circle? Could Steve expect to be a recipient of such force in the future? Yesterday when he held her back from beating upon Sam that look she gave Steve was of such wild savageness it made him think for a second that the next clout was about to be aimed in his direction!

As usual Steve tried to not dwell on such thoughts as not to sully the thoughts and perception he wanted to maintain of Lilian and continue without questions his believe as to what she told him her marriage to Daniel had been like.

She's always declared her husband had been the abuser but Lilian was not coming across as a shrinking violet, especially the longer he got to know her.

Lilian always seemed on edge when he met her but he'd put it down to what she said about her ex-husband, how he treated her, the abuse she told Steve that she received from Daniel which caused her to pack up and run away with her child.

Steve met her using an online dating site, this girl so far from her family, now living alone with a young child, it appealed to a chivalrous side of him, he felt compelled to rescue her, a need to protect her and be her shinning white knight, the damsel in distress mentality.

He'd thought she would settle once her ex was out of her life, once he was truly away from her and Sam, once the dark cloud of possible contact with Sam drifted away, which it had since done. He had no chance to see his son, the court action was signed off but then somehow that evening reappeared.

Steve had hoped that her ex was well and truly out of her life, it did seem he was for a while but even then she only seemed to get worse, her tolerance towards her son even less.

Some days it felt as if she was on a hair trigger and was looking for Sam to set her off, almost with a shaky desire to find an excuse to erupt her temper on him at the least little thing.

Steve was concerned, he felt love for her but this side of Lilian he did not care for.

20

Daniel parked his car against the curb, about 30 meters from the main gate of the school.

It was a straight road and he'd arrived early enough to ensure securing his prime location as the zebra crossing lay ahead of where he had parked on the same side as the school school's open gates and only the running double yellow line streaked up towards the nose of his car before terminating a hand span from his front bumper so no other arriving cars would would park in front of his thus there would be no obscuring his view of the kids departing through the gates.

It would be another 20 minutes before the final bell would sound but already children were slowly filtering through the gate in drips and drabs, most using the crossing directly in front of the gate but some turning left once out or right, a route which would cause them to pass by the near side of his car. He believed Sam's exit would be out the gates then straight ahead across the road at the crossing as this would he the quickest route home to his mum's house.

Daniel was of course taking much for granted. He hoped that Sam would be unaccompanied and not with his mother. In the past she often escorted him to school and collected him after as a deterrent for this very eventuality. But he figured that enough time had passed, almost 4 years since Daniel had tried such a strategy before to make contact with his son. Then, as bad luck would have it, Lilian had also been there in Sam's school, probably having been summoned to discuss something with a teacher, and as she walked through the doors of the school towards the gate with Sam she immediately saw Daniel, who at that time was standing there awaiting amongst a small herd of other parents just inside the gate. She dragged Sam roughly by the hand barging past him whilst loudly, and to cause of much tutting of the other awaiting parents, shouted at Daniel to "Fuck off!"

Daniel did not follow her in the attempt to reason, he knew Lilian was blind to any reason and it would not be a good look for him, a man, keeping pace with a woman and a child racing to almost escape velocity, worst than that, it would only add strength to her refusal of him to have contact by starting a false narrative that he was stalking her, very much a lie but always a good card to play in the court as was the abusive husband card proved to be in the attempt to justify what would otherwise be seen as blatant parental alienation.

Daniel's hopes now were also that Sam would be attending his school this day, he knew from his report card, which he received upon request from the school, that his attendance was not good. Also presuming that once, after the final bell sounded, Sam would not be staying behind for an after school club or something similar. There were a lot of presumptions to be had.

What he did now was that there was a very strong chance this would all be a wasted effort by coming here but even the slightest hope was a candle in the darkness and the night before Daniel stewed over wither he should try this attempt to make contact with his son since that anomalous last text message he'd received.

But here he was, sitting, waiting, watching and butterflies swarming around in his belly intensified with every child leaving through the gate as he scanned their faces looking for his son.

He never told Maria that the was his plan, to turn up at Sam's school and attempt to approach him, she would surely have tried to talk him out of it, probably a good idea on reflection now as he waited, but he had to try, he needed to do something.

More school children continued to drip feed through the gate, mostly solos but some in chatty pairs.

Most were wearing green blazers as were the school colours but some had jackets on as many parents had anticipated rain before sending their kids outside their homes that morning.

A few, all boys just were attired in their jumpers, the odd one just in a white shirt, almost always untucked from the trousers but the weather was still dry and clement which allowed such scant wear, something Daniel was glad the weather was not so cold or raining as pulled up hoods or woolly knit beanies could make identification more difficult, he already had to stare hard at a few kids who seems a similar structure and age to Sam.

It was still five minutes before the bell was due to sound when he saw Sam coming out the gates in a red padded jacket and carrying a sports bag at his side. He was walked by himself, straight out the gate and across the crossing.

The words "stop and look both ways first Sam" were on the tip of Daniel's tongue like a dormant parental instinct arising.

He fastened his seatbelt and started the car sticking it into drive. He could already feel his heart racing and made a conscious effort to control his emotional state which he felt as if being dredged up from his loins to his chest.

He checked his rear view and indicated before departing from the curb.

Sam had already crossed the road and was carrying on with his journey on the pavement of the street opening opposite the crossing. Daniel drove carefully up to the crossing wary of any children and indicated right and drove up the street putting on just a little more speed whilst passing Sam but then stealing a another look at his son through the side window as he overtook him on the opposite side of the road.

Yes, it was defiantly his son. Daniel heart soared with possibilities. He continued ahead on the straight road, it was a residential street, quiet and clear without much through traffic.

Once he had about a hundred meter start on Sam he parked against the curb, removed his seatbelt and watched the progression of Sam as his reflected image gradually grew larger getting closer on the opposite pavement from the offside of the car.

Daniel was nervous but Sam would still be oblivious to his father at that moment waiting in the car parked ahead.

In his mind Daniel had rehearsed this moment one hundred times and now the chance came he could not fumble.

He felt like opening the door and rushing up to his son, scooping his up in an all encompassing hug as if it were the ending of a movie but he must not rush, he must proceed slowly.

Just as Sam was almost parallel on the opposite side of the road to the curb where he'd parked Daniel opened his door stepping out the car onto the quiet road, rested his arm on the top of the door sill and called out to Sam whilst raising his right hand. "Sam, Hello Sam!' he called out. Not exactly a greeting scripted by Shakespeare but served its purpose of stopping Sam in his tracks who then looked across at his father with a almost comical look of bewildered open mouthed surprise.

"How are you Son?" Daniel quickly followed up with.

Daniel analysed every pixel of animation of the face of his Son. Sam's mouth closed and what looked like early dawnings of a smile formed at the corners of his lip, a slight timeout as his mind seemed to be computing what had happened as if processing data.

Daniel's heart increased its tempo within his chest.

"It's been a while Sam."

Sam's face then engaged into neutral followed by a slight shade of crimson from embarrassment as he placed his chin down and restarted walking, now quicker..

He passed his dad at the open door of his car on the opposite side of the road, now an even more determined walk than the amble before the interruption on his journey home.

The butterflies in Daniel's belly turned into night moths rupturing the canvas of their wings battering again a naked lit bulb in an otherwise darkened cavern, he felt crushed at Sam's response.

"It's ok Sam!" he called out as Sam passed him but his son never looked back, he strode on with purpose.

Daniel climbed back in the car, lowered the side window then parted from the curb. When passing across from Sam who was walking at pace he slowed down the car almost to a crawl then called out from the window "Its OK Son. I love you!"

Daniel saw Sam's eyes within his downturned head pivot slightly in his direction but the head remained down and the onward determination did not falter.

Nothing further could be salvaged from the moment so with a heaviness Daniel increased speed and drove on, something which he had to force himself to do as his heart cried out for him to stop and ask Sam why he was forsaking him, it did not seem logical.

Daniel drove on numb for another ten minutes before realising there was a beeping noise due to his seatbelt not being on. He stuck his arm into it without stopping and clicked it in place, a more successful coupling than the briefest meeting with his son had been.

Sam closed the door behind him when he reached home and went straight to the living room to peek out the corner of the window to watch the road outside the house to see if dad was driving past.

His mum was thankfully not at home yet as this was one of her college days which she attended twice a week and Steve would not be finished work yet for another few hours on that day.

Sam used the key his mother had planked for him under the flower pot in the garden to let himself in. Usually on such days it would give Sam a few blessed hours before his mom's return as to when she would expected to then see him doing homework seated in his bedroom at his small desk but he could not relax due to the events which had just transpired.

He was breathing heavily and was very fearful that the black car which he'd saw his dad in would draw up outside and then his dad would come to the door ringing the bell looking for him.

It was not his dad he feared but how his mum would react to such a situation if she was to find out, he did not want her to think that he wad encouraged this to happen.

He was so surprised earlier when he heard his name hailed and then saw it was his Dad standing by a car across the street.

He'd felt frozen like a deer in a spotlight, he felt confused.

At first there there was an elation rising within him followed by an unfathomable awkwardness that there was his dad just across the road calling out his name, but then he thought about the warnings mom had gave him, and the dark blueish message he still wore on the side on his thigh when she found out about his contact by the text messages on his phone just a few days ago.

How she yelled and screamed at him then. Yanked on his ear and slapped the back of his legs, only Steve stopped her hurting him worse. How much worse would it be if she found out he had been speaking to dad in the street, what would be the punishment for that?

He'd had decided to flee, he had put his head down and walk away from the dilemma instead of dealing with it when he saw his dad calling to him.

He had heard his dad call out again saying that it was alright, but instead of comfort this only made Sam feel more ashamed.

More words followed but Sam did not let them register in his mind, as he had walked, he kept repeating to himself Please don't follow, please down come, please no, please don't. He repeated these words like a mantra in his head, a unvoiced plea for his father not to chase after him, not to ask why did he not stop, not to ask why he is running away.

Not running Sam had thought, I'm walking, despite his desperation not to get caught up in that moment he still could not propel himself to kick up heels and run, this was his dad, there was not danger but he

164

would not allow mum to know about this, he could not allow her to know, he had to get away from being in the same vicinity as his dad.

As he'd listened for footsteps falling behind him he'd heard a car engine start up, assumed that it was his Dad's then heard it slow as it was close.

Please don't stop. He had risked a glance from the side of his eye and could see his dad at the car window as he drove past, he heard him saying that that he loved him.

Sam could not respond, he tried to pick up his steps more, hoping he would be left alone, that his father would drive on passing him which he did much to Sam's relief, but still to his concern that he would maybe return.

Sam continued walking quickly for another five minutes before reaching home, both his sanctuary and his cell.

Here he was now twitching at the lace curtain peering between the slats of the blinds checking to see that the coast was clear.

His breathing was returning to normal now but he was shaking. There was a certain excitement seeing his father but it was flushed with the anxiety of worry that his mum may find out that Dad had approached him in the street. Would she believe that Sam did not know this was going to happen today?

There certainly would be a suspicion about the impromptu of his Dad just turning up awaiting for Sam on a day mom would be at her college, and questions would most certainly be asked about if Sam did enough to shun his father.

Sam really just wanted things to die down, when his mum was upset it usually meant bad news for Sam and he knew she was still on edge from finding out about these text messages Sam had sent.

Yet the guilt of what Sam did out there played upon him.

It was hard enough to agree to the slander his mother told Steve night after night then saying that no way did he want contact with "Daniel" but then to put action into play and ignore his dad, that was much harder, terribly harder, brutal! What must he think? Does he understand my reasons thought Sam.

At the end of the day I have to live and sleep under the same roof as my mum, she won't allow me to be impartial, she needs me to take her side to validate all which she tells, my slightest hesitance and I will receive adjustments by the punishment of pain. "Make the skin sing" is what she tells Steve.

Sam usually thought of Steve as having no backbone, like the jelly fish which Sam learnt in biology at school. Steve would curl and conform to his mum in a desperation of the resigned as if he must be on her side if he was to keep her as a partner. Yet it was Steve who comforted him at the nursing home, its was Steve that stopped mom hitting him when she found the text messages to Dad, and Steve who had tucked him into his bed the past evenings talking gently to him when mom was still fuming mad at him.

Sam could remember the raised voices that evening as he lay awake in bed, his leg stinging after Mom beating down upon him when she discovered the texts to his father. Laying there he could make out his mum claiming that it was one massive mistake giving him a phone, and Steve, to his credit that evening stood up for Sam saying it was no surprise that Sam was curious about his father, that it was only natural. He could then hear his mom scream at Steve and Steve would go quiet. She then went on shouting about the mobile phone and how that was a mistake, how Sam could not be trusted.

Daniel returned home Maria called out his name as he closed the door behind him.   She could tell by the pitch in his reply when he acknowledged her that something was wrong.

'What's wrong my love?' Maria asked as she walked up towards him seeing his crestfallen head and the despondence of his stance behind the illusion of normality which he then tried to launch behind it.

'Nothing love.' he answered, 'Just saudade.' he tried to smile but the resistance his heart gave caused a twitch to the sides of his mouth declaring any attempt at gaiety was not a true reflection of the wearer of that smile which was already crumbling to the display of more like a simper as it's scaffolding started to give way.

Maria picked up on this immediately. Holding his hand she walked him to the sofa to give her full attention as to find out what his story was.

Daniel told her the full tale. He told her that he had driven through to Sam's school in the west, awaited his son to leave then was awarded with the first sighting of his child for almost four years as he came out from through the school gates.

Daniel then went on to tell how he had called across to Sam and the cold reception he received in return when rebuffed.

A few days had passed since Daniel had received that final

concluding text message. The words that had been within the message "committed a mistake" and "we don't even know each other." had been tearing at Daniel, grinding him like shrapnel against the bones.

It was first suggested by Maria that perhaps Sam's mother had found out he had been messaging his dad and that final concluding message had been authored by Lilian standing over him. Daniel clung desperately to that mitigating reasoning. The hope flowered within him that this was the most explainable excuse to the change of pace within that last message which he had received.

Daniel had the trinity of hope then, imagination and anticipation.

The hope which Spinoza once called as a feeling of unstable joy but that was what Daniel clung to as unstable as it were.

He used his imagination to develop the narrative fully in his mind how it could be that his mother had caught Sam in contact with him so subsequently blocked off that avenue.

The Daniel fell upon the anticipation of a possible outcome if he were to open another avenue now that Sam had tried for contact.

That avenue would be for Daniel to make contact with his son again but this time physically and outwith Lilian's ability to scupper it. He had foresaw such an opportunity may be had by him turning up to a place he knew Sam would be and at the time he would expect to see him, which was to be at his School.

Daniel told her, describing the look on Sam's little face as he called his name across to him. The animation clockwork which the sighting of his father seemed to set in motion.

For a precious moment Daniel thought he'd broken through to his son, the smile he'd thought that was dawning on Sam's face but never did reach it's zenith as it went off in the other direction as Sam's feet were soon to follow suit.

Maria held his hand and looked to his face with such sympathy and kindness Daniel felt he could let loose his feeling to her with all the candour and never to fear that she would judged him.

As well as the vulnerability that came when his son was born, that one which Lilian had used to her advantage over Daniel, there is also a susceptibility of the heart that comes with love, a trust to open up and spread your most guarded emotions open, display the contents of these inner most vaults of the heart for your loved one to see, your worries, your fears…everything, and Daniel was at that stage with Maria and he had the certitude this was reciprocated from the close intimacy which they shared.

Daniel, when they first met, would tell Maria about the pains he still carried from missing not only his mum but his dad and brother too and then his absent son.

Maria would tell him that it was perfectly normal to feel such loss, and to mourn it still, but she also told him "não morra com seus mortos", don't die with your dead she would say.

She told him that it was alright to cry because he'd lost them and was missing them, but he also needed to know and understand that although they were no longer at his side, he could not allow their absence to control his future.

Life goes on beyond death, and loss is part of that life. By accepting that his dead have died he may not stop grieving for them, but he could find them again in his memories so that they would continue to accompany him with the joys of everything he had, will have and still would experienced in the future as if they were still there with him which in part they were as their influences would always run strong within him, that is the real legacy which the departed leave behind for us.

The memories of his son Sam which he retained was also the same principle but Sam was still of this world, absent just now from Daniel's life but still part of it.

No one could take his fatherhood away from him, his influences would still be sown deep within his boy so he would still be accompanying the child through his young life even now although they were parted, but Daniel needed patience and to live his life building foundations for dreams again to be erected upon, if not, then what would be the use of one day in the future reuniting with his son, what dynasty of their years apart could be gained then shown to him later when they are together again?

Maria spoke these words with love and they were to be ointment to the wounds Daniel carried. Dragons into Butterflies. He loved this lady so very much for what she did for him, the healing through the love she gave him.

She was to be traveling to Brazil next week to visit her family on their farm in São Paulo, she then asked Daniel to come and met her there, it was about time he got to know her family, who she said should also be considered his family, a feeling which comforted Daniel more than she could have known.

Maria also thought, although left unsaid, that the change of scenery would be good for him, especially after the recent false hopes which had arisen but then were so cruelly dashed. The relics of the past had been since removed from the house to help Daniel move on but the ghosts still wandered within its four walls.

21

Daniel sat by himself at a table beside the eatery inside the airport terminal.

It had been more than ten years since he'd last been in São Paulo's Guarulhos airport. Then he was with Lilian and that was also the last time Daniel had eaten pão de queijo, the Brazilian style cheese bread and here he was again, in Brazil, in Guarulhos eating pão de queijo and having once more traveled there to meet with a woman. He never expect to be in this position again.

Maria had flew back to Brazil earlier to spend some time with her parents and Daniel had agreed to follow her later and there, at the airport upon his arrival he waited for her to collect him as he snacked upon cheese bread washed down with a can of fizzy Guarana juice, he fought down the feeling of déjà vu.

He had been excited to see a Casa do Pão de Queijo franchise at the arrivals area of the airport, it had not changed in the past decade and he was content to sit by the glass window munching his snacks awaiting Maria who was about thirty minutes away according to the text message which he recently received.

The past two weeks without Maria being there in his life, as she had been since they'd sealed their relationship with their first night of love making, their first time apart and Daniel felt an immense emptiness without her.

They had phoned each other every night but still he was missing his love so very much, such a short time together yet she was so deeply in his heart.

It was written that the ancient Greek philosopher Plato how emotions interfere with rationality. Plato likened the thinking part of the soul to a charioteer steering two powerful horses each representing an emotional aspect of the self. One is aspirational and tries to fly upwards towards the heavens whilst the other is appetitive and tries to plunge deeper down into the earth. The charioteer should aim to be reason and level these great beasts was the great philosopher's advice but this advice Daniel would never heed. He had jumped feet first into his relationship with Maria and here he was now, in Brazil about to meet her family, her pai, mãe and vovó, father, mother and grandmother who lived on a farm in the countryside of Brazil, a place with a name which sounded strange to Daniel's ears, Caporanga which was in the Santa Cruz Do Rio Pardo area of the São Paulo countryside.

There was a knot of anxiety in his stomach about the prospect of meeting Maria's father, a serious man from the descriptions amid stories he heard, Daniel wondered how his reaction would be meeting the foreigner who was bedding down with his beloved daughter, but even more worrying was to be introduced to Maria's Grandmother, Donna Luara. She was a lady with a reputation to speak her mind as Daniel was told. Maria had described the moment when her gran first met her ex-husband before he became an ex. The man approached her with his hand held out in greeting but Donna Luara just turned her back on him then walked away with obvious disapproval.

By all accounts Donna Luara did seem the type to hold back her tongue or not express her thoughts with actions.

Daniel joked with Maria calling her gran Donna Diablo but under the surface he was seriously worried about the reception he may receive from her vovó.

From Guarulhos it would be a four to five hour drive onwards to Maria's family's farm in Caporanga.

Maria had stayed at her brother's house in São Paulo the night before after arriving from the farm but once collecting Daniel the plan was to drive straight to Caporanga. Daniel suggested that once she had collected him from the airport they could drive into São Paulo city and spend the night in a nice hotel, refresh themselves before the journey to the farm. The actual reason in Daniel's head was not only the overnight blessed interlude he would have with his love but also a days postponement before being introduced to her family, such was his nervousness.

He was desperate to make a good first impression but he also knew he was the type of guy who was never at ease in social situations and this was going to be intense, at least in his mind, meeting the nearest

171

and dearest of the woman he was so very much in love with.

Daniel's phone pinged were it sat on the table alerting him to a newly received text message. It was Maria advising that she had just arrived, was parking up and would meet him at gate four just outside the arrivals hall.

It had only been a short time since he'd last saw her but already he could feel excitement building in his chest at their reunion, absence does indeed make the heart grow fonder he thought to himself.

Popping the last piece of cheese bread into his mouth chewing with haste before chugging some of the fizzy Guarana whilst arising from the table he stood there dusting off invisible crumbs from his thighs. He inserted one arm into his small daypack which he had used as his cabin bag pulling it up onto his shoulder then retracted the handle from the suitcase before proceeding towards the large glass exit pulling the case behind him.

Egressing from the airport the exterior heat hit him like someone had opened an oven door. He screwed up his eyes wishing he had dug out his sunglasses from his daypack. The sun was bright and shinning through the smoggy faded Levi's sky. What a contrast to Scotland, the country he'd left just less than eighteen hours ago flying out to Frankfurt to catch the connecting flight to Brazil, head east before flying west, always a strange thought but to connect in Heathrow was a much more expensive option.

He scanned the stone pillars and found he had exited at gate two, he started walking towards gate four through invites of taxis and guys handing out fliers of hotels to stay in.

It is said that we never quite experience the present, that we only ever see the world as a late arriving projection on the brain one fifth of a second in the past. Our perception of the world is not immediate, but is instead a result after non-sensing parts of our brain's processing and interpret the information first which causes such a delay but in Daniel's mind he had saw Maria standing there awaiting him much sooner than this, so soon it felt as if it were in the future he had saw her image standing there before, long before, almost like a sixth sense. Like a fantasy these past few days be had been visioning this up and coming reunion with a relish that was not any reflection of being away from each other for only a short time, he'd felt they had been apart for much longer and yearned so much to hold her again, taste her lips.

He halted in his tracks, his suitcase thudding but unfelt against his lower leg as he pulled up.

There she was, twenty meters away standing facing him with a smile on her face which dazzled his very soul.

He almost flew the last meters towards her, a grandiose beam on his only face which appeared without any conscious effort.

Nothing in Daniel's heart or mind could be greater to observe than the sight there in front of his at that moment. Nothing Botticelli could produce on canvas or da Vinci with marble could ever compare with the monument of flesh and blood which stood there awaiting his embrace, this was love that stood awaiting him there.

Once love was within his reach his hand released the suitcase grabbing her, drawing her tight against him, locking his mouth upon hers before any words could be parted. His hands were wrapped around her in an embrace as were hers with him. His daypack had slid off his shoulder during the kinetics of their entwining and was then hanging on the crook of his arm but he did not feel its weight.

'Well hello!' Maria gasped out when they broke for air.

'I've missed you!' returned Daniel which was all too obvious from their body language but he felt he still needed to say, then added 'I love you so much!'

Maria's reciprocal statement of her love for him pulled the hair trigger for another crushing embrace. Onlooker would could be forgiven to assume this pair had been separated for years such was the reunion, Odysseus reuniting with Penelope would pale in comparison.

With a salute of thanks the bellman took the tip Daniel slipped into his hand after showing them up to their hotel room and left closing the door behind him.

Maria had already entered the bathroom to freshen up upon their arrival closing the door behind her as Daniel knelt down by his suitcase twisting the central combination dials to gain entry.

He quickly decanted some items from the case into his daypack, the contents of which were now piled unceremoniously upon a chair pulled out by the desk.

Daniel looked across at the bed, it was kingsized with piles of pillows at its head. He harvested a mint from the pillow, unwrapping it allowing it to melt in his mouth savouring the freshness.

Hearing the water from the shower being turned on behind the door to the bathroom he wandered across to the window wall and starred out across the park and the roads and bridges which hedged it.

From the ceiling to floor window of their nineteenth floor room Ibirapuera park sprawled out below in the distance.

It was about five in the afternoon and out in the Paulista world rush hour had began.

The bathroom door opened and Maria stepped out wearing a black lacy nightdress which sent Daniel's heart racing with desire.

She walked up within a few feet of where he stood and stopped with a seductive smile of her face. Daniel placed a hand on each of her shoulders and gentle guided her down upon the bed. Leaning back he kissed her deep and long on the lips savouring the scent of her perfume.

He stood up with some effort to fight the instinct to take her there and then on the bed. She lay on the bed still holding his hands as he backed away until their fingertips parted.

'I have a little surprise for you!' he announced smiling coyly, 'just give me a few minutes to clean up.'

Maria, her curiosity as piqued as her arousal watched him step into the bathroom with his daypack closing the door behind him.

Her commanding for him not to be long delightfully trailing after him.

After quickly showering Daniel unzipped his daypack and removed the items of clothings which were within. He wrapped one of the the garment around his waist wearing nothing underneath which was the true bare-arsed fashion to wear at kilt. He had brought this tradition attire of his country with him to surprise his love with. Maria often hinted that she would love to see him wearing a kilt but like many Scotsmen he never actually owned one but for this very occasion he had purchased a kilt and a Jacobite gillie shirt, which he then pulled over his head, tucking into the waist before fastening the side buckle of the kilt then looping the sporran around it placing the leather belt to top it off with it's shinny silver thistle buckle facing the front.

He silently cursed when he realised he'd left the hose socks and kilt pin in the suitcase through in the bedroom but then had a little giggle to himself when he heard Maria shout through for him to hurry up as she needed him.

He was feeling very salacious for her body too and could feel pressing matters against the Black Watch tartan fabric of his kilt behind the sporran. He splashed on a dab of aftershave and went to open the bathroom door, his pulse racing on how Maria may react at the sight of a kilt wearing Scotsman about to come and ravish her on the bed

Maria exhaled a long lust charged breath upon seeing her man appear in his traditional dress, the pleats of his kilt swayed seductively as he marched over to the bed standing at its side, standing over her. Daniel radiated a fine figure with his wide shoulders and deep chest filling out the linen of the shirt and the kilt sat proud upon his hips.

She reached over and stroked the black calf skin on the facing sporran pouch as if sensing the potency which lay being it awaiting her.

Tugging on the pouch she pulled him that little bit closer to where she now knelt on the bed then reached under his kilt to investigate what he was wearing underneath only to find out the answer was nothing and let out an mm-hmm of pretended surprise at the discovery which Daniel followed with his own sigh of pleasure as she took hold of him underneath the tartan fabric.

In the morning the sun shinned through a gap in the curtains that had not closed flush. Daniel, as gently as be could, removed his arm from around Maria's body. They were both naked lying on the bed, the bedsheets were curled like vines down by their ankles spreading to the floor.

Daniel creeped out of the bed hoping not to disturb the still sleeping Maria. He padded quietly around to the bottom of the bed to untangle the white bedsheet, then as delicately as possible covered Maria's dosing form up just below her shoulders with the linen. Maria let out a dreamy murmur repositioning herself slightly when the fabric touched her body. Daniel nimbly stood back with his palms presented in her direction as if to ward off any rousing emergence from her rest he may have caused by his actions.

He looked down at her sleeping figure and felt a stirring within him. How alluring this blonde beauty was laying down there on the bed, the bed which on the night before they had made frenzied passionate love upon, this goddess, his love. He was beheld by the curvature of her body under the white bedsheet, the moated beam of sunlight which breached the aperture of curtains flared across the room igniting her golden shoulder enchantingly, the tan of her skin a contrast when compared to Daniel's Gaelic derma.

Daniel forced himself to break his trance then silently, conscious of where he placed his barefooted tread to avoid the hastily discarded piece of tartan attire which Maria had unwrapped from around his waist before their night of love making and a black silky negligé which he then picked up holding to his nose smelling the lingering scent of her perfume upon before draping it across the back of a chair.

He crossed to the window then reaching high he attempted to quietly pull the curtains together to unsuccessfully block out the morning light as the fabric separated again when then he heard Maria call out to him.

'What time is it love?' she sleepily enquired.

'Good morning love.' he tenderly replied turning around to greet her,

Daniel approached the desk at the end of the bed and checked his watch which lay there, 'It's seven love, you can sleep on a bit but that's me awake now, I think I will read a little bit.'

They had taken to addressing each other as "love" over the past few months, at first Daniel found it a little clichéd but he did adore hearing her address him as such and soon he followed and soon found it so very natural so call her as such.

'I am going to get up love.' she announced stifling a yawn, 'we have a long drive ahead, best get breakfast then set off with an early start.'

Maria sat upright on the bed pulling the sheet up as not to let it slide and expose her breasts.

Daniel approached the bed and with one knee upon it leaned across and kissed her a good morning. Daniel could smell a velvety lushness from fragrance of her perfume still upon her but also a musk in the air from their love that night before. Daniel climbed further upon the bed, climbing under the covers again conscious of his nakedness as the spotlight of the infiltrating sun ray betrayed any concealment of darkness. He positioned the pillow under his head but still pitched his arm so that the side of his head was supported by his palm at the end of the pillar which was his arm. Maria squirmed her orientation slightly as she lay back to face him mirroring his position. They looked at each other in silence with coquettish smiles which Maria soon concluded asking 'so what now Highlander?' a reference more to the garments Daniel wore to entertain her previously.

'Och aye the noo bonny lass, noo I'll take ye here the noo on this here flair of heathers!' he answered grinning from ear to ear using a elocution that felt foreign to his tongue imitating the parodied Scotchman.

As she laughed He made a grab for her which Maria pushed him off giggling and bolted from the bed into the bathroom pulling the door closed behind her. Daniel laughed, 'come back love!'

'I'll be back!' Maria twittered in return and soon the sound of a tap running and a brushing of her teeth, Daniel, now flat on his back, smiled feeling like at the top of the world knowing what this prelude would mean as did the rising pavilion of the bedcovers at his waist.

Before checking out they both had breakfast, swilling lots of black coffee and consuming breads and fruits to fuel up for the drive ahead.

Once on the road the traffic getting out of São Paulo city was horrendous, the Tietê river, which they drove along the road bordering its banks, gave off an acidic smell which even the closed windows of the car could not keep at bay.

Along the road out of the city Daniel noticed a sign for a turn off towards Osasco which was the city where his ex-wife Lilian came from, a place he had visited in what felt like a formal life. Again that bizarre feeling hit him of history repeating itself, this time with a different character but this was an unfair thought which he pushed put of his mind, Maria was nothing like Lilian, they were chalk and cheese in comparison. Lilian was a spiteful vindictive bitch whereas Maria was a loving caring partner, but still he had once thought of Lilian the same way had he not? Could he be blinded by love not to see the same warning signs? "Gan Canny" was his friends advise, people who knew how he had gotten hurt so much with Lilian after jumping in with both feet, now hearing that he was dating another Brazilian their advice was to proceed carefully.

He looked across to his left in the car, looked at Maria driving, concentrating on the road wearing her sunglasses. To his eyes she was the most beautiful woman on the earth and could do no wrong but was such naivety Daniel's vulnerability when it came to woman? He believed in love, not only that intense feeling of deep affection but also that of true love, that monogamous for life unique and passionate bond. He did feel something with Maria that he'd never felt before with an other. The way they confided during intimacy, discussed their fears and ambitions, never afraid to show their emotions to each other, even resulting tears at time, he did not feel he had to put a macho persona on in front of her. As a sensitive man he had strong emotions that was best shared and she listened never teased or judged. He would tell her everything such was their bond, he told about his love for Sam and how the alienation had effected him, he talked about his mother and their last moments today, teared flowed when he told her, not only from him but also empathetically from her too. She also shared her fears and described her worst moments with him, the death of her beloved aunt and how it effected her, her concerns about her parents getting only older and knowing that they won't always be there. They would common ground with their heart to hearts, they held each other, caressed and dusted each others tears when they ran. Being human comes with it's frailties of emotions and its a release to find someone you can open all your conscious doors to, Daniel had this in Maria and believed she felt the same way, this was true love and something he had never experienced with anyone before, they both carried scars from their pasts but together they found something so very rare in each other.

As Daniel was considering these thoughts Maria turned her head and saw him studying her.

'e aí?' she asked inquisitively quickly following up with its translation 'what's up?'

'Just thinking about how much a love you' answered Daniel honestly.

'Ahhhh love, I love you too'. When Maria said this, as she did many times, Daniel's heart fluttered that bit faster and he felt a warmth, he knew it was the truth, there was an intuition when a couple love each other, something beyond conscious reasoning. He smiled back at Maria with the greatest love in his soul.

22

Once out of the city the roads grew quieter. They progressed east along Castelo Branco highway, only stopping when approaching one of the many toil booths. Along the road there were many trucks driving in the same direction but with three lanes there was no slowing down so they made good time reaching the turning for Caporanga.

The road dramatically narrowed to a single track once they turned off and the surface changed to a rutted track of red soil, terra roxa.

On both sides were fields separated from the single tracked road by wire fences. Grazing within the fields were zebu cows, a breed adapted to the hot south American sun and easy to distinguish with their large hump upon their back.

In the distance at the end of the track they could see a couple of building and sheds.

'That's the farm love!" Maria declared, 'we are almost home!'

Daniel felt his nerviness increase. He forked his fingers through his hair, a final attempt to look presentable to his love's awaiting family.

The last couple of hundred meters of the drive a boxer dog dived out from the side of the fields in front of the car racing in and out in front as if providing an escort leading the way.

'Pablito!' Maria gave out a hearty laugh , 'that's my boy.'

It did not help Daniel's nerves watching the dog in from dart in and out of sight beyond the view over the front hood of the car but it's timings seemed perfectly synchronised and Maria did not have to adapt her speed.

Soon they arrived at the end of the track where her family's farm house stood. Maria slowed to a stop and parked the car at the side of a tree.

She opened the door and started to make a fuss focused towards the dog which danced around her feet lapping up the attention.

Daniel took a deep breath in the attempt to calm his nerves then opened the car door.

The main house was a single storey building with a white sloped roof and terracotta coloured walls. In front was a veranda with a hammock attached to the supporting pillars.

A older woman, short in height with slivery grey bod cut hair who Daniel recognised from photos as Maria's mother was sitting on the hammock, her bare feet on the tiled floor holding a book which, as Daniel looked across, she placed down and stood up before walking across to were he stood by the car.

He started to walk across towards the advancing woman. Pablito the dog came around to his side starting to make a fuss at this new visitor. Daniel was glad of the distraction to bend down greeting the dog fondling its muzzle as a brief interlude to his awkward amble toward the approaching lady, through his nerves he felt conscious about his body language, the social awkwardness of his shy nature always was a blight on his mind during such moments.

'Daniel' she greeted him proffering her hand 'Bom dia!' she smiled.

He gladly took her hand then kissed her gently on both cheeks, 'Bom Dia Célia, Tudo bem?' he replied to her salutation asking how she way.

'Ahhhh…você fala português!' she laughed, of course she knew from Maria that be never spoke Portuguese but was entertained at his reply.

'Desculpe, não fala.' Daniel apologised cheerfully.

As they were greeting each other an elderly lady walked fragilely towards him flattening down her grey hair strands with her palms grooming herself to look presentable. Although diminutive in statue from age she carried herself with an undeniable grace.

Daniel turned to greet her, straightening his posture and attempted to iron out his face trying to look more earnest as he about to receive her.

'Bom dia Donna Luara.' he exclaimed in what he hoped was a respectable tone of voice.

She was smiling and answered in a slow careful cadence with practiced words. 'Hello. Please to meet you.'

Maria and her mother laughed with somewhat astonishment at english words spoken by the grandmother. Daniel felt a wave of relief flood over him but was careful as not to lower his guard. On the journey here he was worried Maria's granny would take one look at him, dismiss then ignore him as just a fleeting foreign boyfriend of her granddaughter and make no effort to know him but here she was, making an effort to speak some english words of welcome to him. He was deeply touched.

'You speak english?' Daniel answered, Donna Luara just continued to look at him with a warm smile on her face not understanding what he'd just said as she'd depleted her english.

Daniel held her hand and kissed her on both cheeks gently whilst proclaiming that he was very pleased to meet her in english. She smiled back at him and Daniel felt all was going to be fine.

They were walking across to the veranda where at that moment Maria's dad came out from within.

He was a tall man, still broad in the shoulders, left overs of how imposing he must have looked when younger. Bare chested only wearing baggy blue and white elephant pants with unclad feet at the ends he displayed himself as a man not interested in the judgment of others. His belly protruded over the waist of the pants with a whorl of grey hairs which extended up his trunk over his chest. His face, heavy with its grey stubbled jowls exhibited the passage of time with its wrinkled skin and deep lines etched across his forehead. Around his eyes emanated wisdom and experience. A bracelet watch was on his left wrist with an analogue face, its losing fitting made it run up his forearm are he reached up to scratch his shoulder as he walked towards Daniel. Despite his casual attire and age he maintained an appearance of someone important and his voice had a deep bass timbre as he called out his greeting to Daniel in an accented english reaching out his hand. He came across very much as the quintessence patriarch figure. 'Hello Daniel!' he boomed with depth.

Daniel returned the greeting by addressing him as 'Senhor Edson.' which felt rightly proper when shaking his hand returning the genuine felt warmth.

Maria showed Daniel to what was to be their bedroom for the next couple of weeks so that he could unpack.

On the wall was a Roy Lichtenstein art in a frame named "We rose up slowly". The painting depicted a square jawed man with a luscious blonde in a steamy embrace in the style of a panel from an American pop cultured girls' romances comic, it looked slightly out of place in her bedroom. The man had red hair and the woman blonde.

'Is that us love?' Daniel curiously enquired with a grin on his face.

'Of course it is!' answered Maria, 'don't you recognise yourself?'

Upon her answer Daniel grabbed her folding her body backwards, holding her below his face then kissed her hard and long on the lips and upon rising up slowly for breath he said 'and there is where real life imitates art!'. She smiled in response pulling his head down for another taste.

Daniel emptied his daypack first by removing the kilt and shirt he had worn for her pleasure the evening before.

'Perhaps I should wear this in the evening and go and say hi to your granny Luara?' joked Daniel.

Maria giggled a response 'you'd give her a heart attack!'

'She is so cute, I love her. I was expecting a demon the way you described her but she was lovely!'

'She is getting milder in her old age. I think she likes you. The first time she met my ex-husband she just looked at him, tutted and turned her back.'

'I remember that you told be that and I was really worried about meeting her. Now I want to take her home with me.' they laughed together.

'Be careful what you wish for love!'

He soon had his suitcase unpacked then went to have another shower to wash off the grime of the road and prepare for dinner.

That evening Daniel sat out back with Maria and her family, he felt accepted, he felt part of the family, part of a family, a feeling which he never realised just how much he was missing until experiencing it again.

The food was a simple but delicious fare of rice and bean stew with shredded spring greens served as an accompaniment. Sliced meat was also served, tender cuts which Maria explained was "picanha", a flavourful cut of beef from the rump of the cow.

Edson, Maria's dad sat beside Daniel at the table. Ever so often he would peel a piece of meat from his plate and feed it to Pablito the dog who'd silently wait at his side for such a treat.

Once the dinner was finished and the plates cleared off the table then woman seemed to gyrate off to the confines of the kitchen, this included Maria who was still catching up on the family gossip with her mum and granny.

Daniel was left seated beside the father. He had been quiet most of the meal, just every so often he would say something in Portuguese and all would laugh, Maria especially who would conclude her giggles with a 'oh pappy', the love surrounding the family was quite obvious.

The evening was getting dark and it's soundtrack was the clicks of the cicadas playing their tymbal to attract a mate with the nocturnal crocks of a frog out there somewhere beyond sight.

Edson looked at Daniel as he asked his opening line 'The food, you enjoyed?'

'Yes, thank you.' replied Daniel and after a few seconds of searching his mind for the words added 'eu gosto comida.'

'Muito bom!' returned the older man with a cackle.

'Maria she tell me you been to Brazil before?'

'Yes, I have been twice to Brazil before.'

'You must really like Brazil?' Edson continued.

'The people are so nice and friendly, very welcoming.' was Daniel's stock answer.

'You like my daughter?'

Daniel looked the father straight in the eyes with all the sincerity that such a question deserved.

'I love your daughter!' he answered sternly with the frankness of honesty, 'I love Maria with all my heart!' Daniel hoped nothing could be lost in translation to what he'd just said, he felt it important that Maria's family knew exactly how he felt.

Edson seemed to search his eyes for a few seconds. Daniel never flinched, he may not have been the most confident of men at times but he stood his ground there strong with the forthrightness of declaring his love for his woman and he was never more sure of anything else in his life.

'Isso é bom!', 'Good!, because I can see that she loves you.'

Both men returned to the night and sat there contentedly in the silence of their company. Questions had been asked and answered. The sounds of the night continued around them peppered by some laugher which would be emitted every so often from the kitchen.

Daniel liked this man's simplicity yet he knew the importance of the sincerity they had both shared at that moment, he knew how important Maria was to her father, but he also knew without question how her love meant everything to himself too and that he had found his soul mate in her.

* * *

183

Daniel returned to Scotland a fortnight later leaving Maria still in Brazil on the farm as she was to spend the remaining next few weeks across there with her family before coming back to Scotland.

Daniel was heralded in with the old familiar glacial blast of chilled morning air welcoming him back to Scotland.

He embraced the chill as it partnered the melancholy within his chest being apart from his love, although it would just be a temporary parting before she would be joining him again, still the aching was there with which an twelve hour over night flight could not disperse in the slightest.

It was almost six ante meridian when he arrived back in Scotland but Helios had not taken to his chariot yet and Selene was still reining the heavens as dawn's first light was yet still an hour away. The morning darkness was a fitting firmament to his arrival back, only sodium vapours from lights gave illumination to the surroundings casting a monochromatic yellow flair on the ground which looked like the pages from an aged book recovered from a house fire.

He hauled his luggage behind him, its wheels ratcheting along the tarmac as he made his way across to where he would find a taxi. Still too early for trams so a hackney carriage would be his only conveyance to the train station which would be his next leg home. "Home" he thought, the word sounded fallacious in context to his head. A home to Daniel was no longer a brick and mortar concept, it was anywhere in this world were he could be with his love. His heart was yoked to Maria wherever she may be and at that point she was over six thousand miles away yet still he felt her deep within him.

23

Sam closed his bedroom door then stood behind it for a while listening. He heard noises coming from the kitchen beyond, his mum was there preparing the dinner from the sounds he heard, the clang of utensils and scrape of a pot.

He hauled his large plastic Lego box across to the bed which he sat upon its edge. Prising the lid off the box he rummaged amongst its content reaching for the smaller cardboard box concealed down at the bottom corner.

It had been almost a month since he'd saw his father as he left the school. Every day since whilst leaving through these same school gates he would scan cars around him wondering if he would see dad again standing there to get his attention. Sam never did see him again as the weeks passed. He was not quite sure what he would do if he did dee him there again, the thought of approaching his father still filled his head with dread, the terror of consequence if his mother was to find out. Perhaps he would give into his fear if the same scenario were to happen, maybe he would just stick his head down again and ignore his dad walking on home, but then this slow burn guilty which he had felt since would accumulate more within him.

The school had just finished for the summer holidays so no more did Sam have that little ember of hope that he felt leaving through the doors that he may see his dad there again, that swell deep within his belly, an excitement of possibilities.

He seemed to rely more upon the reminiscences he had in his clandestine little box which he had planked away in his bedroom, he needed the emotions it stirred within he when he touched the contents within. The memories tamed his yearnings and soothed his remorse even although for the shortest period it still helped him deal, as ameliorative connection to his past.

He lifted it out and placed the cardboard box on his bed opening and removing some of the contents. He fanned the photos over this bed, a count of 12 glossy prints, some of his dad, a few of his granny and others of Sam and his dad together during happier times.He studied the photos as he often did, he closed his eyes trying to imprint what he just saw in his memory.

Suddenly his bedroom door swung open and in stepped Lilian, the forewarning of approaching footsteps unheard by the child so caught up in his reflections of the past .

The words Lilian was about to say, asking him about cleaning up the scattered mess on his bed started to form on her lips but were canceled mid-sentence as she recognised Daniel in the photos.

Despite the obviousness of being found out Sam quickly grabbed the photos up off this bed, shuffling them into his hands as if he could change what his mother had saw in retrospect.

But Lilian had saw the photos, then next she saw red, the crimson mists descended, her anger flared as if a cup of gasoline had been thrown onto an open fire.

She lunged across the room and pulled the stack of photos from Sam's hand as he then sat there looking up at her with a mixture of surprise and gasping fear.

With the photographs in her hands Lilian tore the thin deck in half then proceeded to rip the halves into even smaller pieces.

Sam vaulted upright to his feet and reached across to haul the pieces from his mothers destructive hands, the only thought in his action was to stop theses memories from being destroyed, an instinct without a thought of repercussions.

He'd got a grip on the corners of one of the shredded bundle yanking it back toward him crying out 'don't mom!' when her other hand slapped him with full force across his face on his left side knocking him flying back down into a seated position on the bed again and then with the ripped pieces of the photos scattering around the room like confetti.

'You little bastard!' she shrieked whilst bending down then hauling him back onto his feet by his ear which she grabbed on the opposite side to which she had just slapped.

'Were did you get this stuff?' she screamed the question out.

Sam had taken his hand from the left side of his face which was still numbed from the clout Lilian had delivered, the pain still not registering there yet.

He fastened his hands onto his mother's wrist in an attempt to mitigate some of the force she was exerting prizing him up by his ear as that intense pain was immediate.

She let go of his ear and looked across at what lay on his bed. Sam's gaze followed her's.

She made to seize the cardboard box which was still on the bed. Sam immediately tried to grapple her hands away but he was too small and the box when spinning off the bed scattering its contents over the floor. Sam rushed to his knees to gather the strewn displaced load.

He sensed more than felt his mum bending to pull him upright by the ear again so twisted around then scuttled backward pushing off with his palms on the floor until his back was defensively against the bed.

He scrunched his face anticipating her next attack but she paused, stopped and seemed to go quiet looking at him.

That was when he felt a warmth down the left side of his face and put his fingers up to touch the area below his eye only to see his fingertips come away crimson with fresh blood.

When she had slapped his face the ring she was wearing sliced the flesh along the cheek bone, the blood was running down his face in a rivulets now.

The sight of blood appeared to calm Lilian, she realised just how far she had went with the child, such damage would not be as easy to hide as bruises she'd often left on his legs.

She took a deep breath in an attempt to get her composure back.

'Ok!', she said more levelled as to gain an equilibrium back into a situation which had escalated out of hand.

'Sit on the bed, let me see your face, let me see what you have done to yourself!' she commanded.

What he had done to himself, already the intuitive words of an abuser, blame the victim.

Sam raised himself from the floor and went over to his bed and sat down facing his mother.

She took his chin in her hand turning his face to the light to inspect the injury more closely. There was a shallow plough along his cheek passing out the blood.

'It's just a scratch!' Lillian downplayed. It certainly was not a serious wound, no medical treatment would be required but she had to give it some attention and of course, in her mind, come up with a suitable excuse. He fell and his face hit the side of the bed. He was swinging a cord around the room and he smacked his face. Maybe something in the garden. Fell whilst filling the dishwasher and scratched it on an upturned knife, the fictions were being conceived in her mind rapidly.

She would think better once she had cleaned up the cut, a little plaster over it, perhaps won't look as bad. Maybe some ice as not to swell, her mind was taking over now, planning the deceit.

She let go of Sam's face and went across to his sock drawer. She pulled out a rolled pair of black socks and went out to the bathroom to run them under the cold water tap, then returning told Sam to hold it to his face which he did.

She looked around the room, some dabs of splattered blood would need to be cleaned up before Steve returns. She will change his bedsheets, get these ones into the washing machine.

Once the cold compress of the wet sock had stopped the bleeding and she had cleaned away the smeared blood the cut did not look too bad. Lilian applied a sticking plaster over the wound. The bedclothes were already tumbling within the churning washing machine. Only Sam' s face now would show evidence of what had happened, and of course if Sam was to speak about it then that could bring Lilian plenty trouble.

She studied it closer in the light, the swelling was very obviously, she would need to get that down.

There was no ice in the compartment of the freezer when she looked.

'Sam.', she addressed her son calmly, 'I am going to nip down to the bottom of the road and get something cold to put against the side of your face to make it feel better. You stay here, be a good boy and I will get you some ice cream as a treat OK?, mummy won't be long!'

Sam just sat on his bed looking at her as if it were a rhetorical question. Lilian went to the hall to get her coat and shoes on, she still had a couple of hours before Steve was to return so everything would be fine, the excuse and plan was already formulated in her head and into action.

Sam also had formulated a plan churning it within his head.

As soon as he heard the front door close he bolted upright and got dressed in his jeans and pullover. He slid on his training shoes without undoing the laces and ran through to the kitchen.

He stood on one of the stools there and reached up high for the cookie jar perched on the top shelf.

Within its was a small bundle of ten pound notes, he peeled some layers off without counting and stuck them in his pocket then grabbed his jacket next.

He peered out of the window and saw no sign of his mom, she must be around the corner well on her way to the shops by now.

Sam belted out of the front door and headed in the opposite direction to which his mom went.

After a few rushed minutes he reached the crossroads where a taxi rank waited. He then opened the rear door to the front one, he'd saw his mom do this often returning from the town within when Steve was at work and it was too wet to wait for a bus. He ensured his swollen face was turned slightly as not to be noticed.

'Hiya Son, you just yourself? Where are your parents?'

Sam had anticipated these questions and had his answer prepared.

'My mum sent me down to get a taxi to Falkirk as I'm to stay with my dad the rest of the week, she is choked with the flu so can't come with me but told be to get a taxi to my dad's door as it's safer than getting on and off the train.'

'That it is young fella but its going to cost about £30 to drive you to Falkirk and I will be needing the money before we set off.'

Sam handed across the money and off they set, Sam leaned back in the seat as if to feint tiredness as not to get into a conversation with the driver.

The Taxi driver took the fare and thought nothing else about it only what a polite well mannered kid and an easy fare for himself on what would otherwise be a quiet evening. He stuck the paper notes in his shirt pocket, kept the meter off and headed course towards Falkirk.

Sam's heart was beating in his chest like a bird's due to what he was planning to do. He did not even know if his dad would be at the house or the reception he may be met with but the floating buoy on the waves of his hopes were the last words he had heard his father call which were that he loved him. The power of these words launched more action from the uncertain than any other words that ever could be spoken.

Lilian returned just over half an hour after she had set off, a plastic carrier bag in each hand. One containing the packet of frozen peas she'd got with the idea of using as a cold compress against Sam's face to reduce the selling, and counterbalancing in her other bag was a frozen pizza and a tub of ice cream which she hoped would go somewhat to buy off her son's quietness.

The front door was off the latch. She felt something was not right. Lilian dropped the bags inside the door and called Sam's name.

There was no answer and then she entered through the open door of this bedroom.

On the floor was the baggy jogging bottoms he had been wearing and the the jeans which had been on the chair were no longer there. He had changed his clothes, that was for certain but where could he possibly be? She called his name again, louder this time and entered the kitchen where she saw the cookie jar, its lid laying on the table and the wad of money in the jar looking slimmer so she immediately gathered that Sam had taken some of the money but to what purpose? Was he running away and if so then to where?

Then she knew immediately! He is going off to Daniel's house. Well she'd see about that!

She raced down the road in the same direction Sam had just fled just twenty minutes earlier. Lilian jumped into the back of one of the taxis and directed it to the train station, she was expecting Sam to catch a train to Falkirk and hoped to head him off at the station.

She was angry, she was very angry and could feel the veins at the side of her head throb. She could not believe the audacity of the boy.

24

As his mother reached Glasgow train station in her taxi Sam was already pulling up outside his father's house in Falkirk.

His little heart felt like a jackhammer in his chest. Although he'd saw his dad outside his school a couple of months past it was still about four years since they last spoke with each other with only the few short text messages which he had sent before mom found out. Will his dad be angry that he never made any attempt to see him before this? Did he still even still live there? He must still be here, Sam thought, he recognised the same car in the drive way at the side of the house as the one his dad had when he turned up outside his school.

'Will I wait until your dad answers the door son?' the taxi driver asked as Sam was getting out.

'No thank you, it's ok, he is expecting me.'

After closing the taxi door Sam waved back as he walked down the drive way of his father's house. The Taxi remained waiting as if to see that the boy got in OK.

Once near the bottom of the drive Sam ducked behind the car and peeked at the taxi which eventually drove off after a minutes idle, the driver being satisfied that the child was safe as he never reappeared.

Sam walked up the drive toward the road again then around to the front door. He could see the lights were on behind the closed blinds of the window indicating someone was at home.

Sam stood outside the door hesitating slightly then reached for the bell pressing it once hearing it melody sound from within.

From the frosted glass on the door he could see the hall light illuminate on from within and an indistinguishable shape approach, then the door opened and the figure of a father who the child had so many conversations in his heart with over the past four years stood these looking at him with a certain unbelief.

Father and son stared at each other without a word. A twitching gradually intensified at the corner of Daniel's mouth and the silence was finally broken when he said the child's name 'Sam!', not a question more of a statement after which Daniel bend on one knee, tears already cascading down his cheeks and opened his arms, a safe haven into which Sam fell forward into. They held each other tight, a clutch not to be broken. 'Sam, Sam, Sam!' Daniel repeated as if to convince himself and heard the word's 'Daddy!' being quietly returned to his ears with emotions.

How many times he had imagined this special visitor coming to his door, to open and see his son there and now it happened, it finally came true.

Daniel released his hugging grasp and gently rocked the child back holding onto his shoulders as if to inspect the sight beheld in front of him. So many questions to be asked.

Tears ran down Sam's face too, tears of happiness at this reunion with his dad.

Daniel noticed the cut and swelling on the left side of the child's face and tenderly put is hand up to cup it but Sam flinched slightly so he withdrew his hand.

'What happened Sam?'

The question for now when unanswered only a question from Sam returned, 'Can I come in Dad?'

Lillian scanned around the train station for Sam but there was no sight of him, neither around the ticket office or on the platforms.

Displayed on the departures boards she could she the last train which had left towards Falkirk departed just five minutes before her arrival so it was certainly a possibility he'd have taken that one. She cursed that she'd missed it by such a narrow margin.

The next East bound train which would stop off at a Falkirk station was in another thirty minutes time and she intended to be on it.

She used the ticketing machine stabbing its touchscreen with her fingers entering her destination and purchased her travel, she would get him then back him back home with her!

It rankled her intently what the boy had done. She could not compose herself enough to stand still so she marched up and down the platform waiting for the next train to arrive so she could continue towards he destination, she needed to be in momentum, she felt flooded with a quaking energy.

How could Sam have done this? She milled to herself. He knows that mommy loves him. She provides for him everything he needs she thought to herself yet he had done this against her! The betrayal felt like a stake through her heart! A deep ache coursed through her chest causing her to catch her breath when she thought of the scene she had walked into when she entered her boy's bedroom, all the photos of that man spread out on her boys bed sheets, and then upon her discovery how Sam tried to guard them from her as if they meant something to him! She had saw red! Lilian regretted hitting the boy, she had shocked herself when she'd realised the blood down his face was the result of her actions by lashing out but he'd, Sam pushed her to react the way she did!

She never meant to hit him so hard, it's was her ring she thought, her ring cut his face, she would never have intentionally wounded him as such, it was an accident. But she had been driven to this reaction. This was Daniel's fault, why could that bastard just not leave them in peace. Sam was happy away from him, she and Sam had a new start with Steve but that shit of a man could not let them be happy! The thoughts swelled though her head like breakers hitting against the rocks. There would be no considerations from her for anyone else, no empathy for her son. Her anger eclipsed all else as it had done for years, she needs someone to blame for her own failures and demonised Daniel as the cause of all her woes.

Over a glass of milk Sam told his dad everything which had happened and how he had sustained the injury across his left cheek.

Daniel cleaned it up and applied a clean sticking plaster to the injury, it was not serious enough for stitches but still it made his blood boil how Lilian could have inflicted such pain on their son. He would report this to the authorities later, this could not go unaddressed and god only knows what else she has been doing to his son, but for now the main thing was he was here with him and safe.

'First things first lad!', Daniel said opening the fridge door but not seeing too much offerings for a small child.

'When is the last time you have eaten Sam?" he asked his son.

'So long ago I have forgotten. I am so hungry I could eat a whole cow!'

'Well I don't know where we can get a cow at this time in the evening but what say you and I go out and get a McDonalds?, a celebratory meal. Milkshake, fries and the whole hog?"

'Yes!' nodded Sam rapidly with a big grin on his face, the stress of the day was draining from him such was the resilience of the young but his appetite was growing.

Steve returned to an empty house with the lights off.

When he'd walked through the door he saw two plastic bags on the floor.

Carrying them over to the kitchen work top he extracted their contents. Defrosting pizza and a bag of peas, the ice cream was the consistency of a runny milkshake.

He called out both Lilian and Sam's names but no answer.

The washing machine was still packed full of recently washed clothes he had noticed.

He pulled the phone from his pocket and dialed Lilian's number, it rang a few times before being cut to voice mail, she must be busy to not accept his call he thought, somewhere with Sam but she appeared to have left in such a rush. His mind swarmed for a reason but could come up with nothing.

He sent her a text message **Where are you??** There was no reply forthcoming.

Lilian got off the train at Falkirk station then proceeded to the taxi rank, her steps were decisive and a controlled anger fuelled her path.

In the back of the taxi as it made its way to Daniel's house she sat looking out of the window as it drove through once familiar streets, she felt righteous in her mission to go collect her son from his father then bring him home, the vein at the side of her head continued to throb and the adrenaline of a prospective confrontation coursed through her body yet she felt in control, she was keeping the red mist at bay.

She planned the up and coming confrontation in her mind. She was in the right here, coming to collect her son from a lousy deadbeat father. She intended to knock authoritatively on Daniel's door then file right in once the door was opened and grab her son by the arm and leave with him. Sam would fall in line once he saw her she was sure, she would not expect the slightest resistance from either of them.

About one hundred yards up the street from where Daniel's house was she told the taxi to pull over and let her out, she wanted to walk up to the house to control herself first, get into the right mindset before facing off her ex.

As she was counting out the money to pay the fare her phone rang, looking at the screen she saw it was Steve. Well he will just need to wait she thought terminating the call.

The vibration alert of a received text message juddered against her thigh from the phone which was now in her pocket but the sensation never registered with her as her attention at that moment was drawn the the road from the street side curb where she'd just got out from the taxi as she could see a car reversing out onto the road from the driveway at the side of Daniel's house and from where she stood she could see in the distance a small figure with a jacket she recognised get into the passenger seat once the car was out on the road, there was Sam getting into his car, the red mist descended and she started to stride purposefully up towards where the car was facing. Any lingering rational thought of how to play out the scenes ahead had departed from her body, the Dionysian eclipses the Apollonian, she was determined to drag Sam home screaming and shouting if need be, she was the mother, the boy's carer and how dare him to seek sanctuary with his father, does he not know what she has done for him?

25

It was dark outside when Daniel reversed the car out from the narrow driveway which flanked the side of his house so he could stop in front next to the curb allowing Sam access in thorough the passenger door to sit up beside his dad.

'Seat belt on Sam.' Daniel instructed his son in a fatherly tone enjoying the sensation. The child obliged by belting up, then they were to depart from the side of the road moving forward.

The glow from the sodium street lights were cut though by his headlights as Daniel drove off when he was to noticed someone on the side of the pavement just ahead stepping off onto their path. Daniel's immediate reaction was to slow down, give this person time to cross the road but then the figure started marching with a determined stride on the centre of the road directly towards them blazed by the car's halogen beams . That was when Daniel recognised that it was Lilian and at that same moment so did Sam.

'Daddy! It's Mommy!' Sam shrieked in a panic adding confirmation to the identity of the approaching woman. Daniel steered to the right attempting to progress forward more slowly to pass her but Lilian, anticipating his movement, mirrored him hurriedly moving crab liked to her left blocking the path on his oncoming car.

'Quick Daddy, quick!' Sam yelled out, but Daniel's only option was to brake, stopping the car almost on the middle of the road just as Lilian was to met with it placing both her hands on the hood leaning forward staring at Sam with her twisted up face such was the naked rage upon it.

Daniel, now with the gears in neutral, clicked the central locking, the doors solidly clunked reassuringly locked.

He stuck on the hazard lights.   Lilian was blocking any possible forward movement if it were to move.   Daniel could not try any evasive movement, he pulled up the handbrake, the car was stationary and going nowhere.

'Get out the car now Sam!' shouted out his mother looking straight at the boy through the windscreen, 'Daddy does not love you Sam!' she continued, 'Mommy cares for you, only Mommy!'

Sam was crying such was his panic, 'go away' he cried out between sobs.

'Open the door... Now!' she continued to shout out whilst hammering the hood of the car with both her fists.

'Cover your ears and don't look at her son.' Daniel called out to Sam whilst opening his phone and lifting it higher above the dash board to be observed by the wild woman outside.

'I am phoning the police Lilian, go and stand on the pavement and wait for them, I won't be driving off, I will wait for them here inside the car, I will wait for them to arrive then we can discuss things.' He shouted this out at her through the windscreen, he was surprised how calm and in control he sounded to his own ears, it definitely was not mirroring the fluster he felt within.

Lilian ignored Daniel's announcement of intent and went around to the passenger side running her hands along the car as if holding it in position.

She yanked aggressively at the locked door with frustration calling out for Sam to unlocked it.

Sam, now with his head down and hands over his ears continued to wail.

As Daniel dialled the emergency services and spoke to an operator explaining what was going on and asked for the police as Lillian started started hitting the side window increasing her voice demanding that the child unlock his door. Her anger grew at the boy's refusal to obey her commands.

She took a few steps back and started kicking the side mirror in a frenzy, it soon broke the mount, staying attached to its fitting only by a wire which Lilian started hauling upon with such destructive ferocity that it soon pulled away then fell to the ground.

Lilian started to circle her way around the front of the car to repeat her destruction to the diver side mirror, her eyes with ferrety never leaving Daniel, her face swivelling to meet him as she went.

Once in position, before focusing her destruction on the other side mirror she stomped the car door twice with the sole of her boot denting it inwards. Then she let loose with kicks to the side mirror which soon broke off and hung by a short cable down the side of the door's exterior.

Lilian then started pulling at the hanging mirror adamant to complete her act of wreckage. The rubber covered wire with which the unit was still connected to the car gave stretch but did not break this time. With furious gusto she then planted her left foot against the door for leverage and pulled harder with all her might.

The rubber sealed cable which attached the broken side mirror to its housing on the car snapped and Lilian was launched backwards across the road with the momentum of her exertion from the force she had applied when suddenly the resistance was no more. Her right arm reached out into midair for a balance which she never achieved.

The driver in the white transit van that had approached behind Daniel could see that there was some commotion happening with the car and front and what looked to be a deranged woman pulling at a broken mirror at the driver's side.

He was in a rush to get back to the depo to drop off the van, it was already past his finishing time so he would be late enough getting home without any further holdups on the road.

Cussing the ruckus which was in progress ahead of him he indicated right showing his intention to pass the car which had stopped in the middle of the road flashing it's hazards.

Nothing was coming in the other direction he'd saw as he drove forward so he took the opportunity and pulled out pressing down on his accelerator to get away quicker beyond the scene.

Just as he pulled out speeding up to overtake, the woman shot out in front of him, her body almost parallel to the road with a sprung hurl as the side mirror she was pulling at with her foot up on the car door came away from its tether.

He'd hit his brakes but had already felt the thud of the woman's head hit his nearside corner as the van clipped her just above it's front bumper.

Her skull had hit with such a force he would later discover she had cracked the lens of the headlight.

Now at a stop the driver looked across to the reflection in his passenger side mirror and there he saw a unmoving bundle lying between the side of his van and the other car.

198

* * *

Daniel could see immediately what had transpired. He still was on his mobile speaking to an emergency services operator so changed script and asked for an ambulance explaining quick and breathlessly what just had happened.

Sam had heard the rendering noises as his mom kicked and pulled at both side mirrors but never saw what was going on as by then he had slid forward down into the footwell burying his head down so low as if to escape from the situation which had been unfolding.

Now he started to climb back up the seat when his dad placed a hand gently on the blades of his shoulders telling him to keep his head down for the moment and not to look out the window. He could hear his dad open the car door and get out, there was only the noise of idle car engines, he could no longer hear the screeching shouts of his mother.

As Daniel exited the car he went forward and knelt beside the unmoving form of Lilian where she lay. She was slightly curled lying on her right side facing up the road.

The van driver had left his van and on shaky legs and walked around to where Daniel was kneeling next to Lilian.

'She just flew out in front of me!'

Daniel looked up at him, his face was as white as a sheet under the illumination of the street lighting.

Daniel tried to remember the first aid he had once learnt. There was an acronym of procedures to follow but he could not remember how it went. Assess the situation for danger was the first one which came back into his mind.

'Go back into your van and stick your hazard lights on.' Daniel told the driver then added a "please.' at the end which felt unnecessarily once out of his mouth.

Daniel could see a dark halo expand out from Lilian's head onto the tarmac, the head trauma was obvious.

Trying carefully not to move her he checked that she was still breathing. She was unconscious but he could hear raggedy breaths coming from her when he held his face close.

He felt her head with his fingers, the warm wet sensation of blood nauseating him with its dampness. He could also feel the sickening moment of the bone fragments making up her skull like parts of a jigsaw when lifted from a surface as he probed gently with his fingers, he could not the risk of moving her into a more comfortable position.

He felt someone touch his shoulder and looked over. It was another driver, from a car which had pulled up behind him. He was handing Daniel a red tartan blanket. Daniel looked up at him puzzled at first, a confusion from the shock which was hitting him, he had to shake out of it.

'...to keep her warm off the road mate.' he heard the man finish. Accepting the offered blanket Daniel splayed it out over Lilian's body up to her shoulders. Lilian, although still very much out of it twitched at the touch of the fibres as the edge of the blanket reached her neck. Daniel took his jacket off and folded it into a makeshift pillow which he then tenderly placed under the side of her head which was in contacted with the road, he felt the warm dampness on her scalp as he did so.

Daniel could hear the sirens of an ambulance in the distance, never was a sound more welcoming at that moment.

The white van driver was up front on the road talking into his mobile pacing back and forth. Daniel could also sense the philanthropic blanket donor still standing close behind him talking but he did not hear the words.

He felt a sense of impotency at the scene, a feeling that he should be doing more but more of what? He did not know the answer.

This damaged figure on the road was the woman who had made much of his life a misery by denying him access to his son for no other reason than a pure malice yet here she was, unconscious on the road, he could feel only pity for her.

Looking towards his car Daniel could see Sam had scurried to the drivers side where he now peered out from the open door with pale wide spacious eyes, an image which was to stay with Daniel reminding him of the famous Edvard Munch painting.

Turning his attention back down to the road he softly spoke to his ex-wife although she did not hear 'It's OK Lilian, the ambulance is coming, you are going to be alright.'

Daniel then stood up and went over to comfort his son.

26

He was not able to go to the hospital with Lilian in the ambulance as Sam was there with him and they could only take one passenger, he also was needed to stay and give a statement to the police who had already arrived on the scene and since closed off the road as they were treating it as a possible fatal road accident.

Daniel and the driver of the transit van had been breathalysed by the traffic police following their procedure upon their arrival but both were clear as having no trace of alcohol.

He could see that his son needed him, he tried to console the boy with gentle words and held him tight, the crying soon stopped but Daniel could still feel his son's trembles.

Daniel's request to leave the scene and take his boy the few meters up the road to wait inside his house for the police so he could give his statement there was granted.

He walked Sam along to the house holding his hand, the boy's face was mottled from his crying and was still pale with shock.

This was never the reunion with his child that Daniel dreamt of, not the circumstances of a homecoming either of them would have ever wished for .

Once in his house Daniel took Sam through to the kitchen as the living room window faced out to the road so even with the window blinds closed the blaze of blue flashing lights of the emergency services in attendance penetrated into the room.

Whilst the police attended to the scenes outside Daniel attended to his son inside. Sam's distress was quite apparent as he sat by the kitchen table, an emotional quiver still running through him and his eyes reflecting the shock which the last while had delivered.

Daniel placed his hand on the child's shoulder.

'Are you alright son?'

'Is she going to be ok daddy?'

'I honestly don't know son, but after I have talked to the police we can drive to the hospital and find out a bit more as what is happening.'

This statement did not appear to offer any comfort to the child.

'Can I make you something to eat, I know you must be famished?'

Sam replied that he was not hungry, Daniel could understand his lack of appetite but make him a banana milkshake anyway. It sat mostly untouched on the table.

The police came about thirty minutes later and took a statement from Daniel as to what had happened.

It was a policeman and woman, they seemed satisfied with Daniel's accord of the events as it also was to correspond with what a roadside witness had stated she saw from the front of her house, then also that of the somewhat still shaken van driver.

Daniel had also been on the phone to the emergency services operator at the time giving her a blow by blow account of the destruction Lilian was attempting to the car as he desperately waited for the police to arrive.

The police woman asked Sam if he was ok which he acknowledge he was and then if he was ok to stay with his father which again he said he was, this time with a tiny bit more animation of keenness.

The police left them be saying just before departing that they'd be in touch if they had anymore questions. They did ask if Daniel would want to press charges against Lilian for the damage she did to the car, he found the question strange considering all that had happened but said that he would not want her charged, indeed he never wanted any further problems for her, he had no love for her since all that she'd done, and even less since he discovered how she had hit Sam earlier on during that day but still the image of her lying on that road bleeding from the head brought out the humanity in him and he only had hopes she would pull through, any thought of retribution did not cross his mind.

'I better phone mummy's friend Steven and let him know what is happening.' Daniel said out loud to Sam still strangely not able to refer to Steve her partner.

Sam looked up pale but did not speak up, he was not Steve's biggest fan but still Steve had never really done anything against him directly, he needed to know what was happening.

Daniel never had Steve's direct number for his mobile so phoned Lilian's landline hoping to catch him there, he'd never spoken to Steve before so the prospect did feel slightly awkward but the merits of the situation overrode that.

The phone was picked up on the second ring, silence answered it which made Daniel think that the recipient, Steve?, had saw his name on a caller display panel on the phone.

'Hello is that Steven?' Daniel spoke into the silence.

'Yes!' was the firm one word answer.

'This is Daniel in Falkirk, Sam's father.', perhaps that title was a little uncalled for considering the nature of the call but still it gave him a twinge of childish satisfaction to announce himself as such.

'Sam is with me here at my house, there has been an accident and Lilian has been taken to the hospital.'

The silence on the other end of the phone got deeper as Steve processed what he was being told then after a few seconds he asked 'what has happened, what kinda accident?' There was suspicion in the voice, almost an accusation.

Daniel gave him as much of the details as he could over the phone, he left a few bits out such as her attempted vandalism of his car, just saying that she was on the road when she got hit by a passing van, at this point there was no need to elaborate upon the facts.

Daniel mentioned that he was going to head to the infirmary with Sam to find out more. Steve replied that he too would be heading here right now then terminated the call as if it were a piece of string cut.

The call had went as well as it could have thought Daniel, he did not expect cheer and friendliness but at least there was no shouting or accusations as such. He was a little concerned about meeting him at the hospital which was quite likely, and with Sam there he did not want a confrontation but he had to follow this through and attend, despite all that Lilian had done she was still the mother of his child.

Daniel, with his son drove to the hospital.

They spoke to the lady behind the reception desk at A&E who told them that Lilian was getting prepared for surgery, she said if they'd like to take a seat then a doctor will be along soon and explain things in more detail.

They sat in the waiting room as instructed awaiting further news.

Sam was still very quiet which did concerned his father, he hoped the shock of this evenings event would evaporate from the boy but he knew it was still early yet and a lot had happened, not only with the recent road accident also he had to consider what the child had been through at his mother's house before his odyssey east going to his father's house this very same day.

Daniel asked him if he would like something from the vending machine but Sam declined the offer.

Fishing his mobile out from his pocket he saw there were text messages awaiting him from Maria.

She was still currently in Brazil with her family on the farm which he had departed from just a couple weeks earlier. Daniel had sent her a brief message saying that Sam had turned up on his doorstep closely followed by the mother who had attempted to drag him back but was hit by a car out of the road so was taken to hospital. The most basic of synopsis but said that he would fill her in with the details. There was her messages now, understandably worried and urgently enquiring as to what had happened.

Brazil was four hours behind GMT, Daniel done the quick calculation in his head, it would be afternoon there just now, about Six o'clock, he'd have sent his first message almost two hours ago now, she must be very worried as the replies he received would testify.

Daniel did not want to walk outside and leave Sam there by himself to phone her which would be the better option to explain all so he started to type a more in-depth reply as to what exactly had happened.

As be was doing so he felt Sam nudging him and grunting noisily for his father's attention.

'What's wrong Sam' he asked.

'There's Steve!' Sam pointed directing his father's attention to the back of a tall slim man who was standing at the reception desk assumedly making the same enquires he himself had done just about half an hour earlier.

As Daniel looked across at the man. Just at that moment Steve looked over his shoulder to where they were seated, the receptionist advising him to also sit and waiting further news with the other interested party waiting there.

Steve strode across to the seated pair, Daniel rising to receive him, adrenaline rushing preparing for any oncoming confrontation.

Steve stopped a few feet away, there was a intensity on his face.

The two men seemed to be sizing each other up before Steve broke the tense silence.

'This is all your fault!' he accused of Daniel loudly pointing his finger at him.

'Yeah, I tore her away from Glasgow to come and kick the shit out of my car in the middle of the road!' Daniel answered feeling a turbulence start to pique within him.

'You could not leave her be, you had to keep pushing her!'

'Pushing her?' Daniel exclaimed 'I want nothing to do with that bitch, especially with what she is doing to Sam!'

At that point both men seemed to realise Sam was there beside them privy to their shouting match. Daniel immediately regretted calling his son's mother a "bitch" in front of him whilst Steve then looked down at the now sobbing child and saw the swelling underneath the Elastoplast on the side of his face.

'Were you hurt too Sam?' he asked to the boy lowering to a more gentle voice bending forward with concern to get a better look at his face.

'That was your woman who done that to him!' Daniel answered for him, 'his loving caring mother!'

Steve never took his eyes from Sam then asked him what had happened. Sam summarised how his mum hit him across the face and that is when he ran to Falkirk to find his daddy.

Daniel stayed quiet during Sam's explanation, his temper was abated by the obvious look of genuine upset upon his rival's face.

Steve sat down on the seat opposite Sam and reached across touching him on the knee as a means to comforting him.

'I'd sorry Sam, I am sorry mummy done that!' he said.

Daniel looked at Steve, 'you knew what she was capable of didn't you?, you'd seen her hit him before?' His voice was level which just emphasised the reproof in it all that more.

'Yes, but I love her, I told her not to, I would never agreed with that. She would get very angry and sometimes would lash out at him but I thought she had stopped, I thought she had more control.' he answered to the floor, 'I'd told her that it was not acceptable!' There was contrition in his voice which said Lilian had been out of order.

'Well it does not look like she stopped does it?' Daniel said with a flourish of anger raising his voice again.

The question went unanswered.

Daniel remembered when he was with Lilian, when they lived together with Sam, their little family unit. He'd saw Lilian hit their child then, smack him for the slightest trespass. He told her then that he disagreed but he also knew if he never stood by her he would lose her, she would turn away and he never wanted that, especially due to her much repeated threats she would up sticks and return to Brazil with Sam if Daniel was ever to leave her.

He thought he'd loved her when they were together but later, on reflection he realised he was more in love with the idea of being married, having a little family, a happiness he'd always thought would be in their reach and then to be living a similar fairytale which he saw with his parents marriage but he since knew it was not love, love was what he had found with Maria, that was true love, with Lilian love was just a present, staying with her hoping that she would change, that her temper would somehow abate and she would stop hitting him, hitting Sam but it was a false hope but still he could empathise with what Steve was saying.

He asked Steve in a more flattened tone if Lilian's family across in Brazil knew about what had happened. It was more a rhetorical question as Daniel was already expecting the answer which he received but then also got the follow answer which was what he was fishing for. Steve told him that they were still yet unaware then acknowledged that he would contact them to let them know.

Daniel knew it would be better coming from him, he was their daughter Lilian's chosen partner now, he also felt a somewhat guilty relief that he would not be braking the news to them, why guilty he did not know, maybe because he felt slightly responsibly as she had once moved from her home in Brazil to be with him in Scotland.

As they waited in silence one of the doctors approach them. Both men stood in unison as if a synchronised tandem, they prepared to hear the news.

'Lilian is is a deep state of unconsciousness as she has had severe head trauma. The CT scan confirms our initial suspicions of the presence of a large extradural haematoma which is a build up of blood between the outer membrane of the brain and the skull.'

Daniel could feel Sam pressing in closer to his leg.

The doctor went on to explain that the build up of blood was causing an increased pressure in her intracranial space compressing the delicate brain tissues there and causing the brain to physically 'shift' within her skull. A neurosurgeon had been called out from Edinburgh Royal Infirmary who had since arrived and was scrubbing up whilst Lilian was currently being prepped for surgery where they hoped to evacuate the haematoma as to take the pressure off her brain.

There was also a cervical spine injury but at that moment her head was of more pressing concern and that needed to be seen to with urgency first.

Daniel could feel Sam's hand reaching to touch his and he opened his own to receive it's small presence giving it what he hoped to be a reassuring squeeze.

Steve asked the doctor in a shaky voice how long the surgery would take.

The Doctor would not commit to a specific length of time but did say it would take a few hours to complete. Due to the shattering of her skull they would need to preform a craniotomy which meant that a section of her skull would be temporarily removed so that the surgeon could access and remove the haematoma. Then the pieces of fractured bones would then have to be repaired in hope that they would knit back together once replaced.

Daniel felt strange whilst hearing all that was being explained. This was his ex-wife, the mother of his child yet he could not feel the compassion which he felt he should.

He looked across at Steve's face watching it process all that he was being told, it was ashen with worry, the torment of emotional distress clearly showing.

He did feel a certain affinity with this man now. He realised how much Steve cared for Lillian and the tenderness he obviously had for Sam, although he could never feel the same sympathy for his ex-wife after all she done to keep Sam away and how she had hurt their child but he could still understand how Steve must feel and he could imagine how he himself would have felt if he was receiving such a report on Maria if the situation was different.

As the doctor left with a final promise someone would return later and update them further Daniel looked down at his son. Sam was clinging close to his father for comfort, he knelt down to be level with this son's face and gently held him by his shoulders.

'Let's go home Sam, Steve can give us a call once he hears something about your mum, in the meantime you need some rest.' Daniel looked up at Steve as he said this, looking for some acknowledgment that he would keep them informed of any developments.

Steve took a few seconds to recognise his name had been spoken and confirmed 'Yes, go get some rest Sam and I will phone your dad as soon as I know more.'

Daniel stood up and stared at Steve, he could see the suffering in his face.

'Are you going to be ok? I have a spare room down the road, you can stay there, no need to get back to Glasgow tonight, get some rest and the hospital will call once they have some news, better than sitting waiting in a chair'.

Steve stared at Daniel in silence for a few seconds before conceding that the olive branch had just been offered.

'Thank you.' he replied, 'I'd rather stay here, close and wait for news.'

Daniel stuck his hand out towards Steve. Steve looked at it almost in surprise for a couple of seconds before shaking it then bending to hug Sam.

Daniel felt awkward watching him hug his son yet he could understand the mixture of feeling there must be in this emotional meld.

He left the hospital with his son and headed home to get some rest.

Steve called Daniel's mobile in the early hours of the morning. Daniel answered it before the second ring, he was lying awake, with the events of that evening churning through his mind he'd found sleep eluded him.

Sam was next to him in the bed as his own bed had since been dismantled. The single ring before answer did not disturb the exhausted boy but Daniel walked out of the bedroom upon answering to allow him to sleep on in peace.

'They have done the surgery.' Steve sounded tried and his voice echoed dolefulness on the line.

'She is still in a coma. The damage was worst than they'd thought, they told me they don't expect her to regain consciousness.' He struggled with these last words, his voice braking upon the last and then Daniel could hear only sobs in the silence which followed.

'I'm sorry.' Daniel said, and he was genuinely remorseful that the diagnosis after the surgery was that she would not recover, he was not surprised but still a hollowness shot up from his chest upon hearing it.

'Will you bring Sam to see her and to say something to her?'

'Of course I will.' Daniel confirmed, he knew for his son's sake he had to be allowed to say his farewells to his mother.

Daniel tenderly awoke Sam from his sleep and explained the situation. Fresh tears started running down the child's face.

Daniel helped him get dressed, he thought that they should get to the hospital as soon as possible.

The roads were quiet so early in the morning and upon their arrival to the car park which had been so chockablock earlier but now was almost empty.

Daniel walked with Sam in an almost reverent silence up to the night entrance of the hospital then went up to the reception to explain his late visit.

After a few minutes waiting a nurse came through the double doors and asked the pair to follow her to the ICU where there they both sat in a small waiting area near an empty nursing station.

Steve soon came out from the ward through the doors and headed toward them.

He looked shrunken from when last Daniel saw him just a matter of hours before. His eyes were red from crying and he looked extremely tired.

He immediately bend down and hugged Sam pulling the child towards him, Sam passively stood there limp with Steve's arms curled around him.

Daniel heard Steve emit soft sobs, he felt uncomfortable being present there, as if an outsider yet he knew Sam needed his support during this time.

Steve raised himself up from embracing the boy, Daniel reached out and put his hand on Steven's shoulder when he was coming up as to comfort him, he just done it without thinking. Steve stood up looking at the floor as if ashamed.

'Would you like to see your mum? She is in the first cubicle.' Steve said to Sam, his voice almost just a broken mutter.

'Are you OK Sam?' Daniel bent to address his son, 'are you ready to say your goodbyes to your mummy?'

The child seemed more together now than how he was earlier before leaving the house, he never answered but then walked towards the ward door tugging on his fathers hand to follow.

Daniel looked at Steve as if to ask if it would be OK if he went with

Sam. Steve read this and nodded his consent before taking up a seat in the waiting area which the other pair just vacated as they headed towards the ward doors.

Lilian's cubicle was basically a room with a curtain across the wall where a door would otherwise be.

The lights were dimmed and the pungent smell of hospital disinfect transported Daniel back in time to when he'd visit his mother during one of her many spells in the hospital.

There was a nurse present who was jotting down a readout from one of the machines Lilian was connected to, she turned when they both entered through the curtains, she smiled a smile Daniel had once been only too familiar with, then she left them alone with Lilian. The smile had been one which Daniel recognised from the past when he spend the final nights at his mother's bedside, the smile of shared empathy from the nurses and carers who knew the end which was approaching would be something they all would met one day, that final equaliser.

Lilian looked very waxen lying there on the bed. Her head had a bandage wrapped around it as if it were a turban and she was prompted up on pillows but still very much unconscious and never to wake.

Daniel moved the single chair from the opposite corner and positioned it at the side of Lilian's bed, away from where the drip stand stood.

Sam immediately glided to the chair and sat there as if knowing his spot then reached out and held his mum's hand.

Daniel felt the warm trickle of a tear run down his own face. He wondered how things could have gotten to this stage, when did the dream end and the nightmare start he thought, when did the love turn to maliciousness?

Sam placed the side of his face down upon his mom's hand closing his eyes and wept silently, lamenting the moments of love and ignoring the junctures woven into his too short relationship with her when moments had been more callous and cruel.

During these early morning hours as she passed away, her son held onto not the hand which had struck him, but the hand that once caressed and care for him as a much loved child.

27

After what had happened to his mother Sam had seemed to go into his shell, he was becoming quieter and although he was at ease in the reacquaint presence of his dad he never quite seemed to be the once jubilant joyful, sometimes full of good natured cheeky boy which he once was.

His mother's death from the accident was suddenly and unexpected, the arbitrariness of it just added to the sorrow which shrouded Sam.

It was true that she'd often treated him cruelly, especially when it was in connection with his dad but she was still his mother and it had not always been like that, there were moments, memories which he hung onto where she was tender and loving, times when the sun of the love she carried for her son would shine through the clouds of her darkness.

Sam knew that his dad was very sad about everything which had happened too, the accident and his mom's passing but he also knew, and understood why, he did not feel the same grief which he did. His dad's sadness had since changed into more of a concern about how it had hit his son so Sam felt he could not share his feeling of desolation with Dad, only shallowly explain how he felt when Dad would sit beside him trying to help him through it,

Grief wounds more deeply in solitude Sam felt, and tears are less bitter when mingled with other's.

At the funeral Sam saw the equal of his torment was in the eyes of Steve who hugged Sam tightly to his chest after the cremation of his mother. Sam had returned the clasp in sincerity.

Thought Sam did not feel any deep connection with Steve as to share the affinity brought on by their mutual mourning, he still recognised this man as part of his life, but albeit a part which was no longer there.

His mother's side of the family did not turn up, Sam never asked why.

Only a few of Lilian's friends would show and then they'd stare daggers at his dad during the ceremony and talk behind their hands when his Dad comforted him. This only made Sam feel worse, How could hate still persist after such a sorrow had already resulted from it?

Steve had embraced his dad before and after the funeral which went some way to make Sam feel better to see that amnesty which he'd never would have dared to have dreamt less than a week earlier.

He understood his dad's reasons as to why he never had the same level of heartache over the death of his mom as he did, he felt his father's concern and love for him but still he himself felt the grief to be all consuming and was struggling contending with the sadness.

The evening after his mother's cremation Dad sat down with him then asked if he would like to have a break from Scotland and go across to Brazil with him. Sam agreed but he could not stoke any excitement at the prospect, still he would go along with the plans, for his father's sake more than his own he thought.

.

Even when they arrived in Brazil Sam still seemed subdued, Daniel saw. He had hoped he may perk up a little once in the air but no such luck.

Daniel had been a bit uneasy as to how his son would take to meeting Maria, his dad's woman, the only other woman the son would have, and ever would, see him with since his mother.

It had been Maria's idea, as she was already still across in Brazil so suggested that it would be good for Sam to come across with Daniel, meet with her and the family on the farm to spend the rest of Sam's school holidays across there.

When he initially proposed this idea to Sam he did not seem very enthused, he just seemed to go along with the plans set out for him without voicing any opinions.

Upon arriving Guarulhos airport Daniel walked with his son through to the arrivals where Maria was there to meet with them. Sam was polite enough meeting her when Maria put on a big show about being introduced to this boy which she had heard his dad say so many good things about.

Sam still seemed unresponsive to all the attention he had received the airport as he sat in the back of the car quietly looking out of the window during the drive to the farm in Caporanga.

Once, after they arrived at the farm introductions with Maria's family were made, again Sam would be reserved and just show enough politeness as not to appear rude.

Maria observed Sam's subdued attitude, she had witnessed it during the car journey and understood from a perspective only someone who was at first looking from the outside in would understand.

She saw the gentle tenderness trickled onto the boy from Daniel, she knew this was a father's love with kid gloves on and she only loved Daniel all the more for it, but she also understood that this child's grief should not be so gently prodded, more affirmative actions were needed to build his confidence back up and pull his out of this hole before he was to sink down any deeper. The child had suffered a loss which he will come to terms with eventually in time, but now what he needed was to be a child again, remember how it was to be without fear, remember he was loved without boundaries and experience fund with adventure, so she then and there decided to try something.

Maria bounded up to Sam with an energy that took the boy by such a surprise he'd almost flinched in response.

She took his hand, lifting it from his side and placed it in hers telling him that there were a few other family members she would have to introduce him too. He smiled with the automated politeness he's shown since arriving but there was also a confusion of the situation showing on the boy's face as she walked him over across, almost with a skip in her displayed enthusiasm, to the field where her two horses were standing near the gate of the fence.

She told Sam that the younger horse's name was Pernalonga, a rustic red stallion of quarter horse breed and the older one was Capitan, a dark stallion also of the same pedigree.

This was the first time Sam had actually saw horses close up and would not get close to either horse at first. Instead he stood there rooted to the spot, and Maria did not try to pull him closer when she felt his resistance, instead she let go his hand then bent to pick up a fallen mango fruit from the tree which was beside the fence. She then held it out on her hand to Capitan who received the offering in his mouth and started to crunch it with clamorous delight splattering juice everywhere whilst the skin of the mango hung from his mouth flapping like an orange coloured extension of his lower lip.

Sam forgot himself and let out a giggle at the sight, he tried to straighten his face again but found the scene of the big horse nodding it's head in delight as it pulverised through the fruit's hard inner shell and all whilst straying the juice everywhere was too funny for him not to laugh aloud.

'Does he eat everything?' Sam asked Maria, the first speck of interest he'd shown since arriving.

'Yeah!' she replied as she then bent to picked up another mango from the ground, 'every single bit!',   then she stood handing the gathered fruit over to Sam pointing to Pernalonga.

'That's going to be your mount cowboy, you better make friends with him by offering this mango, you two guys are going to get to know each other pretty well over the next few weeks.'

Sam watched Maria as she instructed him to hold the mango flat in his palm then offer it up to the horse which timorously he did and it was snatched up immediately to which Sam pulled back his hand letting out more chortles with excitement.

Standing back Daniel watched this all with his heart in his mouth.

Sam then asked if he could do it again which Maria agreed and told him the give another mango to Capitan this time which he then did with enthusiasm.

After a bit longer and a few mangos later Sam accompanied Maria back cross to where his dad was standing whilst peeling open a mango himself then trying to sink his teeth into its fibrous flesh.

'Did you see me dad? Did you see me feed the horses?' he excitedly asked with mango juice dripping off his chin.

'Yes son, I saw you, glad to see you are settling into your new job.'

'New job?' he said looking enquiringly at his dad then to Maria.

'Did your dad not tell you that you are now to be a cowboy?' Maria answered him.

'Must have slipped my mind!' chipped in Daniel adding a smile.

Sam's face lit up as he turned his head almost comically switching from one face to the other, 'But I don't know how to ride a horse!'

'Well we are going to change that cowboy, first thing tomorrow morning your lessons begin.' Maria informed him grinning.

'Do I get a gun, and spurs and a hat, a ten gallon hat like on the telly?' he eagerly asked.

'You need a hat for sure, maybe not 10 gallons.' she laughed, 'but as a cowboy a hat is essential and I have one I think that will fit you just fine. Boots too, you will need a good pair of riding boots so tomorrow you and I are going to mosey on down to the store in town to get you kitted out.'

Sam's face was a picture of happiness, the stone birds were leaving his heart, light and happiness started to shine in.

Some days later Daniel sat outside on the verandah squinting his eyes against the bright sun whilst looking across to the field where he saw Maria climb down from her horse before she gave some further instructions to Sam who then dismounting the horse which he had been riding upon too.

It was the fourth riding lesson she had gave the boy since they had arrived and he seemed to be picking up the basics well. She was a good instructor and taught Sam well.

She was proving to be more successful learning his son to ride a horse than he had been when attempting to learn Sam to ride a bike years earlier.

Maria had once talked to Daniel about equine assisted healing and how being around horses could mend the soul after traumas experienced and he was starting to believe this whilst watching Maria give Sam these riding lessons.

He heard Sam giggle as she pulled the tip of his stetson down over his face. It was good to hear Sam laugh again, Daniel had been worried that losing the mother would have a lasting effect on the boy but children were resilient and deciding to spend the summer in Brazil on the farm with Maria and her family was proving to be a good decision.

Daniel was enjoying being a father again although the reason to how he had got to be back in his son's life was never the one he would ever have wished for.

Sun Tzu, the Chinese military strategist and philosopher once wrote in his book The Art of War that "If you wait by the river long enough, the bodies of your enemies will float by." A less confrontational contemporary interpretation of this could be that if you had patience all would come right in the end and who ever wronged you would suffer the consequences of karma.

Daniel would never take pleasure in what happened to Lilian, she did not deserve that, no one deserved that.

She was what Daniel considered a spiteful woman with how she kept him, a loving father, out of his son's life wilfully ignoring the effect it would have on their child and also how she dished out brutal reprimands upon Sam, but still she was a human and as such deserved only pity.

She was loved by Steve, to that there was no doubt. He saw the man's sorrow at the funeral when he attended with Sam and felt immense sympathy for him but still Daniel could not shed any tears for Lilian as there was still a anger in him that what she had done, he was not proud that he still felt that way and still he wished things had not came with such a conclusion.

Maria's father Edson sat on the chair next to him observing the panoramic vista of the fields in front. Daniel had since dropped the prefixed Senhor when addressing Maria's father yet he still felt great respect for the man and would rise to great him whenever he would enter the room.

'The kid rides good!' Edson said to which Daniel answered that he had a good teacher, the old man grasped that this was a compliment aimed at his daughter and smiled back.

The two fathers sat there watching their "kids", it was a good feeling.

'Here comes the desperadoes now!' Daniel said as Sam and Maria moseyed up to the verandah both wearing their stetsons and boots, Sam with a blade of straw in the corner of his mouth, a habit he'd started adopting as his idea of being a cowboy, after the first day of getting his cowboy boots Daniel had to wait until the boy was asleep that evening to remove them from his feet.

'are our ears burning?' asked Maria.

'We were just discussing how well you both ride.' Edson replied in English for Daniel's benefit, 'come daughter, sit here beside your old man.'

Maria lowered herself into the wicker chair at the side of her father and removed her hat.

'When are we having dinner dad?' Sam asked, a typical kid, always hungry.

'Churrasco this evening.' Daniel answered informing his son that they would be having a barbecue, 'have you ever tasted chicken's feet?'

'Yuck!' yelled Sam in mock disgust and pretending to throw up, 'no way!'

'If you are a cowboy you will need to eat like one.'

'Cowboys eat beans around the campfire not chicken feet.' Sam replied.

Edson laughed and proclaimed 'The boy is smart.'

'Too big for his britches!' Daniel laughed out then told his son 'go and help Valdomiro to remove the saddles and wash down your horse.'

Sam left towards the barn with exaggerated drudgery, but he enjoyed working with the old gaúcho farm hand.

Donna Luara, who was sitting at the far corner of within the veranda called out to him in Portuguese 'hey... homem do campoas!' as he passed to which Sam skipped over to the old woman and gave her a kiss on the cheek.

There was a part of Sam which would always miss his Granny and to compensate he seemed to like spending time with the elderly avó. Often in the evening they would talk together in Portuguese which Sam was quite fluent in, something Lilian had learnt him.

Sam would hold her ball of wool as Donna Luara knitted then he would listened intently to what she told him. If Daniel overheard he would not understand what Sam was being told in Portuguese. The old lady was telling Sam about the importance of family and also how he must forgive the bad times and just remember the times of love.

She told Sam that the stupid neither forgive nor forget, the naive forgive and forget but its the wise who forgive but do not forget and one day Sam himself may be a father and it be has children of this own he must always remember how he felt when he was loved and pay that forward to his future children so they will pay it forward one day to their own, that is how love is propagated down the generations. We should not judge those who caused us any suffering, they may have been once a victim of the fist themselves and sometimes history has a habit of repeating itself but the loop can be broken by love, not just the love his father always shows him but also the love his mother once gave him too as surely there would have been such times and that is what needs to be concentrated upon. Sam knew this to be true when he thought back to his mom, he knew love from her but the demons she carried inside were consuming her from within and this produced much of her anger.

28

Maria and Daniel sat out front on the rattan seats upon the veranda. Sitting side by side they watched the evening tide of the sun set. This was becoming a ritual of serene time together where they would just reflect on the day's events and enjoy each other's company.

Spirited laugher drifted out from inside the house and every so often Daniel could make out Sam's howling guffaws.

It's been said that who you decide to give love to will dictate if you are to feel content, whether you feel inspired or whether you feel energised. Sitting there in silence with Maria just watching the sun set together he'd just knew he'd made the right decision taking a chance on love by opening his heart to this incredible woman.

Daniel had made a mistake when he'd married Lilian, he wanted what his own parents had which was their blissful happiness in their marriage, but he'd thought wrongly that Lilian be the one to fill that role with. He since realised it was unrealistic to have expected to achieve such an existence with a personality so removed from his own. He'd long since accepted that when he would tell Lilian that he'd loved her he was really in love with the concept of a happy ever after and he hoped she would change, mould herself to fit into the recess of the role he had expected her to fill but choosing a partner for life does not work like that, we can't configure people to to be how we want them to be, people are already prefabricated by their experiences and influences of the past, we should choose a partner that we know fits with our own needs without requiring any further assembly.

So far with Maria they had not even broached the subject of marriage for discussion. Perhaps he would one day, maybe if they were somewhere really romantic with the red wine flowing, maybe then he would suggest the idea but for him now it would just be a piece of paper as it would not increase the love he felt for this lady one iota. Love can't be marked by a certificate or weighed by a band of gold on the finger, love was effort, commitment and putting someone above yourself.

He had lots of scars from his past which had once caused him concerns about getting so deeply into another relationship and opening himself up to another person as he would do with Maria, no one should worry about the future as if it were the spit wad of Damocles above their head, just live for the present and if there is a love then what what lies ahead will workout, you just needed to keep the faith and hold on to hope.

Daniel thought back when he took Sam to see the unconscious Lilian in the ICU just before she died.

He remembered how Sam, had sat at her side then reached out to take her hand, a beautiful tenderness which absolved the recipient of all her crimes.

It was not with the thoughts of the slaps that Sam had received from her when he reached out for her hand, those moments did not even pass in his mind. It was the moments of the love and caress that he once received from his mum that projected through his memory, these same moments that Daniel had himself remembered whilst holding his own mother's hand as she was passing, it's the love that always floats to the top in the end.

Daniel would try not to think about how Lilian's face looked when she stared through the windscreen at him that night, full of hatred and rage, or the other times when they argued, instead he would make the effort only to recall her as how she was in the maternity ward all these years ago, lying on the operating table after their son was delivered. He pictured her face, a face only of love and concern as the incubator was pulled up close to where she lay, how she then reached out towards their tiny baby son for the first time, that was the Lilian he should remember and mourn.

He made a pact with himself then that he would forgive all else which she had done against Sam and him.

Daniel reached out and held Maria's hand, she looked across at him with a loving smile which he returned.

He then broke the silence by asking 'Do you know that I love you?'
She replied with a question for him 'Do you know that I love you?'
Both these questions did not need an answer.

We choose what we place in our memory boxes, the abstract trunks which we carry in our hearts and minds which go everywhere with us. The bad memories weigh heavy and drag us down, these memories should be discarded. The happy ones float us up like helium filled balloons, it is these memories we should cherish and keep.

Daniel decided he would remove the image of an angry Lilian in his memories and replace it with the portrait of the Lilian when Sam was newly born He also chose the memory of his mum when she lovingly tended to his sunburn with cotton and calamine, not of her lying in the nursing home during these days and nights he had spent there by her side. In went the picture of his brother spinning him as a child above his head around their living room like a helicopter and in went the memory of his dad carrying him downstair on his back, also the memory of Sam's face of concentration as he tried to understand how to peddle his bike.

He looked across at Maria again and wondered which memory of her he would stick in his box, he already had so many to choose from.

She was unaware as he continued to stare at her face. Her golden skin at that point reflecting a rose tint from the setting sun, for Daniel at that moment nothing could look more beautiful.

Sam went to his bedroom that night after doing his rounds saying 'Boa noite!' to everyone.

After he'd got all the lurking mosquitos in his room whacked with a rolled newspaper, he went across to his suitcase and pulled out the old metal tin he had inside which was now his new memory box having since upgraded from the sellotaped cardboard box he once used.

He had found the old tin in his dad's house the day before they were due to fly out to Brazil when he was scavenging for some new photos of his dad and gran. It looked like it was a hundred years old, and the hinges had seen better days but he liked it, it felt special.

In his tin now there were some newly procured photos of his dad also a couple his father together with Maria.

He also had his granny's small comb which he handled with reverence as not to lose any of the long grey hair that were still wrapped in its twines, and her old enamel nurse's badge was in there too.

In his tin was his mom's green emerald ring, the one which Steve had gave for her birthday, and some photos of her, one even of his mom and Steve both smiling at Sam who was behind the camera taking the photograph at the time.

Sam reached into his pocket and extracted a small piece of wool which he'd collected off the floor after Donna Luara had snipped it during her knitting earlier that evening, in the tin it went to join the fountain pen Uncle Edson had gave him whilst showing him how to write his name with a calligraphy flourish, something which Sam found difficult because of his dyspraxia but persevered out of the joy of being in the man's presence.

He'd also earlier that day put in a small snub of a paintbrush which Aunt Célia had held behind her ear when showing Sam how to paint. Her style she claimed was representing nature through repertoires of shapes and colours. Sam had found that the broad strokes she was teaching him was not to be handicapped by his dyspraxia and he could express himself well through the acrylic colours he'd brush onto the canvases and fabrics.

His memory tin was getting quite full so he had to press the lid down but it was so loaded that it sprang open again on it's old hinges, he would have to see if he could get a band to put round it tomorrow, it was so stuffed full of memories. Perhaps he would get one of the elastic hair bands Maria would hold her long hair up with before they went horse riding together, that would certainly be in keeping with the theme of his happy memory box.

The time had just passed midnight when Daniel quietly entered his son's bedroom taking care not to make any nosies as he could hear from the child's deep breathing that he was sleeping.

He used the little light from his mobile to illuminate his way.

Maria had already went to their own bedroom and there she would be lying awaiting Daniel's return once he'd had checked upon Sam.

He was relived to see Sam's cowboy boots were there standing upright by the side of the bed. The past two nights Sam had went to sleep lying on top of his bed wearing the boots which then Daniel had to slide them off him with care as not to wake the boy. 'A cowboy never removes his boots' Sam would later try to explain.

There were two photographs contained within their frames standing upright on the metal framed nightstand beside the bed with its wooden top. Daniel saw them with a strange feeling of a deja vu nibbling at his mind from somewhere in the past.

The photo in the simple wood frame was a picture of the Sam's mum, Lilian kneeling by a green and yellow plastic baby bath which was on the floor,. She was laughing out loud with a massive dollop of soapy foam on top of her head. Daniel remember the scene well, they were preparing baby Sam's bath and as Lilian leaned over to test the temperature with her elbow Daniel had scooped a layer of foam from the water's surface and unceremoniously dumped it on the top of her head. She had roared with laughter and Daniel snapped off that photo with his digital camera before she recovered her composure and removed the foam from her hair to flick back at him with a grin. Daniel had never thought back on that moment for such a while, he smiled at the memories it generated and marvelled how Sam had brought the photo with him in his case.

The second photo, latched within a brass frame was of a younger Maria mounted on the back of a horse, she leaned forward smiling at the camera as she patted the horses neck, the colours had faded somewhat with time. Daniel had not noticed that photo in the room before so wondered if Sam had lifted it from somewhere else. Maria looked as beautiful then as she does now Daniel thought touching his lips softly with his fingers then transferring the kiss to the photo.

There was also a tin on the nightstand. When he shined the beam emitted from his phone onto it he recognised it straightaway, it was the tin his dad Samuel and brother Jimmy had brought up from London after the war, the Pontefract Cake tin, Sam must have taken it with him from home.

The lid was ajar as it was full to the brim, a photo poked out from the side, Daniel gently tugged it out to look at it.

It was a photo of his mother Annie and Daniel together. Both were smiling at the camera. Again he remembered that episode very well, reliving it in his head smiling as he recalled it. It had been Mother's Day and he'd took his mum out for her dinner with Sam.

This photo had also been taken by his son, a simple point and click with his dad's mobile without much effort being required.

Daniel was washed over then by a wave of sentimentality not only by the memories from the couple of photos he had saw but also the thought that how Sam had kept them.

He placed the photograph back, he did not look at any of the other items in the tin, this was Sam's stuff and he did not want to invade his privacy, perhaps on another day he may ask Sam if he would like to show him what he had, maybe talk about these photos and whatever else was in the tin, share the stories.

He knelt by the side of his son's bed and touched the top of the sleeping boy's hand, laying his palm gently over it feeling its heat.

He remembered back when he first touched his son in the neonatal ward, how the tiny fingers curled around his own much larger finger. The words he had said then were "Hello Sam, I'm your daddy.", these words he repeated on his lips now, then he added in a whispered soft voice, 'You are very much loved my son, we all are loved.'

He then kissed his son on his cheek and left the room.

Printed in Great Britain
by Amazon